"Will the Americans attack?"

"The Sword has the best American missiles on board, and advanced, state-of-the-art computers. It will be two years at least before they can put up anything to match The Sword of Allah!"

Salamat smiled and nodded, pleased. "And we will meet our day of power and glory on January sixth?"

Calvin said, "Yes, Your Excellency. You will be master of the world, twelve days from now."

Salamat threw his head back and laughed.

THE SWORD OF ALLAH

Richard Elliott

FAWCETT GOLD MEDAL • NEW YORK

Library of Congress Catalog Card Number: 84-90872

ISBN: 0-449-12604-8

Manufactured in the United States of America

First Ballantine Books Edition: August 1984

PROLOGUE

UBARI, North Central Africa
December 12, 1991

INTENSE, SUFFOCATING HEAT DROVE LYLE TOOKEY TOO OFTEN to his last four-liter canteen. He crouched in his burnoose under a brown-motled camouflage cloth anchored by stones at one end and two aluminum rods at the other.

He was bored and scared. He'd lain half burrowed in the sand and sun-blasted pebbles for two days. Periodically, he listened to military patrol vehicles in the near distance. Sometimes the patrols growled heart-stoppingly close. They seemed on an alert; the patrols had doubled in the past twelve hours.

He wondered if they'd found his camouflaged Land Rover. It was hidden in a small gully three miles out from this perimeter.

He scanned the dials of the opened instrument case before him. The needles ticked and twitched. The multihead recorders made their entries on the sealed, slow-moving microthin tape.

He had four more hours to wait, till dark, and then he had only to bury the directional antenna, which stood a few feet away, disguised as a scraggly shrub, bury the camouflage shelter and his ration cans, and walk back to the Rover.

Provided the directional beeper still worked. Provided the Rover was still there. Provided the damned patrols didn't find him first.

He knew vaguely what the instrument pack was recording: every level of transmission from the secret Ubari scientific installation a mile away. He'd been told the antenna could pick up emissions from electric motors, from computers, even from certain highly sophisticated recorders, as well as the amount of electricity used at every moment. There was even a reading being made of the ignitions of the patrol vehicles that would tell the make and model number to the analysts back at CIA headquarters in Langley.

Lyle remembered his small argument with his section head. "What the hell do we have all those hotshot spy satellites for? There must be one or two that pass over the Sahara. Why can't they make the recordings you need?"

Edward Marin had replied, "We don't have that kind of instrumentation up there, and even if we did, we couldn't get low enough, and even then we wouldn't get but five or six minutes per pass of what we need. Besides, we think they're shutting down when our birds go over."

So there lay Lyle Tookey, sweating blood, sipping hot water, waiting. He had been selected for this shit job because he was dark and swarthy, of Italian extraction on his mother's side and black Irish on his father's side. A dumb twenty-nine-year-old idealist who had probably lost five pounds he couldn't afford from his five-ten, one-forty-pound frame.

Lyle had not been told why the information was so vital or what precisely was supposed to be going on a mile away. But it was something very, very important.

He had entered Ubari as an Egyptian mineralogist employed by an oil consortium based in Oman. He could speak Arabic well and Berber not so well. He could also speak French and Spanish and Italian.

This was spy work: dirty, dangerous, and mostly dull.

It was silent in the desert. The sun was setting. In a few minutes, the heat would melt away, and the air would grow cold while the sand and rocks held their heat for hours.

Lyle sipped hot water from his canteen and decided to take a small chance. He crawled from his low, camouflaged shelter and eased alongside a rounded boulder. There wasn't a sound except his own breathing. He scrambled up the irregular, sand-blasted sides of a slab of rock and slowly raised his head for a look around.

To the west, the sun was a bold orange disc being nibbled to death by a line of far hills. To the east lay Wau el Maradi, an oasis and the site of the low adobe buildings he was monitoring.

He raised his powerful binoculars to his dark eyes and examined the windows of the largest building. Electric lights were coming on. The flat roof showed a large receiving dish pointed up at the darkening sky.

As he watched, a telescope antenna rose upward, higher and higher, until it reached a height at least triple that of the oasis palm trees. The top of the antenna held a pulse-beam dish. The signaling dish turned slightly and reflected orange from the dying sun.

Lyle scowled. That looked like a satellite control setup, which would explain a lot! But it raised other questions. Whose satellite—or satellites—was it controlling? Was this a Ubari operation or staffed and controlled by Russia? By Iran? The French? Why the secrecy?

If the satellite was a weapon . . .

It had become dark and cold in the space of minutes. He felt suddenly lonely as hell. It was so quiet! And except for a few glittering stars overhead and the mile-distant lights from the oasis, he lay in almost total darkness.

Suddenly, vehicle headlights flared on in the oasis, and several patrols headed out into the desert—toward him!

Lyle decided to go to ground again. He crept back down into his shelter and set about closing up shop.

As he buried every trace of his occupancy—even the nearby evidence of his excretions—and finally hand buried the small folding shovel he'd used, the sounds of the all-terrain patrol vehicles grew louder.

Could some instrument have detected him? Some kind of body-heat sensor that scanned the desert when the sun went down and the ambient heat disappeared? From a mile away?

He scuttled away from his campsite, carrying only the ten-pound instrument case, the directional beeper tracer, and a big Smith & Wesson .45 revolver.

He moved carefully. There were too many rocks, gullies, and potholes to beware of; he did not want to fall, twist an ankle, break a leg, a wrist or an arm.

He kept low. Periodically, he got a direction from the beeper and changed his course slightly. The instrument case became heavier and heavier.

He heard engine sounds approaching from behind. He angled behind a man-high outcropping of rock and peered back at the approaching headlights. He pulled his gun and freed the trigger and butt from the thin plastic bag that had sealed the gun from dust and dirt.

He licked his lips. His stomach roiled with fear.

The vehicle was heading straight for his hiding place, slewing away, returning, jouncing, creaking, the engine growling and straining.

As it veered closer, Lyle was surprised to see it was an International Scout. All its windows were open. There were three soldiers inside.

He pressed off the safety on his gun and cocked it. He huddled down against the rocks, his burnoose up. I am invisible, he thought fiercely. I am fucking invisible!

Bright yellow light flared along the jagged boulders over his head. The Scout groaned up a grade and tilted sideways. The driver had to veer left to avoid tipping over. The Scout passed on the other side of Lyle's wall of rocks, then groaned and grumbled away.

He stopped shaking five minutes later. He picked up the precious instrument case with its multiple cassettes and trudged on toward his Land Rover.

Periodically, Lyle heard patrols in the distance. He saw lights flickering, dipping and yawing, but none of the patrols came close. Yet he realized there were at least a dozen patrols out, and most were in his sector. They had to know he was out here somewhere.

He had to reach the Rover before dawn and get away in the darkness. In daylight, he would be doomed.

Then, for a while, the patrols seemed to deliberately close in on him. It took three precious hours of hiding, moving, hiding, to reach the Land Rover.

Lyle was exhausted when he slipped down the side of the deep gully and stumbled to the car. He dragged a full canteen from under the Rover and swallowed greedily of the cold water. He methodically pulled the camouflage netting aside and climbed into the driver's seat.

4

The moon had come up, big and yellow. He didn't want to linger in this area.

He stowed the instrument case in a hidden compartment under the passenger seat and took a deep, sighing breath.

The starter rattled futilely six times before the engine coughed to life and smoothed to a reliable mutter. He switched on the headlights, backed and filled until he had the car turned, and drove carefully out of the twisting, dead-end ravine. He hoped that if a patrol saw his lights, they'd assume he was just another patrol.

He faced a seven-hour drive to Aozid, the fly-ridden capital of Ubari. There he would return the Rover to the used-car dealer from whom he had rented it. The dealer would sell it to a certain professional photographer from Sweden. That photographer would take the instrument-recorder case from the Rover and make arrangements to have the case flown indirectly to the United States.

Lyle's headlights picked up the faint tracks of the wild road linking Sabha to Aozid. He began to breathe easier. The successful completion of this assignment would earn him a jump of at least two grades and fifteen thousand dollars in salary. With that kind of extra money, he and Cathy could begin to think seriously of a house. At last! And a baby or two. And—

A pair of headlights suddenly bobbed onto the twisting road behind him.

Lyle's mouth went dry. "Shit!" He didn't know what to do. He kept on driving at the same pace, hoping the patrol would turn off, drop back. . . .

But the Scout began to gain on him. Every patrol car he'd seen had been a Scout. Funny that the rabid Marxist dictator of Ubari, Abu Ben Salamat, would buy American four-wheel drive, all-terrain cars for desert patrol work.

Funny and tragic! Lyle knew his old Land Rover couldn't outrun a new Scout. But on this curving, rough track, maybe it could outlast a Scout. His gas tank was full, and the odds were the Scout had been on patrol for hours. The Rover's tires were new, and the engine had had a tune-up before he'd left Aozid.

He stepped on the gas and concentrated on staying on the rutted, dangerous road. He began to sweat in spite of the rush of cold, dry desert air. He prayed to God the soldier driving the Scout was new at it.

But it quickly became obvious that the driver was better than Lyle, no doubt from months of experience on night patrols. The bright headlights drew very close. The interior of the Rover was illuminated.

The other driver honked his horn repeatedly.

Lyle drove on. What could he do? He had papers of identity as Henri Pinare, professional mineralogist. A check with Omanco would confirm his identity and employment, but how could he explain his presence out there in the desert so close to that secret facility? He could claim he was on his way back to Aozid from Sabha, but Ubari intelligence had only to call Sabha to discover he'd never been there.

He was a spy! Either way, he was a spy! They'd torture him and throw him into a stinking stone oven to rot.

He almost lost the Rover in a deep natural rut. The old car tried to follow the rut off the road. He wrenched the wheel viciously and rocked free but was suddenly in a too-sharp turn. The Rover's right wheels left the ground. He compensated desperately, and the car thudded down. He instantly had to brake for a terrifying S curve around huge boulders.

He entered a straight, level stretch of road. The Scout behind him had maneuvered the rut and curve nicely. Lyle cursed and floorboarded the gas pedal.

Seconds later, he heard strange popping sounds. An instant later, bullets tore into the Rover.

"Oh, Christ! Oh, Christ!" He hunched down as much as he could. Slugs whined past his head and body. The windshield suddenly splattered with ragged little holes. Slugs buzzed and thudded and clanged into the Rover.

Lyle sobbed with fear. He tried weaving the Rover, but it didn't help much. The terrifying popping sounds continued. An occasional spray of bullets tore into the car. Sooner or later, they'd hit a tire—or him!

If only the Scout would run out of gas!

A fist holding an ice pick slammed into his back. The .23

slug tore into his right lung and nicked his heart. Lyle grunted and spasmed forward, unable to control his body.

The Rover lurched off the narrow road, careened off a rock, jounced high, turned in the air gracefully, and crashed on its side.

Lyle Tookey lay broken and twisted, his head crushed.

PART ONE

CHAPTER 1

THE GOLDEN BROWN EYES OF BRADFORD COLLIER STONEMAN were legendary. It was said he could hypnotize anyone he wished and bend them to his powerful will. Failed competitors swore that was what happened to them.

He sat now in the central chair of his private conference room on the sixty-fifth floor of the massive Stoneman Building. He rested his delicate, liver-spotted hands on a leather folder and directed an intense golden glare at the heavily jowled man on his right. "What about this report from Ubari?"

Lane McDermott, president of New World Consultants, Inc., did not flinch. He had withstood that fierce stare for many years. "Our informant reported that a CIA man was caught spying on the secret Wau el Maradi satellite control station. He was killed."

"What is Salamat going to do about it?"

"Not known."

"What's the CIA going to do about it?"

"Probably try again. They don't like mystery satellites up there, especially when they're controlled by a fanatic Moslem dictator."

Stoneman pursed his thin lips. The grooves above his upper lip became more pronounced. "No. The man who controls that satellite is the man who's in charge at Wau el Maradi. That damned—"

"Calvin Bergendahl."

"Why didn't we get him?"

McDermott said, "He was too hot to touch."

"My policy is to employ every truly brilliant man or woman available."

11

"At the time, four years ago, that didn't seem wise in his case. Bergendahl is a genius in theoretical astrophysics and a brilliant computer man. We had no use for a wild astrophysicist at that time. Brilliant computer people are always available. His personality is warped, and his sexual preferences are social dynamite, at least in this country."

Stoneman snorted. "So he likes little boys."

"The scandal and the trial made it impossible to employ him. We couldn't risk linking him to any of our foreign subsidiaries."

"Nevertheless, he's the one who put everything together for Salamat and got that thing up into space. I want to reach him. I want to control him! Is that thing a weapon?"

Lane McDermott nodded. "The inner circle at the palace call it the Sword of Allah. Our technical experts think it may be a highly maneuverable missile platform. But they also think it's impossible for such a huge payload to have been lifted from anywhere but Kennedy or Baikonur. All Bergendahl had to work with were a lot of old Uranus Two solid propellant rockets Salamat got from Iran, who got them from India, who got them from the United States as surplus seven years ago. They were supposed to be unusable. And at best each one could only put a thousand pounds into orbit."

Stoneman snarled. "So what did he put up?"

"It may be only a propaganda weapon. A symbol of Moslem potency in space."

"Are you joking?"

A red light blinked on the intercom beside Lane McDermott's elbow. He pressed the button. "Yes?"

A high-level assistant's voice said, "Mrs. Stoneman would like to enter, sir."

Bradford Stoneman said loudly, "Of course!"

The light blinked out, and a few seconds later the ornate Philippine mahogany door opened.

Erica Summers Stoneman entered, a smile quirking the corners of her full red lips. She carefully closed the heavy door before speaking. She knew the room was soundproof. "Am I interrupting the running of the world?"

"Only a small part of it." Stoneman admired the tall, slim,

12

yet sensuous beauty of his new young wife. Very young, for a man his age.

Her short silken blue dress rippled on her body as she moved—so gracefully!—to sit beside him. She crossed nylon-clad legs and asked, "Am I privileged to listen?"

Stoneman nodded. "And contribute, if you wish."

Lane McDermott, next to Bradford Collier Stoneman, was at present the most powerful manager of the vast, multilayered, multiarmed octopus of money and power that had been built carefully and boldly for more than one hundred years by the Stoneman family.

Yet he knew his place: He was at most only an extremely well paid right-hand man, a man who carried out orders, a gatherer of secrets. And he knew that Erica Stoneman, besides being one of the most beautiful women in the world, was a woman of extraordinary intelligence and—lurking in the depths of her character—steel ruthlessness.

He knew, without anything ever having been said, that Brad Stoneman was grooming her to assume total control of the empire.

Lane said to her, "We're going over the Salamat satellite problem . . . if it is a problem."

Stoneman said, "We don't know what they've got up there. Does anyone besides Salamat and the people at Wau el Maradi know?"

McDermott shook his head. "Not yet."

Erica placed her small, smooth white hand on Stoneman's wrinkled, spotted hand, on the arm of his chair. Her long blond hair shifted entrancingly on her shoulders as she turned her head to ask, "How is Salamat spending your new loan to him?"

Stoneman smoothed his few strands of white hair across his skull. He was seventy years old and showing more age than he liked. Younger men were subtly beginning to treat him as a senile relic. They couldn't help it; society had preconditioned them to think that old men couldn't think straight.

Whenever he detected that attitude, he had the younger man discharged. To hell with them! He had the power! He had Erica!

Lane had answered her question: "Guns, military equipment, supplies. He's training squads of terrorists and assassins."

Lane rose from his leather chair and asked, "Would you like a coffee, Mrs. Stoneman? A pastry? Brad?" He walked to a serving cart that had been wheeled in before the meeting began.

Erica said, "No, thank you, Lane. We're having lunch in a few moments."

McDermott brought a cinnamon roll on a napkin and a cup of heavily creamed coffee to the highly polished table. In his late fifties, he kept trim by heroic exercises and periodic starvation. This week he was indulging. He said, "I'm getting noises from Newco in England about some serious prying into their loan portfolio."

Stoneman came alert. "Who? Why?"

"Our informant in the CIA called me last night. He had just learned the name of the Newco employee who is selling the firm's loan files."

Stoneman grimaced. "You know, there was a time when I owned the CIA, from the director on down. Now . . . Damn Barr! We should never have reelected that man."

McDermott continued. "The CIA agent in London is John Norris, likely the best field man in the agency. He can't be reached. He's the loan information buyer."

Puzzled, Erica said, "I thought that investigation had been quashed."

"It was, for a while. But the director was told by President Barr to find out who funded Salamat's satellite program, and no excuses. Barr knows Bergendahl had the use of some very secret Defense Department advanced computer technology and hardware. Now that Salamat has that satellite up, somewhere, with god knows what on it, the director is putting on the pressure for results. He personally assigned Norris to London."

Erica asked, frowning, "How did they get close? How did they know about Newco?" Brad had slipped his hand onto her thigh and was sliding her blue silk dress to and fro. He seemed to have lost interest in the discussion.

Lane answered, "They had help. The Russians and the

Israelis and the French are all worried about that thing. They managed to trace the money flow backward far enough to implicate Newco Associates. From Newco they might isolate First Trust in Singapore, then up the line to TUK of Panama . . . and finally good old Eastern-Wenn, the notorious Stoneman bank.''

Bradford Stoneman said abruptly, coldly, "Stop the leak."

McDermott nodded.

Erica looked startled for a second. She glanced at her husband thoughtfully, then smiled. She murmured, "The end does justify the means, hmm, darling?"

"Damn right!"

McDermott sipped his coffee. He made an entry in a small leather notebook. He polished his gold-framed glasses.

Stoneman resumed fondling Erica's thigh. The moving silk of her dress hissed softly over her nylons. She was curious about something. She asked, "Lane, why can't that satellite be destroyed in space? We and the Russians both have hunter-killer satellites, don't we?"

McDermott looked up. "Yes, but Calvin Norman Bergendahl has somehow packed enough fuel and state-of-the-art computers and god knows what else into that thing to allow it to change orbits, laterally as well as vertically. The thing is unfindable."

"How do you know there's anything at all up there?"

"Let me amend. We and the Russians run across it once in a while. Understand, there's a computer-directed search going on twenty-four hours a day. It's found—and lost again. There aren't enough telescopes. Bergendahl got something big up into orbit. What it is—what it can do—we may just have to wait and see.

There was a short silence in the richly appointed room. McDermott sipped at his coffee. "We may have unknowingly funded a monster."

Stoneman laughed. "I'm used to creating monsters—and dealing with them. I can name five presidents—''

Erica said, "What if Salamat has a nuclear missile on that satellite? That would explain why they call it the Sword of Allah."

15

Stoneman snorted. "Who'd give that madman an atomic weapon?"

McDermott answered, "No one. And he didn't buy one. The intelligence nets are sure of that. No nukes have been stolen. He doesn't have a nuclear power plant in Ubari, or a breeder reactor. Nothing. No atomic installations whatsoever."

Erica was fascinated by this top-level discussion, by the use of men and nations, by the manipulations of vast financial power. Brad had shown her secret documents and had matter-of-factly discussed with her many of his plans and current international maneuvers.

At first, soon after their marriage, she had been surprised, puzzled, amazed, by his openness. But as time had passed, she realized he was testing her, training her.

She had entered this secret meeting expecting that it would end with her arrival. Instead, she was participating. This was headier than lunch in the penthouse suite.

She ventured a joke. "Maybe his satellite will broadcast to all the world, twenty-four hours a day, some of his most rabid revolutionary speeches."

Brad Stoneman grunted, not amused. Jokes were a waste of time. His golden brown gaze shifted to McDermott. "Is the timetable for his invasion of the Azouad Republic still on track?"

"Yes. June tenth, after the spring rains and after the crops are sown."

"Crops! If he knew that little clutch of tribes are sitting on five lakes of oil!"

Erica was puzzled. "If he doesn't know that, why is he interested in taking over that area?"

Stoneman answered harshly. "He doesn't care about that scrub desert. He wants people dead. It's a blood feud. His cousin rules Azouad and ten years ago financed an abortive coup against him. Salamat lusts for revenge."

She said, "That seems foolish."

Brad Stoneman pulled Erica close and kissed her lightly. He smiled. "My dear, he's insane—by our standards—and in many ways a fool. But in many ways he is not a fool! He spent three years at Cambridge, remember, and he's read

Machiavelli at least once a year. We pay him an average of thirty million hard dollars a day for his oil, and he buys arms. We made secret loans to him to build strategic roads and airfields—and he diverted some of it to build that damned satellite. We have a secret protocol with him giving us exploration and exploitation rights to all territories he controls or in the future may control, but how do we make him keep his word? We've given him—or sold him—some of this nation's most secret military technology—a mistake!—and he has apparently mounted it on that damned satellite!''

Stoneman shot a malevolent glare at McDermott. ''Our intelligence failed.'' His gaze softened as he turned back to Erica. ''But Salamat does not know of our secret funding of Sudan's military and the millions we pay to Sudan's Committee of Three. We effectively control the United States' military and foreign policy to the extent of assuring Sudan unlimited arms and even an American expeditionary force if Salamat becomes too big to control or reneges on our 'understandings.' ''

Bradford Stoneman warmed to his topic. His powerful eyes flashed. ''The oldest rule of moneylending and power brokering is always make sure you have the power to collect on a loan. If you raise up one ruler, you must prepare another to bring him down if necessary. There must always be a sheriff with a gun to enforce foreclosure or the collection of debts. In this world, that is and always has been the iron law of survival for us.''

Erica nodded. She had heard variations on this theme from him dozens of times. She kissed Brad sensually, with parted, warm, soft lips. She felt him resist briefly, then yield to her tongue. She knew better than to continue the kiss too long. He was beginning to tremble when she pulled her mouth away. She whispered, ''Darling, don't we have a special lunch planned?''

She saw Lane McDermott sitting still, silently eating his cinnamon roll, eyes neutral. She wondered what went on in that large grayed head? Lane was only fifty-seven, she knew, and unmarried.

Brad Stoneman leaned back, flushed. ''Yes, we do. You go on up and get ready.''

Erica rose smoothly and moved to the door. "Good-bye, Lane. Perhaps I'll see you again next week."

"I suspect you will, Mrs. Stoneman."

Bradford watched her leave. When the big door snicked shut, he said to McDermott, "Nothing shocks her. She's coming along very nicely."

Lane nodded. He drained his cup of coffee.

Stoneman said, "This time next week, as usual, unless an emergency develops. I enjoy these face-to-face meetings. I can never fully trust a phone line to be secure."

McDermott smiled. "With good cause now'days." He rose. "Good-bye, sir." He left the room, using a door at the far end of the room.

Alone, Bradford Stoneman pulled a hidden drawer from the conference table before him and checked the glowing green telltale lights on the secret control panel.

Hidden cameras and sensors in the room's paneled walls, ceiling, and floor—even in the chairs and table itself—had detected no tape recording or transmissions during the meeting. McDermott had not carried a gun. The pastry on the serving cart had been checked after having been purchased at random from one of twenty bakeries in the city. The coffee had been prepared by Stoneman's long-time personal cook. But Stoneman rarely ate or drank during these meetings with his top aide.

He flicked switches and closed the drawer. He rose slowly from his thronelike leather chair. Pain in his arthritic right knee flared as if a vise had tightened on the joint. His doctors wanted to do something about that, but the alternatives to pain were heavy medication, injections, or an immobilizing operation.

Stoneman hated to limp. People lost respect if you limped. But he hated hospitals and doctors and medication even more. He even refused to take his high blood pressure pills. They made his brain feel as if it were full of cabbage. It was easier to endure the frequent pain and occasional spells of dizziness.

He took up his ivory-handled cane and tucked the leather folder from the table into his coat pocket.

He limped out of the conference room and down a short,

deeply carpeted hallway to a private elevator. It was ready for him; Erica had sent it back down for him.

He entered, folded out an upholstered seat near the control panel, and sat carefully. He stabbed the penthouse button with a bony finger. As the elevator surged upward, he began to consider the dalliance he had planned with his beautiful wife. She knew what he expected.

Erica was waiting by the elevator doors when they opened. Her full red lips curved into a genuine welcoming smile.

"Would you like some wine?"

He nodded. "The '74 Sauvignon." As he got to his feet and left the elevator, he watched her walk gracefully to the bar. There was something hypnotically attractive in a beautiful woman's walk. The sway of Erica's slim hips under her short blue silken dress, her tanned nyloned legs, the sensuous brush of her thighs, the swing of her slender arms, the gentle bounce of her long, wavy blond hair. . . .

He followed the temporary tracks her shoeless feet had crushed into the deep-pile white carpeting and settled into a loveseat facing the floor-to-ceiling window. It was snowing heavily in New York again. Another convincing bit of evidence that the Northern Hemisphere was sliding into a long cycle of severe winters. But New Yorkers had learned to live with constant blizzards, as they had learned to live with ever more frequent power outages, strikes, shortages. He smiled as he remembered something he'd read in the *Times* a few days ago: New Yorkers were a ten million man and woman rat pack.

Erica sat beside him and handed him a small crystal goblet. "Here you are, darling." She sipped from an identical goblet.

He tasted the expensive white wine and savored the subtle flavor. Thank God his taste buds hadn't deteriorated much with age. He leaned back in the cushions, sighing.

She asked, "Want me to take off your shoes?"

He nodded and watched her kneel before him. The scoop bodice of her shimmering dress fell outward to give him a tantalizing view of her large-nippled breasts.

Erica was the daughter of Randolph Yardley, U.S. senator from New York. Stoneman had married her almost a year

19

ago, after having divorced his first wife over five years before. In the interim, he'd used a series of mistresses and exceptional call girls.

Erica had all the qualities he had belatedly realized he wanted and needed in a woman: extraordinary physical beauty, high intelligence, breeding, taste, education, and a strong element of submissiveness in her character. Erica had been married once before, to a wimp who wrote a bleeding-heart, nationwide syndicated column. They had tried to outsubmit each other and had failed miserably. She had seen the problem and gotten the divorce. Under her surface compliance and self-effacement lurked a great deal of hidden determination.

Erica looked up, blue eyes sparkling. "Are the problems of the world giving you a bad time?"

He laughed. "There are always problems. I'm glad you're not one of them."

Erica laughed. She sipped from her goblet, then resumed massaging his feet. "I'm one of the solutions."

Stoneman agreed. She knew what he needed and was willing to serve him, to adorn power, to learn the uses of nearly supreme power, and to enhance, in her way, his power. It was a perfect marriage for her, too.

There had been a flurry of criticism in the lower-level media over his having taken for a wife the daughter of a U.S. senator. The charge had been the "capture" of Senator Yardley by the Stoneman financial empire, and there had been complaints that he had no right to marry a woman younger by forty years. But a simple statement by Erica that had been broadcast on the cable nets and on radio had squelched it all: "Brad Stoneman is more than enough man for me, and I married him in spite of my father's opposition."

The truth: Randolph Yardley had been owned body and soul by Stoneman for fifteen years and had been delighted when the world's most powerful man had chosen his daughter for marriage.

The truth: Stoneman was more than enough man for Erica, because she wanted a man in only one special sexual way. When Stoneman met Erica at a Washington, D.C., party, there had been a strong, instant mutual attraction. Their needs had communicated by means of odor and subconscious body signals. He had had McDermott run a complete investigation of her, especially of her personality and character. The resulting dossier confirmed his most ardent wish: She was extremely oral. He had discovered the joys of oral sex in his sixties. His demands and "impositions" on his first wife, Marsha, who was puritanically religious and opposed to such activities, had made their divorce inevitable.

Erica sat back on her bare heels and said, "I've been invited to Los Angeles to speak at a banquet to launch Gary Baker's gubernatorial campaign. We were close friends at USC."

Stoneman grunted. "The hotshot liberal Democrat."

"I could do some good. I could go there against your wishes." She smiled.

He nodded. "And show I cannot control even my own wife. And prove again indirectly that your father isn't in my pocket."

"Um-hmm." Her blue eyes sparkled. "And Gary is being supported by the United Citizens for Tomorrow, which happens to be largely funded by the ABT Foundation, which in turn is funded by grants from Sufibre Corporation, which is owned by Interco, which is owned by—"

Stoneman laughed. "Yes, yes. We've had Gary Baker since he ran for councilman in Santa Monica. He might be president someday."

"Many are owned, but only one can be president at a time." Erica's full lips quirked. "We've got politicians lined up for the next twenty to thirty years, don't we?"

"Of all persuasions."

"Then I should go?"

"Of course. It's a fine tactic. You have a cunning Machiavellian mind. I'm proud of you." And he was. He had arranged for the invitation to test her insights and cunning. He had plans for Erica beyond the bedroom and as hostess of social affairs.

Erica stood up slowly and reached to unzip the back of her slinky dress. "Darling, shall we eat before we eat?" Her eyes were suddenly hot.

Stoneman drained his goblet. His mind filled with memories of her enclosing silken thighs, the humid muskiness of her pink center, and the violent undulations of her sleek belly as she cried out in orgasm. He said hoarsely, "By all means."

CHAPTER 2

LONDON
December 22, 1991

JOHN NORRIS WAS HAPPY TO LEAVE THE BITTER, WET DARKNESS of Knatchbull Lane when he entered the Needle Marks Record Shop. His digital watch showed 7:55. The shop closed at eight.

His informant stood browsing in the Classics section, the only customer besides himself.

The man was short and chunky, a blond bear in a heavy brown overcoat and a six-foot green-striped muffler. He pretended not to see Norris. He snuffled with a cold.

The clerk looked up from his preliminary cash register count. "We close in a mo', sir."

Norris nodded. "Just want to check if you've got a certain record." He unzipped his blue White Stag ski coat halfway to make easy a quick reach inside. His 9-mm. Benelli automatic hung heavy and cold in its holster under his right armpit, near his waist.

The clerk smiled. "Look all you want, sir." He now knew Norris for an American by the accent. Expensively outfitted Americans usually had lots of money. But that was as far as the clerk would go to make an extra sale; damned if he'd fawn over this big, tall capitalist mucker.

Norris walked down a narrow aisle past Jazz, Instrumental, and Hot Rock Vocals. He paused a few feet from the other man and began flipping albums in the two American Folk bins.

After a minute, the man, Neal Konowsky, said, "Bloody awful weather this week." He snuffled and reached into his coat for a handkerchief. He wiped his pug nose.

Norris asked, "Isn't it always this bad in December?"

23

He took a nearly empty pack of Players kings from his shirt pocket, shook the last one up, and offered Konowsky the cigarette. Also in the pack were ten thousand-pound New Pound notes. They showed clearly in the ragged hole. "You can have the last three if you want. I hate bent smokes."

Konowsky brightened. "Thank you, sir." He took the pack and stuffed it into his inside coat pocket. "Can't afford to pass on anything free anymore, what with the bloody inflation and the bloody government lifting taxes every six months." He fished in another pocket for a cheap butane lighter.

As Konowsky lit up and drew deep, satisfying lungfuls of smoke, Norris resumed his album flipping in the American Folk bins. He glanced at the clerk, who was intent on counting shillings and crowns. He said to Konowsky, "No Baez records."

"That a group?"

"No. Joan Baez. Singer."

"Uh. Might try the recycle bin over there, if you don't mind used records. People are selling anything they can. Bloody fucking government!"

Norris moved to a section marked "Preowned Records— All Purchases Final." He found an old copy of *Diamonds & Rust*, an A & M 1975 release. He looked inside the sleeve and saw a computer floppy disc beside the record. He nodded. "Very good. Thanks for the tip."

"Thanks for the smokes." Konowsky looped the long muffler around his neck and carried two Beethoven symphony albums to the clerk.

Norris followed. It was 8:02.

The clerk looked up. "Found two more to your liking, eh, Neal? You must have every Beethoven symphony ever recorded by any orchestra."

Konowsky grinned. "Close to it. Close to it. I listen to them all day while I'm slaving over the bloody computer."

"They let you have a player where you work?"

"Not bloody likely! I work in my flat. They put a station there for me." He grinned with pride. "They value me, they do. I told 'em I had to be home to take care of me mum, and

24

THE SWORD OF ALLAH

so in went the cable and in went the 50K Mitzu." He paid for the records with a ten-pound note.

As he made change, the clerk glanced at the record Norris carried. His lips twitched with contempt. "A pound even for that one. That's a rare one." He met Norris's gray-green eyes and looked away.

"They're all rare. Disc recording is a dying industry."

Konowsky stood at the door, hesitating before plunging out into the cold, dark night. "Truth there. But tapes and digital cost too bloody much, and they'll never get everything on tape that's on discs."

The clerk took a pound note from Norris with a grudging nod. He said to Konowsky, "Who would buy it all? Ninety percent of it is pure shit. Shouldn't have been recorded in the first place."

Konowsky laughed, in good spirits. "Listen to him! A man says that who goes home to play Klee chants."

As Norris waited while the clerk reluctantly put the Baez album in a flimsy bag, with a receipt, Konowsky said angrily, "Look at that! Half the bloody streetlights went off! And there wasn't but a few to begin with."

The clerk said indifferently, "Another outage somewhere."

"Another bloody Skinner's likely thrown another cobblestone into the works, you mean."

But Norris frowned and looked out through the heavy steel grillwork over the dirty shop windows. The narrow commercial street was almost blacked out. Only a tobacconist's shed faint yellow light a block away. He noticed a scurrying shadow across the lane. Another.

Konowsky obviously had not noticed them. He had been half turned toward the clerk. He shrugged. "Got to get back to mum." He opened the heavy door.

Norris called, "I think there are—"

But Konowsky had darted out into the night. The door hung open.

Norris said, "Shoelace . . ." and dropped to one knee, his broad back to the clerk, below the level of the window display shelf. He quickly slipped the flexible computer memory disc from the Baez album to inside his pale blue arctron

25

shirt. He pulled the Benelli and pressed and locked a silencer onto the barrel. He turned and called, ''Hey!'' He let the clerk see the automatic.

The man paled. .

''Turn off the lights!''

''Why . . . why scuff me? I don't have—''

They heard Neal Konowsky scream. His agonized shriek echoed in the silent street.

''Turn off the fucking lights!''

The clerk ran to a nearby circuit box and pulled the main switch. The shop was plunged into darkness.

Norris heard the clerk drop to the floor and begin crawling toward the rear of the shop.

Did those in the street want Norris dead, too? Probably yes. Someone at Newco Associates had discovered that Neal Konowsky was selling high-level, very secret international loan information. Someone even higher up had decided to have Konowsky monitored until a meet was set up and a buy was made. The orders had to include killing the buyer, too, and recovering the information.

Norris hoped they'd wait a few more seconds, until his eyes completely adjusted to the darkness. The killers weren't true professionals if they'd let Konowsky scream like that.

Now they had a problem.

Norris called to the clerk, ''Is there a rear door to this place?''

The man answered in a shaky voice. ''No. There's a loo, and I'm going in, and I'm locking it!'' A door slammed. A bolt slid home.

Norris knelt, facing the half-open door, and smiled. The inside of the shop was still black, but when he cautiously lifted his head enough to look over the window shelf through the glass and grillwork, he noticed that the thousands of tiny puddles in the cobblestone-paved street reflected the soft light from the tobacconist's and from distant upper windows and streetlights.

There was a man in a dark car coat standing behind a lamppost directly across from the shop. There was a driver in a small sedan a hundred feet to the left. The car emitted a purring exhaust.

Norris couldn't see anyone else.

But they had to come to him or give up, and they couldn't know where he was in the shop. They couldn't know for sure if he had a gun or not.

A soft male voice with a Jamaican accent came from just outside the door. "Come out, mahn. We no hurt you."

Norris didn't answer. His right leg below the knee began to go numb. He shifted position slightly. The leg filled with pins and needles.

"All we want is what you got from de other mahn."

Norris caught a gesture from the man behind the lamppost.

The man by the door said, "Naw, you be de brave one."

The man across the street called, "Five thousand," in a cultured British accent.

"That make me brave."

Norris smiled cynically. He waited, the silenced Benelli cocked, steady in his left hand.

A slim man edged silently into the shop doorway. He kept his right hand hidden behind him. He gently pushed the shop door wide open. "Just throw me de thing you bought. That's all we want."

Norris, in deep darkness, could now see the man held a thin double-edged boot knife. The blade glistened dark and wet.

The man slipped inside the door and tried to flatten against the wall. He knocked back a tape display and lurched sideways, off balance.

Norris squeezed the trigger. The Benelli jumped and coughed twice.

The slim man jerked from the impact of the 9-mm. slugs and sagged to the tile floor. He tried to froth words through a ruptured throat but then abruptly stopped breathing.

Norris lurched to the door, handicapped by his blood-starved leg, and used the door frame as a shield. He took careful aim at the man in the dark car coat by the lamppost and fired four times.

Two bullets hit the post and ricocheted. One shattered a

window. The other hit the man. He staggered back, clutched his left arm, and ran for the car.

Norris emerged from the shop and put three quiet slugs into the car, but it pulled away once the man had clambered in.

Norris holstered his gun and walked quickly in the direction Konowsky had taken. He found Konowsky's body on the sidewalk half a block away. A final, mortal stab between the ribs to the heart had done the job after at least three to the abdomen had failed. The very sharp knife had easily ripped through the heavy brown overcoat.

Norris retrieved the Players kings from the inside pocket.

He rose and continued on. It was shockingly quiet again on the lane. As he walked, he wiped the Benelli clean of his fingerprints and threw it onto a steeply pitched roof of a two-story building. He heard it clatter down into the rain guttering.

He unsnapped his holster and straps and pulled them from his jacket. They immediately found a resting place in a trash can.

Norris blew his nose in his handkerchief and casually ditched the handkerchief in another trash can.

He zipped up his expensive ski jacket and walked a bit faster.

CHAPTER 3

KIMBERLY BEALES PUSHED THE MAN'S BIG, STRONG HAND OFF her thigh. "Hey, keep both hands on the wheel, okay?" She shifted even closer to the passenger's door on the front seat of the old Ford pickup.

The driver had offered her a ride at the café in Wolf Camp and promised he was going all the way to Gull Junction. He wore a heavy plaid coat against the near-freezing weather. He was bearded, sweat smelly, and turning mean. "Shit, what's the matter with you? Don't I get nothing for giving you a ride?"

She nervously licked her lips. "Listen, I appreciate it. But I don't pay with sex. I've got a couple bucks I can give you to help with the gas. Okay?" She zipped up her heavy, quilted ski coat even though the heater in the pickup was blowing a steady breeze of warm air against her booted feet and jeans-clad legs. It was comfortable in the cab, but she knew her heavy breasts had caught his eye, and the bulky sweater she wore under her coat only made them seem larger. She remembered another big-busted girl saying to her in premed last term, "These ten pounds of tits are the worst things about being a woman!" They were magnets for men's eyes, and men couldn't or wouldn't take her seriously as a future doctor.

The driver shifted into second on a long grade. It was beginning to snow again. He said, "What'd you expect, for Christ's sake? Think I offered you a ride just out of the kindness of my heart? Out of charity? You want a favor, you give a favor."

"You didn't say you wanted sex for the ride. I didn't agree to it. That's not free market."

"Oh, shit. You're one of them libertarians. You a fucking survivalist, too?"

"My brother is." Kimberly shifted her backpack onto her lap from the floor. She defensively wrapped her arms around it. She watched him from the corner of her eye.

"Where you from, around here?"

"Portland. I'm going to medical school. I'm visiting for Christmas and New Year's."

"You should've taken the bus. Hitchhiking this time of year is the shits."

"I didn't think it would be this bad." She watched the narrow two-lane highway and checked her watch. Almost three in the afternoon. Low clouds were enveloping the tops of the fir-covered hills. She asked, "How long will it take to get to Gull Junction?"

"Not long, even in this weather. But I'm not going that far unless I get something for it. That's just it. That's the goddam bottom line." He laughed. "I've got a rubber if that's what's bothering you."

"I've got six dollars." Kimberly fumbled with the buckles on her pack.

"I don't want your lousy six bucks. I got my welfare check yesterday and my food stamps. I don't need your stinking six bucks! I want to get my hands on those big jugs you're carrying, and I want to fuck you. That's worth a trip to Gull Junction and back."

"I thought you lived there! You said—"

"I live in Elking, about five miles from here. If I'm going out of my way and using up my gas, I want some good feeling and fond memories in exchange. Understand?"

She thrust six new dollars at him. "Here! This is more than worth your precious time and gas. Especially since you won't report it to your welfare worker."

His bearded face twisted with anger. He snatched the red-backed bills from her hand and stuffed them in his torn jacket pocket. "You're a fucking libertarian, all right!"

"And you're a fine, upstanding, typical citizen of the United States of Something for Nothing!"

"Goddam—" He braked hard. The pickup slewed drunkenly on the icy, snowy blacktop and skidded to a stop. He turned to her. "Listen, you snotty bitch! You put out or you get out! Right here and now!"

"I won't!" She glared at him. She delved in her pack for her knife.

Before she could find it, he reached past her, unlocked the door, and flung it open. "Then hike it! Up to you."

Kimberly sat, feeling the cold air from the open door. She stared out at the snow, at the deserted highway, at the frigid, empty forest. A ball of fear slimed the pit of her stomach. She wasn't a virgin, but she would be damned if she'd submit to this sour-smelling, freeloading son of a bitch!

"All right, I'll walk. Give me back my six dollars."

"That's my pay for taking you this far. Out!" He gave her a powerful shove sideways.

Kimberly tumbled awkwardly from the truck. Her right foot turned on the slick blacktop, and a flare of hot pain lanced up her leg. She screamed. Her backpack landed beside her.

The man slammed the door shut. The pickup growled forward.

She yelled, "Hey, wait! I hurt myself! *Hey!*"

The pickup disappeared around a curve.

Kimberly shivered even though the biting cold hadn't fully penetrated her clothing. She bit her lip as she tried to move. Her ankle was either broken or severely sprained. She pulled her backpack into position and struggled to her feet.

Her ankle pulsed with squishy-hot pain. She tried walking and could only hobble a few steps before giving up.

God, it was quiet! She listened, holding her breath, but there was no sound. She flipped up her hood and zipped tight. She would never make it the five miles to Elking by herself.

She stood, swaying, most of her weight on her left leg, and looked back along the desolate, iced, whitening highway. The minutes dragged by. Fear ate into her mind. The silence became terrifying.

Her feet were beginning to get very cold. She kept her hands in her coat pockets. A crust of snow was forming on her coat, on her jeans and boots. Her left leg was starting to tremble with exhaustion. To make matters worse, she had to go to the bathroom.

Somebody else had to use this state highway!

Ten minutes later, she collapsed. She moaned with the pain. Her right ankle had swollen up to twice its normal size.

Finally, she heard a car. She struggled to her feet, gritted her teeth from the knifelike agony, and watched a gray Jeep wagon with a blue top round a curve. She flipped back her hood so the driver could see she was a girl.

The headlights were on. The swift-moving windshield wipers showed two bulky figures in the front seat.

Kimberly waved her arms and painfully stepped out onto the snow-covered blacktop. "Hey! Stop! Stop!"

The Jeep slowed carefully, and the passenger rolled down the window. It was a man in some kind of winter uniform. He was thirtyish, clean-shaven, and he grinned at her as the Jeep, slowing, passed her by a few yards.

She limped to the door, crying out with anguish, desperate lest they change their minds. "God, thanks for stopping! I can't walk. I've got a sprained ankle or something worse. I need a ride to somewhere."

She bent to peer into the car. Both men were uniformed, but they weren't army or air force. The thirtyish man, blond, crew cut, asked, "You have a wreck? Where's your car?"

"No, I—I hitched a ride with a guy who wanted sex, and he dumped me here when I wouldn't do it."

The driver, dark haired, in his early twenties, said, "We can take her into Elking, can't we, Jerry?"

Jerry checked his military-style digital watch. He made a face. "We've got to report in by three-thirty. If we're late again, we get d-marks and an official entry in our files. We don't have time to get to Elking and back."

Kimberly said, "But isn't Elking only five miles?"

He snapped, "It's more like ten miles, and in this stuff that translates to forty minutes going and coming back."

She asked, "Can't you take me with you to wherever you're going? Can't you check in and then maybe—"

"No, you'll just have to hike it." He started to roll up the window.

"I can't! My ankle— I can't walk ten steps! I'll die out here!"

The young driver said, "We can let her stay in the guard-house entrance lock till somebody drives out."

Jerry sighed angrily. He stopped raising the window. "You asshole! You know security regs."

"But sergeant, we can't just leave her! Shit, she'll freeze to death in this weather. It's gonna get worse."

Jerry glanced at his watch again, looked up at Kimberly, said, "Jesus Christ!" and twisted to unlock the back door. "Get in!"

"Thank you!" She climbed painfully into the back seat and pulled the door shut.

The driver gunned the wagon. Its studded snow tires dug easily through the inch of snow on the narrow highway.

Kimberly unslung her backpack and settled back into the cold leatherette seat. She asked, "Is there a base near here? That where you're from?"

Jerry answered, "Just don't ask questions. Don't see anything, and don't hear anything. Our asses'll be in traction if anybody finds out we're doing this."

"Oh. Okay. I'm just very grateful."

"Yeah."

They rode in uncomfortable silence. The blond man radiated seething irritation. He was mad at himself for giving in.

Abruptly, the driver turned off the highway onto a barely visible track. He engaged the four-wheel drive, and the tough vehicle jolted up a steep, twisting, rutted road.

Kimberly wondered where in hell they were going. This didn't seem a likely road into a military base. And, come to think of it, this Jeep wasn't painted like a military car.

She said warily, "Hey, you're not taking me off some-where to rape me, are you?" She carefully unzipped her pack and took out a gravity knife.

Jerry said disgustedly, "That's all we need, a rape charge on top of breaking security."

The young driver said, "Don't give us ideas."

She kept quiet. She looked over her shoulder at the small cargo compartment and saw three bulging mails sacks.

The car entered a small, tree-shrouded clearing. The driver parked in a low wooden shelter next to a big green van with black side stripes.

Jerry said to Kimberly, "Keep low. Don't make any noise. Ron'll come back for you in a few minutes."

Ron, the driver, said, "We have to relieve—"

"Shut the fuck up!"

The two men trudged away. She watched them fade into the swirling snow. She kept the knife in her fist. She passed some time by pressing the release button in the handle and flipping out the long, sharp blade. Then she pressed the release again, held the knife vertical, and watched the blade slide down into the handle. Her brother had given her the knife five years ago, in 1986, the year of the mass riots and all those huge business collapses.

Kimberly felt scared again. What was this place? Who were those guards? The biting cold began to really penetrate now as the residual heat in the car melted away. It was a lot colder up here in the hills than down on the highway. She began to regret asking so desperately for a ride.

She was shivering violently, later, when she heard footsteps crunching in the snow. She ducked below the window level. There was nothing to see; it was snowing very heavily now. Her breath steamed before her. The air was so cold it was painful to draw it deep into her lungs.

The footsteps approached the Jeep, the door opened, and the young driver said, "Jerry says you'll have to stay out here in the car."

Her teeth chattering, shivering, Kimberly said, "I c-can't. It's t-too cold."

The youth knew it. He could feel it through his heavy wool coat. He hesitated. "God. I don't know what to do. I guess we shouldn't have picked you up. We've broken so many regs now—"

"I don't understand what the b-b-big deal is. Can't you ask somebody to come and g-get me or drive me to Elking?"

"No. No. This is a—" He hit the top of the Jeep wagon with his gloved fist. "Damn it!" He turned away, then turned back. He stared miserably at her.

"My feet are getting numb. My fingers, too." She felt only dull, pulsing aching from her sprained right ankle.

"Damn it! We shouldn't have stopped! I'm the one who wanted to stop."

"I'm glad you did. I would have frozen to death if nobody else had come by."

"Yeah, maybe." He took a deep breath. "I can't let you die out here. We've gotten in so far now . . . Come on!"

He helped Kimberly out of the Jeep and supported her as she hobbled through the swirling, blinding snow. She dragged her pack. "Th-thank you for doing this"—she remembered his name—"Ron. That Jerry wouldn't have."

"Oh, Jerry's okay. He's just too strict sometimes."

A concrete bunker loomed up ahead. There were no windows. The gray steel door had no handle or keylock.

Ron pressed his left hand against an orange plate inset in the heavy metal. A tiny shielded TV camera Kimberly hadn't noticed peered down at them.

The door didn't open.

Ron began cursing. "Come on, Jerry!" He looked up into the TV camera. "Let us in!" He was shivering now, too.

Finally, the door opened silently.

They entered a small anteroom with a solid blue metal inner door. A single wire-caged bulb glowed in the low ceiling. Jerry's heavy gray parka hung from a metal peg on the unfinished concrete wall.

The outer door closed. Ron hung his coat next to Jerry's and said, "You have to stay here! We can't let you into the other rooms. And you have to stay on this side of this room. You're not to look in when the door opens for me. Understand? This is serious. This is the way it's got to be."

It was cold in the small entranceway, but not below zero, as it was outside. She nodded. "Sure. I don't want to get you into any trouble."

Ron smiled. "I'll be right back with some hot coffee and a sandwich for you. I can probably find a cushion or something for you to sit on."

"How long am I going to be here?"

"A couple hours, maybe. Jerry thinks he can insert an entry in the— Well, I'll probably be able to drive you to Elking in a while, that's all." He paused. "I—we have to look through your pack." He smiled an apology. And Jerry wants to see all your ID."

"What for?"

He was embarrassed. "You might be a spy."

"Well, in that case, I'd better tell you there's a Nikon in my pack, and it has half a roll of pictures of beautiful downtown Roseburg in it." Kimberly handed over her wallet and backpack. "Is this some kind of top-secret government research station or what?"

"Just don't ask."

"Okay. But I do have to ask to go to the bathroom. My back teeth are starting to float, and I need to do some other things."

Ron scowled. He rubbed his neck. "Jesus! I don't know . . . I'll ask. Stand over there."

When she had moved so that a view into the inner room was impossible, Ron pressed a yellow button in the jamb of the blue inner door. The door clicked and opened a few inches. He pulled it open and passed through with her things. A second later, it clicked shut.

"Huh!" Kimberly fingered the knife in her coat pocket and sat carefully on the cold concrete floor. Her ankle was hurting again. She waited.

Ron returned ten minutes later with her pack and wallet. "Jerry thinks you're probably okay." He pulled a scarf from his pocket. "I had to really argue for you to get him to let you go to the latrine. I have to blindfold you. And I'll lead you to it and wait outside. When you're finished, you call me in, and I'll put the blindfold back on and lead you back here."

She nodded. "Anything." She struggled to her feet. Her ankle nearly gave way. She grabbed him for support.

He tied the scarf around her head, covering her eyes. He took her hand. A few seconds later, they passed through the blue door.

Kimberly felt warm air and heard a low power hum. Suddenly, a line printer machine-gunned a message. She knew that sound; she'd worked part-time in the Oregon Medical School registration office.

They moved slowly. Ron walked beside her, guiding her, one arm around her waist. She limped badly.

Then her right boot caught the leg of a metal chair. She stumbled and involuntarily put a lot of weight on her right foot. Her ankle exploded in pain, and she lurched forward, pulling from his arm, off balance. The chair back hit her in the stomach. She tipped it over. Her arms flew forward reflexively to protect her face and head as she fell. The movement of her fat, quilted coat sleeves brushed the scarf upward from her eyes.

She struck the floor heavily on her hands and knees. "Oh!" A sharp pain lanced up her thigh. She looked up at Ron, who was gaping down at her. She held up a hand. "Help me. I think I cracked my kneecap or something."

She heard Jerry yell, "Close your eyes! Ron, you fucking moron! Get that blindfold back—"

But Kimberly had automatically turned her head to look at Jerry. He was seated before a console of TV monitors and switches. A big metal desk partially blocked a complete view. She did notice he wore sergeant's stripes on his gray shirt.

Jerry sat back in his swivel chair. "Oh, Christ! What a fucking mess!" He glared at Ron and Kimberly. "Get her into the latrine, asshole!"

She managed to get to her feet with Ron's help. The pain from her knee receded to sharp twinges, but her ankle continued to be agony. She hobbled beside him across the room and down a hall to a bathroom. They passed what appeared to be closed elevator doors.

As she relieved herself, Kimberly heard the men talking. Jerry was furious. "We've just bought ourselves twenty years in the stockade!"

"We were only—"

"Shut up, you fucking imbecile! I've got twelve years on the line here. I've got a cushy, premium-pay post for the first time in my life, and you—you fucking bleeding heart—"

"I only suggested— You made the decision to bring her up here! Just because we might be a few minutes late relieving Donaldson and Zilker—"

"Yeah! Yeah! I'm the rank here! So I have to make another decision, don't I? You sit there and think about what we've got to lose, and I'll make the fucking decision!"

"Let me call the lieutenant."

"Shut up! Let me think!"

After that, their voices got low—impossible to understand.

Kimberly took off her boot and examined her ankle. It was swollen and very tender to touch. Her knee ached but seemed okay now. She wrapped a wet, cold towel around her ankle and sat combing her brown hair.

She thought she heard Ron say, brokenly, "Oh, shit!" Then Jerry mumbled something more. . . .

She unwrapped her ankle, slipped on her sock, then, carefully, her boot. She found she couldn't lace tight the top hooks. She stood up and found she could put a little weight on her right leg. She washed her face and hands with paper towels and hot, soapy water. When she had her coat back on, she rapped on the wall and called loudly, "Hey, I'm finished."

A few seconds later, the bathroom door opened inward, and Jerry stood in the hallway gripping a long, thick military police truncheon. His blue eyes were terrifying. The end of the heavy club twitched as if alive with deadly purpose.

A chill of terror came to Kimberly. She lurched backward. "Am I under arrest or something?" Her hand crept into her coat pocket to grip the knife. He was going to hit her with that thing! He was going to kill her!

He said, "Come on out of there. I've got to take you to see the lieutenant." His voice sounded funny. Tense.

"Where is he?"

"About half a mile west of here."

"But I can't walk. I don't believe you. You get him to come here. Get him on the phone so I can talk to him." She was scared! Something deep in her mind was screaming for her not to trust this man. She could almost smell his fear. He was ready to kill her! She called, "Ron? What's going on?"

Ron answered from the main room. "Go with him. It's okay." But there was something wrong with his voice, too.

Kimberly asked desperately, "What's going on? Is this part of some secret missile base? I won't tell anybody! I promise!"

Jerry's voice shook as he said, "It's even more secret than that. I'm sorry. Jesus Christ, I'm sorry." He lunged through the doorway and swung the truncheon at her head.

She ducked, screaming, and jerked her hand from her coat. She lurched forward and dodged sideways, her throbbing, uncertain ankle making her moves extra erratic as she tried to get around him. She pressed the release button on the knife and whipped out four inches of two-edged steel blade.

The truncheon clanged off a floor-to-ceiling pipe six inches from the painted concrete wall, throwing Jerry off balance.

As she passed him, Kimberly sobbed and slashed backhanded at his arm. The gray cloth of his shirt parted, and the blade opened a red gash in his flesh.

She was abruptly in the narrow hallway. She cried, "Ron, help me!"

In the main room, Ron stared at her with suddenly lifted, tortured eyes. He was sitting in the chair she had earlier tripped over. He didn't move.

Kimberly saw a pink elevator button beside the inset elevator doors. She frantically hit the button with her fist. She put her back against the doors as Jerry emerged from the latrine, gritting his teeth. Blood trickled down his arm, staining his shirt, but he still gripped the heavy truncheon. As he came for her again, the elevator doors suddenly opened.

Kimberly fell backward and cracked her head on the linotile floor of the cage. She lay dazed, unable to move, the knife loose in her hand.

She saw the control panel. There were two vertical offset rows of numbered floor buttons. The lowest button was numbered twenty-four.

Then Jerry came into the elevator and viciously swung the truncheon downward. Her consciousness exploded into fire and blackness.

Kimberly's awareness of self returned faintly, episodically, as her head bounced on the floor of a fast-moving car. Her head hurt terribly and felt weirdly bloated. Each jolt of movement caused a hammer blow of agony, but she couldn't even moan. Everything was disconnected. She passed out.

Her dark mind swam up to semiawareness as she was dragged from the car. A male voice was cursing. "The sonovabitch didn't have to kill you. He didn't have to kill you!"

Then she was rolling down a rocky, snowy incline. She came to rest against a young fir tree. She welcomed the lack of movement, the quiet, the peace. The terrible pain in her head faded. She lost consciousness again.

Her body's uncontrolled shuddering brought her up from the soft darkness. The pain in her head was dull and heavy. In addition, there was pain in her left cheek.

She managed to open her eyes. It was deep twilight. Snow covered her outflung arm and both legs. The young fir had sheltered her torso and head. She was still dressed. Her coat was open.

She discovered she could move her legs. When she lifted her head, she shrieked from great throbbing lances of excruciating pain.

But she had screamed. She could move. She could think. She remembered. The bastards!

Kimberly managed to sit up. She grimaced and turned her head slowly. Her eyes kept going out of focus. She raised numb hands and felt the hurting place at her cheek. She gasped as she touched a jagged tear in her flesh. She discovered she could move her tongue tip through the gap.

She lifted her hands farther and felt of her head. Her hair was crusty and stiff. She cried out with sudden agony and horror as her clumsy fingers found a terrible oozing dent in her skull.

She wept for long minutes. But she didn't die. Gradually, a fierce rage came to her. She slowly changed position and began a laborious, painful crawl upward over the sharp, freezing-cold rocks.

An hour later, in full darkness, she feebly inched her way onto the glazed surface of the highway. She could go no farther.

A National Park forest ranger found her forty-two minutes later.

CHAPTER 4

CIA HEADQUARTERS, VIRGINIA
December 24, 1991

"YOU SURE YOU DON'T WANT SOME TEA?" EDWARD MARIN glanced at John Norris but didn't wait for an answer as he poured steaming water into a large "M"-initialed mug.

Norris slumped deeper into the steel-and-leather armchair next to Marin's large steel desk. His gray-green gaze drifted around the three-window, fifth-floor corner office of his section chief. He said patiently, "I shouldn't have been pulled out of London."

Marin smirked. He dipped a bag of mandarin orange spice herb tea into his mug. As he carried the mug to his desk, he said, "But your informant was killed, and you left his killer dead. The record-store clerk could easily identify you. And British intelligence was embarrassed."

"There is a hell of a lot more data needed on Newco's loans. I could have recruited somebody else."

"Perhaps, in time. But M-5 wanted you out. We have to cooperate with our allies, you know." Marin took a small white bakery bag from a lower desk drawer. "Maple bar?"

Norris shook his head quickly, disgustedly. He despised Edward Marin, a man one year older than he, at thirty-eight, but so pudgy and self-indulgent he looked ten years older.

Marin bit into a frosting-laden pastry and ignored Norris for a moment. Then he said, "They were angry. The problem was bucked up to the director, and he personally decided to bring you home."

"Then send somebody else back. I was just beginning to get a lead on where all that Salamat money is coming from. Newco is only a conduit."

"Ummm. A laundry. Yes, we'll follow it up. Don't worry."

Norris watched the fleshy tip of Marin's nose move as the man chewed another greedy bite of the maple bar. Norris stood up abruptly and walked to a large window. His heavy corduroy jacket shifted on his big shoulders as he ran long fingers through dark blond hair. He stared down at the parking lot. "Why am I being assigned to Ubari?"

"That will be fully explained downstairs on the morning of the twenty-eighth. You'll receive a full briefing. Until then, you have three full days of Christmas vacation. Enjoy yourself, John. If you know how."

Norris turned, tall and powerful, and smiled. "We have different luxuries."

Marin chuckled as he sipped his tea. "And different lusts." For an instant, his soft brown eyes turned cold with envy and hate.

His gaze met hot contempt in return.

CHAPTER 5

WASHINGTON, D.C.
December 24, 1991

VICE-PRESIDENT OF THE UNITED STATES JULIA WAGGONER stalked angrily into her suite in the Senate Office Building.

Brenda Ingram, an aide, looked up from a desk and said, "Mr. McDermott is in your office. He's been waiting about ten minutes."

Julia made a face. "I forgot. What does he want with me?" She didn't expect an answer. She instructed Brenda, "Call Wygant and tell him to never, ever ask me to talk to Roland Lewis about anything again! That old bastard— I don't care how badly the president needs votes for continuing our 'presence' in southern Mexico. Tell him the sexist and infinitely stupid speaker of the house won't listen seriously to anything a woman has to say, even if she is the vice-president."

Julia turned away and then added, "And tell him I want daily intelligence updates again. I want to see the same information the president sees. If they're trying to freeze me out or send me a message, they're going to have to tell me to my face."

Brenda nodded, making quick notes, smiling.

"Now go in and tell McDermott I'll be with him in a minute. I've got to go to the bathroom. And bring in some cheese and crackers . . . and some Tiger's Milk for me. Did he want anything?"

"I offered coffee and cookies. He declined."

Julia nodded and went through a doorway into a short hallway. She took a key from her small blue leather purse and unlocked a door. She entered her private bathroom.

Three minutes later, as she stood before the lighted mirror combing her graying blond hair, she wanted a drink. Some-

44

thing to slow her down, relax her for a few minutes. But wanting was not getting. She'd had her brush with alcoholism and heavy tranks twenty-two years ago, after her baby boy had died. Not even David's fatal heart attack seven months ago had been enough to tempt her into that numb existence again.

She sighed and put down her comb; she was losing too many blond and gray hairs. She examined her chin. Getting a bit droopy under there. She liked her pale blue eyes but not her thin, "aristocratic" nose. At five feet five inches, she was too short and at 113 pounds too slender to impress men. She hated to admit she looked older than her forty-four years.

She'd come a long way since her marriage to David, just out of UCLA. City councilwoman of Riverside. State senator. The first woman governor of California. And now the first woman vice-president of the United States of America. The big time. Hardball with the big boys. But they didn't really want her to play with them.

She applied a fresh coat of pale pink lipstick, fluffed her blond hair, tugged her skirt, tucked her blouse, slipped on her coat, and turned to the door that opened to her private office.

Lane McDermott put a sheaf of papers into his briefcase and rose from his chair when she entered. "Ah, Mrs. Vice-President." He appeared tall in a loose-fitting tweed suit that disguised his potbelly.

"Mr. McDermott. Sorry I had to keep you waiting. Roland Lewis can be difficult at times."

"No problem. I understand. I've had frustrating conversations with the speaker myself."

Julia sat at her desk and buzzed for Brenda. As the plump, sharp-eyed young woman entered with a tray, Julia asked, "Would you like a refreshment, Mr. McDermott? I'm forced to squeeze a nibble lunch into my schedule today, I'm afraid."

"Thank you, no. I've eaten." He smiled. He waited for Brenda to leave before speaking again. "I'll take very little of your time. I'm here to informally offer you memberships in the Foreign Affairs Council and the Transnational Committee." He took a small pack of lens tissues from his inner breast pocket and began polishing his gold-framed glasses. He waited for Julia's response.

He knew many things about Julia Fielding Waggoner: that she had played nearly world-class table tennis in her youth, that she had broken her right arm in a rock-climbing fall, that she loved medium-rare steaks, that her belly was marred by a ragged scar from the nearly botched cesarean delivery of her only child, and that when her blue eyes turned cold—look out!

Julia thought, Well I'll be damned! She said, "I'm flattered. But why am I offered these prestige memberships now? I'm in the third year of my term, and it's doubtful President Barr would pick me to run with him again even if he could run for a third term, which he cannot."

McDermott smiled and put his glasses back on. "This has nothing to do with politics. The membership committees have wanted to invite you to join for six years, but as you may not know, the memberships are strictly limited. Tremayne Harding's death allows us to now come to you."

Julia nodded. "It would be nice to be among the elite. The official Stoneman establishment."

McDermott looked pained. "That is one way of describing it."

She nibbled a cheese-cracker sandwich and sipped from a glass of Tiger's Milk. She knew there was a price to be paid for the memberships: following, overall, the Stoneman line, Stoneman policies. She would be expected to subtly and indirectly work for Stoneman. There were rewards: assured high-paying positions in Stoneman-controlled corporations, enormous consulting fees . . . And if she "worked out," it was possible the Stoneman economic and political power could be used to advance her political career—into the presidency. If that wasn't possible, she could be slated for a high cabinet position in the next administration. She would be taken care of handsomely for the rest of her life.

It was very tempting.

"Am I to be the token woman, Mr. McDermott?"

"Of course not. We value achievement and character. You have demonstrated a great deal of each. You are an exceptional person, Mrs. Vice-President, and we would like very much to benefit from your knowledge, experience, and if I may say it, your unique perspective as a woman.''

She smiled. ''You are a master complimenter.''

He cocked his head slightly and returned her smile. ''In this instance, it is sincerely sincere.''

They both laughed.

''Does Bradford Collier Stoneman have plans for me?''

''Mr. Stoneman does not control the council or the committee. We are groups of public-minded—'' He saw she didn't appreciate being fed the official PR line. He shrugged and smiled.

Julia said, ''This conversation is not being taped, Mr. McDermott.''

''I did not imagine it was.''

A silence lengthened.

Julia said, ''Thank you very much for the offers, Mr. McDermott. There are many aspects of these memberships I'll have to consider very carefully, as you know. May I let you know later what I decide? Is there any time pressure?''

''Of course, of course, take your time. But we would like some word—some indication—by the end of January.''

''Thank you. I'm very pleased to be offered such an opportunity.'' She stood up.

McDermott also rose and took up his briefcase. ''Thank you for taking the time to see me, Mrs. Vice-President.''

As she watched him depart, Julia saw him as an emissary from the devil. If she sold out and joined the hidden power structure, she knew she'd suddenly be treated with extreme respect, be listened to during cabinet meetings and National Security Council meetings. Even that old bastard Roland Lewis, a longtime Stoneman cohort, might listen to her.

If she joined ''the team,'' she could probably influence policy in many areas. If she refused the offers, she would be iced out and would disappear after the 1992 elections. At forty-four, she was too young for that kind of oblivion.

Vice-President Julia Waggoner was tempted. She felt slightly sick to her stomach.

CHAPTER 6

CALVIN NORMAN BERGENDAHL, LEAN, WIDE-HIPPED, SPINDLY legged, dressed in an open shirt and lavender slacks, ruffled the twelve-year-old boy's curly black hair as they sat at the low, ornate wooden eating table. He leaned back against fat brocade pillows and murmured in halting Berber, "I have a pleasure night planned, Fari."

He slipped a fat purple grape into the boy's eager mouth, then slid his hand into the child's loose white robe. He caressed a rounded arm, the butterly skin of the waist, a plump silken thigh.

The boy flicked a wise dark-eyed glance up at Calvin's pale, self-indulgent face, at Calvin's long, straight white-blond hair and waxen skin. He nodded and smiled widely, letting juice from the grape dribble from his lips.

Calvin's gray eyes flared with sudden lust. He bent to kiss the boy's seductive mouth.

A yellow phone at the end of the table chirruped softly. Bergendahl froze. He jerked his head up and glared at the instrument.

The phone chirruped again.

He snatched it up and said in a deadly voice, *"What?"*

Colonel Djabo's rough voice blurted in clumsy English, "My low radar possesses five attack helicopters approaching from the south. They're away eleven minutes."

"Eleven minutes! Are you sure? How could they get so close?"

"All the way low behind the Tibesti Mountains."

Rage and fear coiled in Bergendahl's guts. Was this an attack by CIA mercenaries? The Russians? The Israelis? Bitter-

48

tasting fluid surged up his throat from his clenching stomach. He swallowed it back. His brilliant, warped mind lost focus for long seconds. He sat, paralyzed, refusing this reality.

Finally, he managed, "Whose are they? What type?"

"The . . . umm . . . the profile is for Russian Cherzov Z-3s. They may carry each twenty men plus four crew. That model is armed with sixteen Katruski rockets, five ninety-millimeter cannon, two waist sprayers."

Bergendahl felt a surge of confidence. A shiver of strange delight prickled his skin. "Only five copters? They must think us fools! Alert our soldiers. Arm the missiles. I'll be there in a few minutes." He tabled the phone and turned to Fari, who had listened uncomprehendingly but knew something important had happened from Bergendahl's tone and expression.

Calvin said in halting Berber, "I must take care of intruders. Do not be afraid when you hear explosions and shooting. Do not leave our rooms."

The boy nodded, wide-eyed.

Bergendahl pulled on boots, took a heavy plylon bullet-proof jacket from his closet, and hurriedly left his luxurious living quarters.

Six minutes later, when he burst into the small defense center in the basement of the satellite control station, he was a different man. His face had hardened. His eyes glittered in the harsh light, the gray irises flared and dark.

Colonel Djabo was speaking quickly into a radio, setting out defense positions for his highly trained squads. He saw Bergendahl and pointed to a radar hologram sweep. The screen showed five blips moving apart from a tight formation.

Djabo put down the radio phone. "Where have you been?"

Bergendahl snapped. "Don't question me! I am in full command here. I've been in the control room checking on the location and security of the Sword. We tried to send an orbit change, but it was out of range. If there is a coordinated attack, it will fail up there, at least. The Sword has defenses against anything in space." Bergendahl studied the radar hologram. He touched the shoulder of the youth manning the instrument. "How close are they?"

The young technician said, "They are sixteen klicks far. Fourteen. They try to disrupt and fool our radar." He adjusted a dial and snapped in a second, then a third radar scan mode. "I have them. They fly slower than Z-3s' attack-only capability. They must be possessing full loads."

Bergendahl nodded. That implied a full complement of attack troops and their equipment. But how many?

"They land at twelve klicks. Three separating."

The two down helicopters were undoubtedly carrying a cargo of return fuel for themselves and the other copters. That meant sixty assault troops in the other three. The low-flying copters would land and disgorge their commandolike squads for a three-pronged attack.

He moved to the missile console and watched the American-trained young man lock onto the approaching, heavily laden helicopters. He said, "Let them land. Wait until they begin to rise again, then destroy them."

Djabo overheard and asked, "Why? Why not kill them in the air?"

"I want some prisoners, if possible. I want information. They are undoubtedly Cubans from the Russian base in Madama. There may be a few Russians along. It depends on their objectives."

Djabo snorted. "They are giving our leader reasons to invade Niger. Gangara is a fool to allow this."

The young tech said, "Positioning. Ten klicks. Very low."

Bergendahl watched the advanced hologram screen, fascinated, as the three Russian copters converged on Wau el Maradi. He replied to Djabo, "The world is full of fools. But Gangara may not even know of this. The Russians want more than simply to destroy this place. See? They are landing! *They* want prisoners. *They* want information. They want *me*!" He laughed wildly, an edge of madness in his tenor voice.

"Seven klicks. Two landed. Three."

"Now, in a moment, the copters will rise to attack our perimeter. Then we will hit all the copters and leave those soldiers on the ground without retreat, eight hundred miles from their base!"

Colonel Djabo smiled. "A good plan. My men have their M-21s equipped with starlight scopes and heat-sight lasers."

Bergendahl looked around at his defense commander, grinning. He squeezed the shoulder of the missile tech man. "When the copters rise—"

The young man tensed. "Their number one is coming up." He flicked two switches and pressed a red LAUNCH button. The roar of the Panther missile leaving its tube penetrated solid ground and thick brick walls to the basement defense room.

The missile tech loosed five missiles in quick succession.

Bergendahl and Colonel Djabo watched intently as the large radar depth screen tracked the missiles toward their targets.

A third technician had turned on television screens monitoring every quadrant of surrounding desert. He called, "East!"

Bergendahl flicked his gaze to the dark east screen and caught a white and red flare beyond the low, nearby hills. His gray eyes flicked to the other dark screens and saw similar silent, colorful, distant explosions.

Then, in the south screen, two golden red balls of fire lit up the far night sky.

He felt a fierce, swelling exaltation. A glance at the radar screen showed all five blips had disappeared. The tech switched through the four highly sophisticated radar modes to make sure the copters were gone. He was grinning.

Then the rumbling of the missile strikes reached them. Bergendahl laughed in triumph. He clapped Djabo on the back and pranced around the low-ceilinged, brightly lit room. "We've got them! Their ground force is doomed."

Djabo said warily, "They are now fifty to sixty desperate, well-armed men, with nowhere to go—except here."

Bergendahl sat cold and bored in the command Scout next to Colonel Djabo and listened to the officer direct mop-up operations against the scattered few Cubans remaining alive and mobile in the frigid night desert. It was three A.M.

He wore headphones and heard all the reports and orders

but could make little sense of them; the crack Berber soldiers spoke their language so quickly he couldn't follow.

Periodically, Djabo translated in short bursts of awkward English. "They use obsolete infrared equipment for targeting. It makes them the targets. . . . Fifteen killed of them in R-6 wadi. . . . Seven dead on the dawn ridge. . . . We haven't lost a man. . . . Nalut's squad has a Russian prisoner!"

Calvin said quickly, "I want him brought in. I want to question him!"

Forty-five minutes later, he strode cockily into the base garage and spotted the slumped Russian tied to a girder post next to a damaged Scout. Two Berber soldiers accompanied Bergendahl. They carried no weapons.

The Russian was a small, slender man. His Cuban army uniform was torn and soiled, but a Soviet science officer insignia had survived.

There were six other prisoners, Cubans, two of them wounded, bound with wire, sprawled on the filthy concrete floor. Berber guards stood alert nearby.

Bergendahl stopped six feet from the exhausted Russian. "Do you speak English?"

The man slowly lifted his head. A purple bruise mottled his high forehead. A trickle of blood from a scalp wound stained his thin blond hair and darkened the collar and left shoulder of his jacket. Wire-rimmed, round-lensed glasses hung askew on his nose. He answered, "Yes."

"Ah." Calvin nodded. "That speaks volumes. Do you know your force has been wiped out? Only you and these few Cubans are left alive."

"I know."

"What's your name?"

The Russian licked his lips and kept silent.

Calvin waited a few seconds, then turned away. He said in Berber to the two soldiers who had entered with him, "Make him willing to talk."

Seconds later, the Russian began screaming. Metal clanged on metal. One by one his fingers were being smashed on the girder post by large ball-peen hammers. Finally, he screamed, *"Yes, yes!"*

Bergendahl turned from contemplating a Scout whose engine hung from a chain hoist above the gaping, wire-strewn cavity. He signaled the men to stop the torture. He watched the Russian's twisted, agonized face. The man quivered helplessly, drooled saliva, and sobbed with shock and pain. Strings of snot hung from his nostrils. Blood flowed from his mangled fingers.

Bergendahl picked up the man's glasses from where they had fallen to the concrete. They weren't broken. He toyed with the wire stems. "What's your name?"

"Os—Oskal. Boris."

"Boris Oskal. Boris, your leaders are so stupid! We're working to help the socialist world. We're working to wipe out the capitalists."

"I follow orders."

"And I give them. You were sent to capture me, weren't you?"

"If . . . possible." Boris snorted and coughed. Extreme pain trembled his voice.

"Are you a specialist in satellite computer technology?"

"Yes."

"And what was your mission? What was your timetable?"

"Capture . . . capture the station . . . and you . . . and your team. We were to take command of—of the satellite and discover the programs and codes." He fell silent, then whimpered, "M-my hands . . ."

"Your hands are bleeding badly. What was planned for me after *my* capture?"

"I don't know. Please—"

"How many Russians were there on this stupid attack?"

"Fourteen. A computer team. Technicians." Boris sagged. He went to his knees, screaming as his bound, ruined hands were dragged down the steel post behind him. He whispered brokenly, "I . . . can't . . ." He knelt in a pool of his blood.

"Amazing. A full computer team. Were they in one of those Cherzov Z-3s that landed first?"

"Yes."

"So. I see. You wanted the Sword! You wanted to take it over! And *I* would have been the one tortured! Yes. Once you had the codes and frequencies and possessed a printout of the data matrix, you could have programed computers in Russia—and controlled the Sword from there! Was that the full plan?''

Boris gasped weakly, ''Yes. . . .''

''Very good. Bold. Clever. But we had far superior weapons, didn't we? *Didn't we?*''

Boris Oskal didn't answer.

''You Russians! Except for brute-force operations, you are incompetent. It must be your Mongol heritage.''

Oskal tried to say something.

Bergendahl squatted in the dying man's blood to better hear. ''Are there backup forces on the way? Boris? Is another attack coming? How many long-range copters are there left in Madama?'' Bergendahl lowered his head close to the Russian's. He lowered his voice to a gloating whisper. ''I'll tell you something, Boris. Something. . . . Do you know, even Abu Ben Salamat doesn't know the real capabilities or the final purpose of his wonderful Sword of Allah!''

But the Russian was unconscious, breathing very faintly.

Bergendahl spat at him. He stood and turned to the watching torturers. ''Do we have a soldier who can speak Spanish?''

One said, ''It is a second language for most. And French.''

''Good. Learn from these others, these Cubans, everything they know of the attack, of their base at Madama. Then kill them. Let this Russian die, if he isn't already dead.''

''We don't have a hospital.'' The soldier shrugged.

Calvin smiled. He walked out of the garage.

CHAPTER 7

WASHINGTON, D.C.
December 25, 1991

Sandra Timmons jerked awake when John Norris rolled onto his back and his left arm dropped heavily across her small, naked breasts. She glanced at the luminous clock on the night table beside the king-size water bed. Only three A.M.

Norris breathed slowly and deeply. But an occasional faint, protesting groan marred his sleep. Occasionally, a muscle twitch curled his fingers, tensed his belly, or moved his head.

She reached over and tapped the base of a lamp. Twenty watts of light came on. She turned slowly to the right and watched him. Some of the lines in his forehead smoothed when he slept. His mouth relaxed, too.

She watched the rise and fall of his deep, muscular chest. Dark blond hairs grew around his tiny nipples. Her blue eyes were caught again by the bullet-wound scar on his powerful shoulder . . . and again by the long, jagged knife scar running from left elbow to wrist.

She kissed his shoulder lightly. She loved this big, dangerous man. But she couldn't let herself love him totally. Someday he would be killed on one of his dirty, secret assignments. He wouldn't quit.

She knew he'd awaken soon. He rarely slept for more than three hours at a time. She didn't like that. She was a normal day person, an eight-hour sleeper, and he was like a tiger. He didn't even like to sleep under a sheet and blanket. He kept the thermostat of this expensive, luxuriously furnished apartment at a constant seventy-four degrees.

Sandra yawned and turned back to press off the light.

"Leave it on." He had awakened. His big left hand closed gently on one of her warm little breasts.

"I was thinking of taking a shower." She hadn't been, but the contrary, rebellious element in her character made her say things like that. She needed to oppose people, to frustrate them sometimes, in order to feel part of their world. To make them stop taking her for granted.

With John Norris, the impulse came to her frequently, because he was such a quietly overpowering, self-contained man.

His hand was capable of crushing her flesh, yet he had never hurt her in the slightest. She had watched him in his exercise room, wearing only a jock strap, his magnificent male body sheened and dripping with sweat, grunting and hissing with weights, trembling as he reached his limit, determined to extend that limit.

His hand caressed her breast tenderly, bringing the soft inner heat of arousal to her. He kissed her, and she shivered and met his tongue. Her nostrils flared as her lungs were suddenly starved for air. She felt the urgent size of him pressing against her naked hip and wanted him.

Sandra was ashamed of her quick response, her quick lust. It came from their year-long relationship since she had met him at a debriefing at CIA headquarters. She was a CIA analyst specializing in world political and economic affairs. She had succumbed to his silent, commanding need that first night.

She realized she had been conditioned to his voracious, sensuous lovemaking. When he returned from an assignment, he was greedy for everything—sunsets, fine food, music, the good new films and dramas, exhilarating sports like skiing and mountain climbing . . . and her slender body, her welcoming arms.

She yielded willingly as he came over her. Her resentments and embarrassments faded in the tide of her own need to give and to be possessed. She gasped as he entered smoothly, easily, and thrust so wonderfully deep.

She had no resistance or need to resist the wild pleasures that followed. He was both selfish and considerate, somehow always bringing her along, propelling her into the golden spasms of orgasm before his own shook him and forced guttural cries from clenched jaws. He was savage then. Had she not been in ecstasy, she would have been terrified.

When their breathing had slowed and his weight became oppressive, Sandra whispered, "I really do need a shower now."

"Okay. You first." He left the bed, picked up his robe, and padded into the living room.

She went quickly into the marble-walled bathroom and into the marvelous three-nozzle shower enclosure.

Ten minutes later, Sandra joined him in the kitchen. He had a pot of thick, rich Arabian coffee ready. She wore a short, white-ruffled blue calico nightshirt he had given her on her birthday in August.

She knew she would be awake for the rest of the night but didn't really care now. It was Christmas. She had brought along three presents for him when she had come over yesterday afternoon, after his call.

She sat at the butcher block table and slowly combed out her long, silver blond hair.

John stroked her head briefly before pouring her a small china cup of the syrupy coffee. "Your hair is like silk."

"It's too fine. I can't control it worth a damn."

He smiled. "I know." He pushed aside a tumbling cloud of hair and kissed her right ear. "And your breasts are too small, and your ears are too big. Poor flawed Sandy."

"I don't know why you have anything to do with me. You're so perfect—I mean it—and so demanding of yourself for perfection. Why do you want me? Why am I starting an argument?"

He sat opposite her, chuckling. "You don't want to be too happy with me."

She made a face and sipped the hot, heavily sugared coffee. "I'm going to need something to go with this dynamite." She went to a cupboard and took down a package of thick oatmeal cookies. "Want some?"

"Yes." He opened the thin blue venetian blind covering the wide kitchen window and stared out at the city. "Great. Freezing rain."

She returned to the table with some cookies on a plate.

"I'm glad I don't have to drive to work today. Tomorrow, though—"

Norris said wryly, somewhat bitterly, "The world never stops doing stupid, dangerous things that require constant recording, filing, and analysis. Your job is secure."

"And you keep trying to undo the stupid, dangerous things." She fed him a piece of cookie. "Which means dealing with stupid, dangerous people."

He nodded, chewing.

"Why?"

"It has something to do with compensating for being a second-class child. I never told you I was an orphan, did I?"

"No."

"It's an experience every child should miss. Especially in Sioux City. It makes you keenly aware of injustice, and you grow up either doing it or fighting it."

Sandra felt her throat tighten and tears start. She blinked rapidly and said, "Wouldn't it be nice if we could pick a few good people, go into space, and start over again on another planet?"

"Sure. Trouble is, good people don't always stay good. And the usual proportion of their children grow up to be stupid and dangerous."

"Well . . ." She tried to change the subject. "Even space is dangerous now. At least for Russia."

Norris looked curious.

She continued, happy to divert him with shop talk. "We received a report from our Horasan tracking station yesterday afternoon before I left. One of the Soviet Kazan-class killer satellites broke up—probably exploded—over Volvograd. Parts of it rained down on Orsk."

"Do we know why it exploded?"

"Not yet."

Norris grunted. "The Russians have been littering the rest of the world with pieces of failed satellites for over ten years. There's some poetic justice for you."

CHAPTER 8

WAU EL MARADI
December 25, 1991

BRILLIANT MORNING SUN GLARED OFF THE SIDES OF THE LARGE descending helicopter. The swirling sandstorm created by the hurricane downdraft from the two sets of powerful vanes caused Calvin Bergendahl to turn away and shield his face.

He was sweating in the ninety-five-degree morning heat, and he was very tired. The adrenalin high, the ego high, from the total defeat of the Cuban and Russian assault force had faded. Not even the Sword's successful defense of itself an hour after the ground attack was enough to keep him revved up. That additional triumph-induced flush of pride had melted, too.

Colonel Djabo stood proudly beside him, facing the abrasive blast of air, eager for the arrival of his commander and leader, Abu Ben Salamat.

The American GD-306 passenger copter touched down and settled on its wide, heavily shocked landing gear. The engines became a coughing mutter, and the rotors slowed, lowering the vanes to become menacing blades that swooshed low over the heads of Bergendahl and Djabo as they came forward to the opening door.

A set of steel steps slid down, and four elite Berber palace guards armed with M-18 auto-rifles darted out to flank the doorway.

Calvin and Djabo waited. The suspicious palace guards raked them with hard black eyes.

Finally, Abu Ben Salamat appeared. He wore a tailored camouflage jump suit with a holstered sidearm. His black boots shone with a high polish. He extended his hand to Bergendahl as he stepped down. "I viewed the wreckage of the Russian helicopters. Very fine. Very fine.'' His piercing dark eyes crinkled with pleasure. His salt-and-pepper beard was perfectly trimmed. His thin lips spread in a smile.

"Thank you, your Excellency." Bergendahl was surprised again at how short was the savage dictator of Ubari.

Salamat nodded. "And the Sword? Safe? No more attacks upon it?"

"No, your Excellency. It would take the Russians days to maneuver another hunter-killer satellite into a proper orbit for another attack. The United States may be about to try, however."

"The Sword blew the Russian satellite out of the sky! Eh? Very fine! I must meet your team and congratulate them."

"We are at your command, your Excellency." Calvin hated this subservient role, the constant smiling, the bridle on his own importance. But that would change! Soon the entire socialist world would hail him, fawn over him! Salamat would crawl to him and kiss his feet! Calvin Norman Bergendahl would be recognized as the savior of mankind!

Salamat turned and embraced Colonel Djabo. "My friend. My third arm! My new general! Eh? You like that? You are now a general!" He laughed. "You and your men deserve a reward!"

Calvin was quickly ignored as army officers descended from the copter, followed by government officials in suits and ties.

Seething, Bergendahl followed Salamat and Djabo toward the garage where the few Cuban survivors were imprisoned and guarded in a lube pit.

Calvin knew why he was being treated like camel dung: It was because of his love for Fari. He was viewed as unclean, as a violator of fundamental Moslem law. An exclusive user of boys was not considered a man. A man fathered sons! A man kept a wife. A man might occasionally discreetly seek pleasure with a boy, but it was not love! It was insignificant unless the man preferred the boy to women!

Calvin kept his resentment and hate carefully hidden. Salamat was using him, but above all, he was using Salamat.

One of Salamat's uniformed aides dropped back in the

procession and said to Calvin, "The leader wishes to inspect and question the prisoners with only his general and advisers present. He knows you are tired from the long night and will call you to him in the afternoon. You may rest until then."

"But I'm the one who directed the defense! I decided when to attack with the missiles! I defeated the attack! And there are things to be said about the prisoners. I—"

The aide said fiercely, "You will obey the leader!"

Calvin took a deep, quivering breath. "Yes. I'll be in my apartment."

But he went first to the satellite control room. The two Berber guards at the door stiffened slightly to greater attention at his approach. They kept their eyes from him after that first recognition.

He pressed his right thumb to a sensor plate and then directly faced a ruby light laser scan for a computer match of the recorded patterns of the blood vessels in his eyes. The door clicked open, and he entered air-conditioned coolness.

Hans Lichtner sat before a long bank of television monitors and computers. His moustache drooped over the corners of his mouth. His brown eyes showed weariness. He gestured loosely at a TV screen. "Self-important swine, isn't he?"

The color screen showed Abu Ben Salamat looking down at the huddled, bound Cubans in the lube pit. He was flanked by his entourage.

Lichtner asked, "Want to listen?"

Calvin crossed to the padded swivel chair farther along the extensive console. He slumped down and replied, "No. Anything new?"

Hans flicked his gaze at rows of instruments and checked a printer. "Should be over Melbourne by now. It'll be forty minutes before we can get a status check. Everything was perfect the last pass."

"Anything interesting on the USAM bands?"

Lichtner shook his head. "The usual weather data. No heavy military squirts. They're counting down on schedule for their new space shuttle launch." He got up and went to a refrigerator in the corner. "Want a Coke?"

Calvin nodded. He caught the cold can Lichtner tossed to

him. "They could launch with a thousand pounds of extra fuel. They could have installed a missile."

"We'll know if they are mounting an attack if they go to a low orbit."

"Tape the launch broadcast." Calvin popped his can and swigged the cold, throat-burning drink. It refreshed him. He rolled his chair to the TV monitor controls and switched to the secret cameras in the special apartment maintained exclusively for Abu Ben Salamat's occasional use.

Soldiers were busy searching the rooms. Calvin laughed. "The bastard doesn't trust anyone."

Hans said, "Neither do we. That's why George runs a scan of this place every day."

Calvin switched from room to room in Salamat's apartment. The hidden pinhead cameras and mikes all worked. He said, "Program taping for every one of his rooms from the moment he enters. Tell Jonas to personally monitor Salamat as much as he can." Then Calvin asked, "Has Pedro finished the Theta Pinch field math yet? I'll need it soon."

"He's on schedule. It's in the Z-15 bank if you want to check it over."

"I'm too fucking tired. I'm going up and get some sleep."

"I will, too, as soon as Jonas relieves me."

Calvin yawned and stood up. He raised his right fist. His eyes glittered. "Fifteen days!"

Lichtner's languid manner changed. He grinned ferociously and raised a fist. "The death of capitalism!"

Fari shook Bergendahl awake when the yellow phone made its funny sound, as he had been told to do. Calvin rolled over and fumbled for the extension on the wall over the low bed. He slurred into the receiver, "Yeah?"

A strict male voice—the military aide—said crisply, "The leader will speak with you in ten minutes. Come alone."

"Ummm. Yeah. Okay." Calvin lay staring at nothing in particular for a moment. Finally, he noticed the deepening yellow light that filtered through the closed drapes over the bedroom's west window. He glanced at his watch. Almost four o'clock. He muttered, "Shit!" and struggled to get up.

He was dopey from having been abruptly awakened from a profoundly deep sleep.

Fari handed him a clean white shirt. Calvin smiled and kissed the boy as he briefly fondled the youth's firm, round bottom. "Tonight, sweet one."

Eight minutes later, Bergendahl was ushered into Salamat's apartment.

Salamat waved away all the military men and advisers. "I will speak with Mr. Bergendahl alone. Out. Out!"

When the last of them had exited and closed the door, Salamat motioned to Calvin to sit in a high-backed chair close to him. "I know you were the—the mind behind the defeat of the Russian attack last night. General Djabo was generous and honest in his praise of you. You are the master of the Western technology we possess."

Calvin glowed. He smiled and decided to be diplomatic. "The primary credit is yours, Excellency. You provided the equipment and, above all, the magnificent fighting men who learned quickly to use the equipment and the weapons. Because of you, the Russians and Cubans were totally surprised. They didn't have a chance. Just like that CIA spy we killed on the twelfth."

"Yes. But I would prefer to keep CIA spies alive for my private questioning in Aozid. And I am disappointed in the death of the Russian science officer last night."

"Excellency, I made a full report of his statements."

Salamat folded his arms. "Yes. I have questioned the guards and the soldiers who applied the torture. They confirm your report. But they are being punished for choosing that fatal, crude method. I cannot punish you, Mr. Bergendahl, because you and your team are too valuable to the operation of the Sword and to the plan. But you are too . . . ruthless. There is that in you—a fanaticism—which is not at the mercy of your mind."

"I am a scientist, Excellency. I use my science in the furtherance of our common goal."

Salamat nodded warily. "I find I must trust you and your team of ideologues, and I do not like it. I do not like your insistence that only you and the six other foreigners are permitted in the Sword control room.''

"My team and I are the only ones qualified to be in that room, Excellency. I cannot permit ignorant soldiers in there touching computers, looking through papers, disturbing our concentration. Why should they be there? To spy on us for you? How would they know what we were doing?''

Salamat grimaced sourly. "Very well. Let us talk of the plan. Is the Sword ready?''

Calvin nodded. "It's on schedule, your Excellency. We're testing the capacitors, the plasma systems, the command cycles. And we know the Sword can defend itself. We know we can alter its orbit by program or by direct command from here, to make it nearly impossible to find.''

"If that is so, how did the Russian hunter-killer satellite find it?''

"That was our error. We were trying to save maneuvering fuel and kept it in an unaltered orbit for three days. The Russians have thirty-four operational armed satellites in near space. I think they were lucky, and I think they coordinated with the United States in the attack. They had to have been fed information from the U.S. military tracking network.''

"What will happen next? Will the Americans attack?''

"I think so, in space. But the Sword has the best American missiles on board, and advanced, state-of-the-art computers. It will be two years at least before they can put up anything to match the Sword of Allah!''

Salamat smiled and nodded, pleased. "And we will meet our day of power and glory on January sixth?''

Calvin said, "Yes, your Excellency. You will be master of the world twelve days from now.''

Salamat threw his head back and laughed.

CHAPTER 9

JOSEPHINE COUNTY, OREGON
December 25, 1991

IT WAS SNOWING HARD AGAIN. AT LEAST A FOOT OF SNOW HAD accumulated in the looming, ghostly, forested hills. Winds of twenty-five miles an hour built high drifts. The state snow plow had scraped the highway the day before, but in another hour or so the blacktop would be invisible and driving extremely dangerous.

Josephine County Sheriff Jackson O'Brien peered out through the flake-spattered windshield of the patrol car. He asked Deputy Bill Rouse, the driver, "You sure it was around here?"

Rouse slowed the car. The rattle of tire chains lowered in pitch. "Yeah. About a mile past Big Bear Creek bridge. The girl remembered the bridge. At least that's what she told the ranger who found her, and that's where I found the old side road yesterday. I followed it up— Damndest thing I ever saw in this country. Looked like a blockhouse up there, like some of those pictures of World War Two."

"Well, we'd better find that road"— O'Brien checked the three following county cars filled with deputies—"or Judge Culda'll have my ass for supper."

"It's just around this curve, I think. Shit, all this plowed snow on the shoulder is going to make getting—"

In the swirling white gloom ahead, red flashing lights appeared, and then a solid roadblock of six state police cars.

O'Brien said, "What the hell is this? Did you tell—?"

"Shit, no! Maybe that ranger reported to somebody after he called us. Or the hospital."

When Rouse stopped the car close to the wall of state cars, O'Brien zipped up his blue parka and got out. His three carloads of deputies had braked in a line. He motioned the men to stay inside.

A state police officer emerged from one of the highway patrol cars and clumped over to him. "Go on back, O'Brien. We've got jurisdiction here."

O'Brien recognized Capt. James Ferris, in command of the southern Oregon division. "Yeah? You mind telling me what's going on?"

Deputy Bill Rouse got out of the county car and joined the sheriff.

Ferris said patiently, "I told you the state's taking over here. My orders are to turn you back."

O'Brien was baffled. "From what? Since when do you guys interfere with county felony crime?"

"My orders—"

"Fuck your orders, Ferris! You can't prevent me from investigating kidnap and attempted murder in my own county!"

"That's what I'm doing. And I can't tell you why. So get back in that car, drive back to Grants Pass, and forget this."

Bill Rouse asked angrily, "How did you know we were on our way out here?"

Ferris ignored him and said to O'Brien, "Call Salem if you want to."

"I will; depend on it! But right now I've got a search warrant and two arrest warrants in my pocket signed by Circuit Judge Culda that say I have a right and a duty, according to the state constitution and state criminal law, to go up a road off this highway and look into a serious crime. So get the fuck out of our way!"

Ferris shook his head. "We have jurisdiction."

Bill Rouse snarled, "You got something proving that? All I hear is a big mouth."

O'Brien used his arm to move Rouse back a step. "Take it easy."

Rouse gritted his teeth. "Christ's sake! I was up there yesterday. There's some kind of fort up there! Two guys in some kind of uniforms I never saw before came out and played dumb-shit games with me. Wouldn't give me their names, who they worked for . . . nothin'!"

Ferris folded his arms across his heavy jacket. He said, "I can't let you go ahead, sheriff. Under no conditions. So let's break this up. I don't know about you, but my nuts are starting to freeze."

O'Brien took a deep breath, looked around, past the blocking patrol cars, then met Ferris's gaze. "Have you been up that road?"

"Can't tell you that."

"Who ordered you to do this?"

Ferris hesitated. "One of my superiors."

O'Brien said, "Listen, two days ago, a girl was taken up that road to some kind of military base, and she was assaulted with intent to kill. She was then dumped further down this highway. They thought she was dead. Now, we've never heard of any base around here, so what do you know? What's going on?"

"I can't tell you. I have strict, specific orders. Maybe they're mistaken orders, but I'm following them to the letter. So just cooperate, please."

O'Brien counted the state highway patrolmen in the six cars. Twenty-two.

Ferris seemed to read his mind. "Don't push it. I'll order my men to shoot if I have to."

"That would make interesting headlines."

Beside him, Bill Rouse muttered, "If it was allowed to make the headlines."

O'Brien made a decision. "Okay. I'm sending my deputies back to Grants Pass. But me and Bill here are going to drive on to Twisted Creek Hospital. Would that violate your orders?"

Ferris shook his head. "Just so you don't try to go up that road."

"Agreed."

An hour later, Sheriff O'Brien stood beside the desk of Howard Franks, chief surgeon and director of the thirty-bed Twisted Creek Hospital, and asked incredulously, "Why in hell didn't you call me?"

"Why should I? She was remarkably coherent, lucid, and sane. I was assured—"

"A half-frozen girl is brought in here with a severely fractured skull, the victim of kidnaping, assault with intent to kill, and you let her sign herself out of your hospital the next day?"

"Wait a minute. She didn't tell me she'd been assaulted. Her lawyer said—and she confirmed it when I talked with her—they both said she'd slipped on ice beside the highway and fallen on some rocks."

"That isn't what she told the ranger who found her."

"Well, I didn't know that. She arrived here unconscious. The ranger didn't tell any of that to the emergency-room nurse."

"Wait a minute! What lawyer?"

"I told you, there was a high-powered lawyer here this morning representing her. I didn't have any choice. He was quoting law at me like—" Franks rummaged in the center drawer of his desk. "I've got his business card here." He found the card and read, "Arthur Webber Albertson of Albertson, Benter, Keller, and Petroski. San Francisco." He handed the card to O'Brien. The card was heavily embossed and expensive.

"So who hired him? How come this guy showed up so quick?"

"He said he was engaged by her brother in Gull Junction. I don't know why he flew up so quickly."

"You just let an expensive lawyer come in here and take a critical patient from your hospital? Didn't she need medicine and constant attention? Hadn't she lost a lot of blood?"

Howard Franks took up a folder from his desk. "Kimberly Ellen Beales. She needed two pints of type O blood. She had a badly sprained ankle and a severely torn left cheek, a lacerated right ear, various abrasions. The traumatic compound fracture of her right frontal cranium required extensive team surgery to relieve pressure on the brain and to prevent further hemorrhage. We stabilized the—"

"And you just let her walk out?"

"Don't be absurd! She left in an ambulance and was taken to Carter's Helicopter Service. There—"

"What?"

"—she was placed on a very impressive ambulance helicopter and flown to Grants Pass. At Grants Pass, she was transferred to a medical jet and left for San Francisco Memorial where she will be given the complicated, specialized surgery and treatment she requires and which we cannot perform here. I was going to send her to Grants Pass today, anyway."

O'Brien stared down at Franks, speechless. Finally, he asked, "You checked on the jet? Did you call San Francisco Memorial?"

"Of course. They were expecting her. I talked with Dr. Daniel Butteridge, the chief surgeon, and filled him in on her condition as fully as I could. I also called her brother to confirm the arrangements. He is her legal guardian until next year."

O'Brien gestured in frustration. "Jesus H. Christ! This stinks. The whole business—"

Franks said defensively, "The severe skull fracture did not affect her mind. She was able to think and speak clearly, sheriff. She signed herself out. She did not appear to be under any duress. She was apparently very happy with Albertson."

"Yeah. Big money buys a lot of happiness." O'Brien turned away and left Franks's office. He stamped out of the small hospital to the car.

When he got in, Bill Rouse asked, "Were you able to talk to her?"

"Nope." He told Rouse what Franks had told him.

The deputy was enraged. "You know what that sounds like to me? It sounds like we've got some kind of high-level conspiracy going on here. If they've got to the state police—"

O'Brien nodded. "Yeah. The federal government . . . or some big, powerful corporation. This really gets me. I've got a good, clean little county, and now this comes down. Some lousy cover-up . . ."

"I'll betcha they've gotten to that ranger by now, too. He'll probably change his story now."

"Wouldn't be surprised." The sheriff rubbed his eyes. "Come on . . . back to Grants Pass. I've got some phone calls to make."

CHAPTER 10

KIMBERLY KNEW SHE WAS FULL OF PAINKILLERS AND OTHER drugs, dripped into her veins from two IVs. Her mind was like a soup—a mixture of pain, whooziness, anxiety, tranquillity, and anger.

Her head was bandaged heavily from the skull-repair surgery the day before. She hated the fact that her lovely brown hair had been shaved. Her left cheek felt weird from the inside as she constantly tongue touched the sutures that held closed the awful wound inflicted when she had been dumped out of the Jeep wagon and rolled down that icy, rocky slope.

She liked Dr. Butteridge, the grandfatherly surgeon who had answered all of her questions fully and honestly before and after her six hours in the OR.

She did not now like the too-charming Arthur Webber Albertson, the lawyer who had conned her into leaving Oregon. He stood beside her hospital bed now, obviously impatient at this waste of his time but trying not to show it. He didn't have to be as smooth and charming now.

He shifted his briefcase from one hand to the other. "If you're not feeling well enough to talk, Miss Beales—"

"I can talk. I can think. I wanted you to come here so I could find out when I can go home." Her speech was slurred by her cheek and its tight bandages.

"Oh, well, that will depend on how soon you're able to travel."

"No kidding! I'll be able to travel in a week, if I go by medical jet. I want to stay with my brother."

"I seriously doubt—"

"I don't care what you doubt. I've talked with Dr.

70

Butteridge, and I know enough medicine to know I can convalesce at my brother's place if I have a visiting nurse check in on me every few days.''

Albertson tapped a finger against his worsted wool pantsleg. He looked about the private room. He finally met Kimberly's resentful brown-eyed gaze. "There are problems with returning you to that area.''

"What do you mean?''

"There are national security considerations. Josephine County has become a hotbed of antigovernment, anarchist activity, and your brother, Darrell Beales, is a leader of that activity.''

''You're crazy. All he and his friends do is live free. They live without taking handouts from the government and advocate others do the same. Since when is that anti-American?''

Albertson refused to argue. "We're not sure you'd be able to keep your knowledge of that secret government installation to yourself in that libertarian environment. We'd prefer you recuperated in Salt Lake City, with your parents.''

Kimberly shook her head as vigorously as she could. "We don't get along very well. They're brainwashed statists. I'm more at home with Darrell. Besides, he's the one who's putting me through medical school.''

"Nevertheless—''

"Listen, I don't know anything about that place! All I remember now is being picked up by two soldiers and given a ride up a mountain to some kind of pillbox—like the old Maginot Line of World War Two.''

"Kimberly, you were inside, and you saw equipment and facilities which signify a host of conclusions about that place. It would be best if you stayed here for a full recuperation and for the cosmetic surgery required to restore your cheek. After that—''

Kimberly felt cold rage. "Can I go back to Oregon or not? Am I a prisoner?''

"Of course you're not a prisoner. But you signed an agreement giving us medical guardianship and promising silence about your experiences at the installation in exchange for full medical coverage and a settlement of one million dollars. It's in your best interests to abide by that agreement.''

"I will abide by it! I won't tell anybody about that place. I'll tell Darrell and everybody what we agreed I'd say—that I was struck by a hit-and-run driver while I was hitchhiking. I'll keep my word! But I didn't agree to never see my brother again! Or never to go back to Oregon!"

"There's a fine medical school in Salt Lake—"

"No!"

Arthur Webber Albertson pursed his thin lips. He contemplated her for a silent moment. "If you violate the terms of the agreement, you will lose all the stipulated benefits. The money . . . and the plastic surgery. You could go through life with a very ugly, disfigured face. You could be blackballed from medicine in a way you could never prove."

"And you could probably kill me, too, just like Jerry tried to. To protect yourself and your precious secrets. Governments love final solutions like death. Your kind love to use absolute power over people."

He said, "Governments exist for the benefit of all the people."

"Please, don't try to make me laugh. It hurts me to even smile."

Albertson pulled a chair close to her bed and sat. "Kimberly, you're intelligent, young, and you'll be very attractive again. You have a fine future. Don't ruin your life. What happened to you is terrible, and your government accepts full responsibility for what happened and is more than willing to compensate you with the finest medical care and a handsome financial settlement. You're fixed for life. But in exchange you absolutely must stay silent about what happened and where."

She asked, "What are you going to do about Ron and Jerry?"

"They are in a special military stockade. They'll be court-martialed and imprisoned . . . for decades."

Kimberly frowned. After a moment, she said, "I'll keep my contract. I signed, and I knew what I was signing. But I'm going back to Oregon as soon as possible, to stay with Darrell. I'll fly down here for my facial surgery later, and it better be at government expense."

"It will be handled by a private medical insurance company whose premiums will be paid by a special military disbursement.''

Her eyes widened. ''Wow. Layers and layers . . .''

Albertson smiled. ''We'll take a chance on you, Kimberly. I hope you'll keep your word.''

''As long as you keep yours.''

CHAPTER 11

PRESIDENT WILLIAM T. BARR LIKED A NAKED FIRE. HE LIKED TO feel the heat of it and to hear the pop and crackle of burning wood. He loved the faint aroma of woodsmoke.

He nudged a flaming log into better position and racked the fireplace poker. He reluctantly turned to deal with the two men seated on the high-backed sofa.

Richard Soble, director of the CIA, and John Norris, top-grade field agent, waited for their president to respond to their arguments.

He said, "There's no proof. It could have been a Russian killer satellite."

It was Norris who said calmly, patiently, "The odds are a thousand to one the Salamat satellite got our h-k with a missile."

The president didn't like that. The man did not say "Sir" or "Mr. President" before speaking. And there was something in John Norris's gray-green eyes that disturbed—a deep self-assurance, a steel core—that made William T. Barr unconsciously aware that this man had killed too many men, had seen too much, to be impressed by any politician, no matter how high the office held.

The president said, "I don't like to think that a renegade Moslem dictator in northern Africa controls a sophisticated, armed satellite superior to our own."

Richard Soble said, "Neither do we, sir, but facts are facts. We put our hunter-killer in the area of space where our best people estimated the Salamat thing would be, and our satellite was blown to pieces."

"Speculation. Damned little hard information." The president returned to his chair. He picked up his coffee cup from the massive coffee table between him and the sofa.

Soble spread his hands. "I have soft information. Stories out of Niger are that about a week ago a group of Russian assault helicopters left their base at Madama loaded with Cuban commandos and didn't come back."

Soble continued. "Subsequently, there was some excitement in the palace at Aozid, and Salamat and a few of his top military men and cabinet officers flew down to the Wau el Maradi base on the morning of the twenty-fifth. They appeared very happy."

Norris added, "And the probability is that a Russian h-k was destroyed on or about the twenty-fourth." He gazed steadily at the president.

The president avoided those eyes. He grimaced. He pushed up the right sleeve of his cable-knit sweater and scratched a hairy forearm. "I put all that together, and I get a hell of a geopolitical headache. The implications are that if that satellite—what do they call it?"

Soble answered, "The Sword of Allah."

"If the Sword of Allah—Jesus!—if that thing has missiles capable of hitting American cities—and if it can't be destroyed—that suggests some international blackmail soon."

Soble responded, "Sir, if that satellite did possess such weapons, I'd think Abu Ben Salamat would have made his demands by now. The longer that satellite stays up, the longer we and the Russians have to shoot it down."

John Norris abruptly stood up, startling the president. Norris strode to the french doors to stare out at the countryside. He was unaware of being watched by both his director and the president. He said, "We could, like the Russians, mount an attack against the control base."

President Barr nodded. "True. In fact, gentlemen, if that madman attempts to force United States policy changes by threats, I will order a nuclear strike against that base, and to hell with Moslem goodwill, oil cutoffs, international financial consequences . . . whatever!"

Richard Soble nodded. "A threat of attack from space by

missile is a virtual declaration of war. That response would be justified, sir.''

The president smiled. "He must know that. Any president of the United States would act. I couldn't submit to blackmail. My party couldn't elect a dogcatcher if I surrendered. My God, Congress would impeach me!''

President Barr also rose from his chair. He paced toward the fireplace. "Can you see Julia Waggoner in the White House? I took her as my running mate out of political necessity, and the conservative wing of the party—and the nation—accepted her because I'm young and healthy. But I'm not about to hand her the presidency.''

John Norris turned and spoke. "More speculation.''

President Barr managed a laugh. "Right, Norris. I get lost in iffy crap sometimes. I'm going to get specific now. That's why you're here.'' He switched his gaze to Richard Soble. "Dick, I want to send Norris into Ubari. I want to give him a chance to find the recorder Tookey had before he was killed. The data on those tapes could tell us everything we need to know about Wau el Maradi and that damned satellite.''

Soble ran long fingers through graying hair. "That's a long shot.''

President Barr grinned. He cocked an eye at Norris. "Yes, but Norris has an exceptional ability to somehow perform miracles when necessary. I've read his record. An amazing man. That Riyadh mission of his two years ago, for instance.''

Soble was reluctant. "Sir, the risk—''

Barr was enjoying himself now. He liked discussing Norris as if the man were not present, listening. He liked the idea of sending the man into a very high risk situation. Something in him liked the prospect of sending the arrogant John Norris to his death.

Soble shook his head. "Sir, the satellite has been up there for at least seven weeks. If it had anything but short-range defensive missiles, Salamat would have acted by now. Our analysts don't think it possible that Bergendahl put anything really dangerous to us into orbit.''

Barr countered, "From your intelligence reports, the man is a genius.''

"Yes, sir, possibly in theoretical astrophysics. But as an engineer . . ." Soble shook his head.

President Barr crossed the room to his desk. He leafed through a sheaf of blue-paper reports. "You say here . . . Bergendahl recruited a team of brilliant revolutionary scientists four years ago and has had billions of dollars to work with." He let the papers fall back to the desk. "Now you're denying this? Why are you changing your tune?"

"Sir, I agree John should go into Ubari and try to recruit more agents. We do need more inside information from the palace. But to send him to Wau el Maradi is a virtual death sentence."

The president turned to Norris. "What do you say, John?"

"I'll do what you want."

The president would have bet he'd get that response, but he felt cheated at having gotten it. There was an undercurrent of contempt in Norris's tone. Barr turned back to Soble, smiling. "You're outvoted, Dick. It'll be John Norris to Ubari until or unless Salamat forces other moves. That's the decision."

Richard Soble said, "Very well, Mr. President."

John Norris left the room without speaking.

CHAPTER 12

AOZID, UBARI
January 4, 1992

Nahud Zella again shook his grizzled head. "I won't rent anymore." He crossed his arms and squinted at John Norris as they stood in the sun-baked shadow of the whitewashed office shack.

Norris pointed to a battered Scout on Zella's used car lot. "That one." He was being deliberately persistent.

Behind Norris, wearing wraparound sunglasses, April Weaver stood holding a thick green document file. She appeared bored and petulant as she constantly patted her long, beautiful brown hair and shifted from one sandaled foot to the other. Puffs of dirty desert wind fluttered her short white dress against her lush, perspiration-damp body.

Norris took out his wallet. He displayed an international credit card. "I'm Martin J. Singer. I'm with Vestel Films. See? I need a four-wheel-drive car like that Scout, to go out on the desert."

Nahud Zella nodded. "I understand. But I will not rent them anymore. I lose them that way."

"How do you lose them?"

"A month ago, a man, a mineralogist, he said, rented a Land Rover from me. My best. And he was a spy for your country, a CIA, and he was killed. My car was shot up and wrecked on the road to Sabha. The government even forbids me to tow it in for parts."

"Well, I'm not a spy! We're here to look for good filming locations for an Arab war movie. This is my assistant." Norris snapped his fingers at April. "Give me those Ubari permission papers."

She delved in the folder and pulled out government documents.

Norris took them and waved them before Zella's face. "This one—see?—is a permit to hire a Ubari guide for driving in the desert. This one and this one are permits to interview Ubaris for jobs in the film. We will use many Ubaris as soldiers in the film and a few others in small speaking parts. We will spend millions of dollars here. Your government approves my renting a car from you. You will make a lot of money renting us cars."

Nahud Zella remained adamant. "I do not have insurance now for renting. I lose too much. You must buy."

Norris turned away in apparent disgust and frustration. He handed the papers back to April. He glanced across the ill-paved street and saw a familiar dusty van with what he knew to be a shotgun mike mounted on the roof, pointed their way. The van had been following their taxi all day.

He said to Zella, "All right! How much for that old wreck over there? The Scout."

"Wreck? Wreck? It is in excellent condition! A new battery last month, a new wires set, a tune-up. It is worth much more than what I will ask from you. You insult that fine machine."

Norris noticed Zella's eyes flick at the van across the street. He said, "I don't insult the machine. But you insult my intelligence. How much?"

"In American dollars . . . in American dollars . . ." Zella scowled in concentration. "I ask six thousand dollars."

Norris rolled his eyes. "I can get a new Scout in the States for less than that! There's been a deflation on for eight years, you know."

"Then buy a new one—in the States."

Norris ventured, "Five thousand! But only if you agree to buy it back for forty-five hundred."

"Impossible!"

"We're only going to be here a week or two. Five hundred dollars is a good profit for you."

April Weaver asked plaintively, "Marty, how long are you going to argue with him? I'm sweating like a pig. Let's just pay that government man at the ministry to loan us a government car.''

Zella said quickly, "Government cars always break down. They never change the air filters.''

Norris said in exasperation, "I'll change the damn air filter, then.'' He turned away.

"Ah, American! Don't be so impatient. But I understand you are not used to our heat. It shall be as you wish. Five thousand, and I will repurchase at forty-five hundred—but only if the machine is returned undamaged!''

"Okay.''

Twenty minutes later, as Norris drove the weary Scout back to their hotel, he said, "That's a smooth old fox. He doesn't have Tookey's Rover, can't get it, and doesn't know if the recorder box is in the secret compartment or not.''

April wiped her forehead. "The way you men play at telling things. What now? I could use a cool bath.''

"I'm going to have to tap a source in the Ubari military. I've got to know if that box was discovered.''

"Isn't that risky?''

"We're in a high-risk profession.''

April said sarcastically, "Oh, very profound.''

"So is 'Isn't that risky?' '' Norris checked the rearview mirror. The van was following. "Our tail is still wagging.''

"And I'll bet our hotel rooms have more bugs than when we left. Do they know we're CIA?''

"They might. We have to play our cover, though.''

"Of course, but why is my cover always a mistress or an easy-lay secretary?''

Norris grinned. "You look the part.''

April nodded sourly. "When I was recruited, I expected more than bed and bored.''

"You may get more than that this time. Listen, I'm going to park at that French bakery in the next block. They have a phone. You go in and buy some obscenely sweet, gooey pastries, some cream puffs, if they make them. A small variety of stuff to eat in your room. And while you're in there, call seven-six-four-one, extension nine-two, and say you're calling for Martin Singer and try to set up an appointment for me to meet the defense minister. It'll be the wrong office in the ministry to have called. The man will give you a number to call. Remember that number! Thank him and hang up. Then come back to the car with your goodies."

April repeated, "Seven-six-four-one, extension ninety-two."

When she came out of the bakery, she was eating a long, golden-crusted, jelly-filled creation and was enjoying it immensely. She swung a white paper bag in her other hand. Her long bare legs whipped her short skirt. The sweat-dampened area of her bodice clung to her prominent, jiggling breasts. As she climbed into the old Scout, she said, "I like your assignments, Marty."

"You're a slut. A beautiful slut but still a slut." Norris started the noisy engine and pulled into the street. The trailing van had parked three spaces behind. They had been able to listen until the Scout's engine drowned their shotgun mike's reception.

April swallowed her mouthful of pastry and, laughing, offered Norris a bite while saying, "The number he gave me is five-three-two-eight, extension ten."

"Thank you." He stopped to let a string of heavily laden donkeys and their owners complete their crossing of the major Aozid street. He took a bite of the confection. "Ummm!"

The meaning of the numbers was this: Five meant tomorrow, the fifth of the month; three-two-eight—three meant a specific location, a brothel, two and eight were throwaway numbers; ten was the time of the meet.

When John started the Scout forward again, shifting noisily through the gears, he said, "Tomorrow night, about twenty minutes after nine, I'm going to make a pass at you. Give me an argument. Too tired, it's too hot, you're angry about something, whatever. I'll get mad and tell you off and say there's plenty of local talent around, and I'll leave the hotel."

"How long will you be gone?"

"I don't think over two hours."

"And if you don't come back?"

"Go to Marhut. And make damned sure you're not followed."

CHAPTER 13

NEW YORK CITY
January 5, 1992

HE STOOD FIVE FEET THREE INCHES TALL, WORE TWO-INCH heels on his black shoes, affected a gold-inlaid cigarette holder, disdained the "weak Western coffee" offered by Erica Stoneman, and kept his dark eyes almost exclusively on Bradford Stoneman. His name was Jebel Nukheila, and he was a secret emissary from Abu Ben Salamat.

He said softly, "I must speak with you alone, sir. It is a message of highest import and restrictedness I have to impart to you."

Bradford Stoneman studied the man further, lifted a trembling cup to his lips, and mentally cursed the nervous affliction that had in the past three days plagued his right hand. He nevertheless sipped the hot chocolate laced with brandy he had come to love every afternoon and motioned Erica to stay in the electronically secure conference room. It was the same room used for his weekly "insider" meetings with McDermott. He replied to Nukheila, "I choose to have my wife share the message, whatever it is."

"Sir, it pertains to the Sword of Allah, which rides in the skies of the world at this moment. It is a most significant event which is to come. I was instructed to speak of it only to you, alone."

Stoneman's fierce golden brown eyes narrowed with anger. "I will hear it with my wife present."

Erica stood calm and quiet beside Stoneman's thronelike chair. Her beautiful face was impassive, but her eyes danced at the Moslem's discomfiture. In Ubari, women were lesser creatures, never allowed in high councils.

The small man finally bowed his head. "As you wish. I

must first identify the Sword of Allah. It is a magnificent satellite thrown into the sky by Abu Ben Salamat to change the world. It is provided with weapons to defend itself against the attacks of the bear and the eagle. It has met these attacks and killed the devices of the bear and the eagle. The Sword of Allah reigns supreme in the skies.''

Stoneman nodded, his lined face a mask, giving nothing. He waited.

Nukheila continued. ''You may know this. You have fingers and ears in many places. But you do not know this: The Sword of Allah carries a supreme weapon never before seen on the earth or in the skies. That weapon is a beam of fire so powerful it can pierce the atmosphere as a needle pierces cotton, and it can burn a swath of destruction many meters wide on the earth below. Nothing can withstand it! Nothing can prevent it! It is invincible!''

Erica asked, ''A giant laser beam?''

Nukheila would not speak to her. His glowing black eyes remained on Stoneman.

Bradford Stoneman sipped his chocolate again. ''Go on.''

''Because of the great love Abu Ben Salamat holds for you, he has instructed me to inform you first of the Sword of Allah and its terrible weapon. When I leave you, I will fly to Washington and tell of the Sword to the highest officials of your country.''

''Your leader's consideration is appreciated.''

Nukheila bowed his head. He resumed. ''The great event will occur in two days, on January seventh. The beam of fire will strike an abandoned settlement in the Sinai, Sharm el Shula, as a showing . . . a demonstration, as you say, of its irresistible power and accuracy. The benevolence of Abu Ben Salamat is great. He does not wish to harm anyone. He does not wish to do great damage to an important place.''

Stoneman smiled. ''He only wishes to control the world.''

Jebel Nukheila shrugged. He carefully inserted a Turkish cigarette in his holder and lit up, using a gold-plated butane lighter.

Erica slid into the leather chair closest to Stoneman. She asked, ''What concessions does Salamat want from—'' She amended, "Are there other emissaries going to other capitals around the world?"

Nukheila flicked a shocked glance at her. She was sitting unbidden in the presence of her husband! And in the presence of a man of high standing in the councils of the mighty Abu Ben Salamat! He would never understand Western men. He chose to pretend Stoneman had asked the question.

"Twelve such as I are about to speak as I speak to you." He looked at a diamond-encrusted watch. "In four hours, our words will tell the highest of the high of the world of the Sword and of its power. Then they will know of Abu Ben Salamat's supreme power."

Erica said, "And what will Salamat ask of them?"

Nukheila asked angrily of Stoneman, "Does she speak for you?"

Amused, Bradford said, "Yes. Erica knows my mind."

Nukheila permitted himself a full stare at the Stoneman wife. She was strikingly beautiful with her long blond hair coiled in braids atop her finely modeled head, a diamond necklace at the throat, wearing a cool, mint-green silken dress. She sat proudly erect and, smiling, met his eyes.

He permitted a vision of her to briefly fill his mind: naked, on her knees before him, begging for his pole.

He wiped his mind clean. This old man was a fool to allow such a woman to intrude into crucial matters such as this. The leader would be interested in the senile decline of the great Bradford Stoneman. But he could not now offend this old fool. The humiliation must be endured. He puffed fretfully at his cigarette before speaking again.

Finally, he said, "I must speak bluntly. It is important to avoid confusions. Once the leaders of the world have witnessed the power of the Sword and are convinced of its invulnerability, Abu Ben Salamat, in his wisdom, will ask that the United States, Germany, France, England, Russia, China, India, Brazil, Argentina, Mexico, and Japan stop all financial and military support of Zionist Israel.

"Further, it will be asked that Zionist Israel yield all of its occupied and annexed Arab lands. This is the primary request. It is the most important and urgent request."

Bradford Stoneman squinted suddenly as a stab of pain lanced in his skull. It dulled quickly to a vicious ache. His vision blurred. He managed to ask Nukheila, "What other demands are there?"

"There must be a new policy favoring the holy war of Allah against the remaining dogs and infidels of Arabia. The shah of New Persia must be given arms and money in the forging of the new Moslem empire."

"That's asking a lot." Stoneman knew it was useless to argue with this self-important, arrogant little shit. Nukheila was only a fanatic messenger.

Stoneman's headache grew worse.

Nukheila carefully stubbed out his cigarette and inserted another in his holder. "It is considered a righting of wrongs. I am here first saying these things to you, things that will not be said to the leaders in Washington, because it is known that your power can help in these matters in Washington . . . and in other governments. It is recognized that your policies are often the policies followed in Washington."

"You flatter me."

"No, I think not."

"Are there any other 'requests' from Abu Ben Salamat?"

"The leader will require more money. After the great event at Sharm el Shula, other emissaries expert in money matters will visit you and arrange new loans at different rates of interest than presently apply. There will be a revision of the oil royalty scale. These are not my primary purpose. I simply alert you."

Stoneman pursed his thin lips. He raised his left hand to rub his liver-spotted temples. "That will have to be one hell of a convincing demonstration."

"Of course. The world will quail before the might of the Sword of Allah."

"If there is a demonstration. Has your leader considered the possibility of a first-strike demonstration by the United States or Russia?"

Nukheila smiled. "From this moment on, any—*any*—military move against Abu Ben Salamat or against the Wau el Maradi base of any magnitude—or *any* magnitude, I repeat—will result in the fire beam of the Sword of Allah being turned upon the major cities of what is so quaintly called the civilized world. The most populated areas of the United States and of Russia and of Europe would be burned.''

Erica said, "But if the control base is destroyed—"

"Stupid woman! The Sword is preprogramed! Now! Now! Now it is preprogramed! Unless our scientists at Wau el Maradi are alive to cancel certain parts of the program, the fire beam will burn this city—mighty New York—and destroy perhaps this very building!"

Nukheila's black eyes drilled contemptuously at her unperturbed gaze. "Do you think we are such fools not to know the first thoughts of the Israelis, of you Americans, and of the Russians? If we are attacked, the Sword will burn Israel a dozen times in a month! And Moscow! And London! And Paris!"

He paced beside the mahogany conference table. He calmed and addressed Stoneman. "How much do you love the Zionists? How many Americans will you sacrifice to allow them to keep the Arab lands they have stolen? How many before your people rise up and force you and your purchased leaders to do as we request?"

Bradford Stoneman said quietly, "There is great doubt among our military that your satellite is capable of anything but some degree of self-defense. And I personally wonder how long it can continue."

"Naturally your generals say that. They are so smug and superior in their delusion that no other people can surpass America. I can say to you as I will say to those I meet in Washington—the Sword of Allah has fuel and armaments to destroy all of your vaunted hunter-killer satellites. Its fire beam is fueled by the sun! It will rule earth for five years. In three years, Abu Ben Salamat will have a second mighty Sword in space. And any nation which attempts to test new space weapons of any kind will feel the leader's wrath!"

Stoneman felt dizzy. He closed his eyes, but the vertigo grew worse. He managed to say, "The base at Wau el Maradi was attacked the night of December twenty-fourth by a helicopter-borne force of Cubans, with a few Russians. They were wiped out. But why didn't your Sword of Allah retaliate against Russia?''

"It was not ready. It had not been fully programed and tested at that time with the proper attack sequences. It is now so programed, and the period of our vulnerability has passed. The fire beam has been tested twice on the endless dunes of the Sahara, and there is no doubt that the Sword will perform as instructed, in code. The new reality is about to begin!''

Erica noticed her husband had paled. He was massaging his forehead, and his right hand shook worse than before. She leaned to him. "Brad?''

Stoneman opened his golden brown eyes. He felt nauseous. Grimly, he exerted all his willpower to maintain a stable, normal appearance. He motioned Erica back. What am I having, he wondered, a stroke? A heart attack? He focused on Nukheila. "Will there be rewards for us if we assist Abu Ben Salamat?''

"Of course. The leader is generous. He understands the need for servants of great experience, skill, and managerial resources. Your various corporate arms will be awarded even more fabulous concessions and privileges in the development of the new Africa.''

Stoneman's headache and nausea began to fade. He wondered if his chocolate-and-brandy had been poisoned somehow. That possibility had to be looked into. He said, "We will be glad to cooperate with the new reality.''

Erica watched Bradford carefully.

As did Jebel Nukheila. The old man was maybe dying, he thought, and had no son! To have lived so long and never to have sired a son! Western men were fools, and they deserved to lose everything.

Nukheila said smoothly, "The leader will be pleased. I must now leave for my hotel, and then to my flight to Washington. I have many calls to make.''

Stoneman nodded. "I thank you for your directness and honesty in everything you have told us. I value straight talk.''

Nukheila bowed and left the conference room. When the door closed, Stoneman opened the control drawer in the table and pressed buttons and switches.

Erica asked, "Brad, are you ill?"

"I think I had a touch of migraine for a few minutes. I'm going up to the apartment to lie down. I want you to stay here and learn this console. Then get the tapes of this choice little meeting and bring them up with you. And arrange a scrambled call to McDermott beginning . . . an hour from now."

Erica felt a thrill of joy. He was bringing her into the center of the power structure in a real way. She rose to help him to the near door.

He brushed away her hands, used his cane, and wobbled slowly out of the room.

CHAPTER 14

IT WAS THE BEST BROTHEL IN AOZID AND CATERED TO LOCAL and foreign businessmen, tourists, diplomats, and high-ranking Ubari government and military men. It occupied a former French governor's mansion that had been sacked by rebels during the colonial uprisings in the 1950s. In 1963, the French returned with foreign aid, an ambassador, and built an embassy on the far side of the fly-specked city. The French politely never claimed ownership of the ten-bedroom, three-story mansion. A relative of Abu Ben Salamat now owned the brothel, and it operated above the strict Moslem law enforced on the lower classes.

John Norris sat at the cedar-paneled bar and sipped a complimentary glass of champagne. The first drink was on the house. His watch showed 9:52 P.M.

A hostess slipped into the bar chair beside him. She was a slender, sinuous black girl with large eyes and full, tempting lips. Her pointed breasts wobbled enticingly under a semisheer white linen dress. She said, "Would you like me as company?" She spoke French-accented English. She looked up at him with genuine admiration, for he was a very large, handsome man who subtly radiated power.

"What's your name?"

"I am Daniele." She turned to fully display her body to him. The glow of brown skin through linen showed no undergarment.

"My name's Marty." Norris smiled and nodded approval. "You're a beauty."

"Would you like to buy me a drink, Martee?" She leaned close and grazed a breast against his plaid coat sleeve.

"Hey, whatever you want."

"Thank you. From me you can have whatever *you* want."

Norris grinned as he signaled the bartender. He checked the back-bar mirror and, in smiling at Daniele, flicked glances past her to the doorway.

The fat, red-vested, dark-skinned bartender took Daniele's order and served her a very weak whiskey sour. He charged Norris ten new francs, the equivalent of three hard dollars. Norris paid with a new redback hundred-dollar bill.

A tall, lean Berber in traditional tribal clothes, accompanied by a stunning, voluptuous blonde, entered the bar and imperiously claimed a table occupied by a stylish European. A violent argument began.

During the uproar, a thin young man in slacks and a wrinkled blue blazer eased into the chair to Norris's left. He fumbled out a pack of American cigarettes and lit up. He leaned around behind Norris and said in French, "Daniele, will you be long with this foreign dog?"

She laughed and replied, "This dog has much American money."

Norris patted his coat pockets, looked up and down the bar, and asked Daniele, "Where can I get some cigarettes?"

She stroked his cheek. "I can get them for you, Martee."

"Okay." He handed her a five-dollar bill. "Camels or Winstons, king size."

She smiled wickedly. "You are a king-size man, eh?" Then she slipped from her bar chair and walked gracefully past the clustered men and women at the long bar.

The bartender served the young man a glass of champagne. Norris turned and asked casually, "Have you used Daniele before? I heard you use her name."

The young man shrugged and said in English, "Yes. She reminds me of a woman I knew in Algiers." The recognition word was Algiers.

The bartender moved away. Norris asked quietly, "Was a black recorder box found in the CIA man's Land Rover after he was killed near Wau el Maradi?"

"I don't know."

"What happened to the Land Rover?"

"It's still where it turned over, beside the road."

"What condition is it in?"

The young man shrugged again. "It's full of holes. But it didn't burn."

"The man is really dead?"

"Yes."

A lithe, young black-haired girl walked over and lightly stroked the young man's back. She asked, "Hello, are you lonely?"

Norris said to him, "I don't like what you call football. Soccer."

The young man put his arm around the girl's waist. He said contemptuously, "You Americans are too much excited by violence! Your football is like bulls and mad dogs fighting. There is no skill in it, no grace or subtlety. He fondled one of the girl's plump little breasts through her flimsy orange blouse.

Norris turned away. He sipped champagne and waited for Daniele to return with his cigarettes. He was sure he was being watched.

A bald fat man in a blue pinstripe suit touched the back of Daniele's bar chair. "Taken?"

Norris spotted the bulge of a shoulder holster. He had not himself come to the brothel armed. He answered, "Not really. Take it."

"Thank you. The bar is crowded tonight." His English was almost perfect.

"Drinking is always popular." Norris took the man to be Ubari intelligence. Was this encounter a test? This man may have listened to his argument with April in the hotel room.

The man said, "And if you add the women, eh?" He chuckled and pushed Daniele's drink out of the way.

The bartender appeared very quickly to take the man's order of scotch and water.

Norris said disgustedly, "Women! I've got a beautiful girl back at the hotel, and you'd think I'd be dipping into her instead of paying for it here, wouldn't you? Wrong. She's a prick-teasing bitch."

"Wives can be difficult."

"She's not my wife. She's a goddam location assistant.

She knew up front her job included prod time. First class all the way, high salary, and now she's not in the right mood, or it's too hot, or it's too cold, or she's got jet lag!''

"Here at least you will not be refused."

"Damn right I won't. Next trip I'm thinking of picking a hooker off Santa Monica Boulevard and taking her along. Probably be cheaper and more fun."

Daniele appeared with two packs of Winstons. "Martee? Now you can smoke."

The fat man swiveled. "Ah, I have taken her chair."

Norris waved for him to stay seated. "We're going upstairs." He took Daniele's soft, bare arm and guided her out of the bar.

Norris called April an hour later from the large downstairs living room of the brothel. He had just left Daniele, who had been everything he expected.

April answered the phone. "Yes?"

"Hey, bitch! I just had my ashes sorted, sifted, deposited, and hauled. And better than you ever did it."

"Marty? Listen, I'm sorry. I—"

"Shut up! I'm going to take a drive. I've got thinking to do." He hung up on her. He knew she'd stay put for twenty-four hours. "I've got thinking to do" was a code phrase. He hoped by now Ubari intelligence was convinced he was a legitimate advance man for Vestel Films. They certainly had had enough time to check out Vestel and his and April's employment by them and their intent to make an Arab war film.

Vestel Films was an indirectly controlled CIA operation, a legitimate production company that had in the past made a few movies, one of which, *The Glory Hand*, a high-grossing horror feature set in England, had made huge profits and funded many other CIA-front operations worldwide.

Unless there was a high-level leak in the field operations division at Langley there was no way Ubari's intelligence service could know Marty Singer and his assistant, Donna Schachter, were CIA. Employment records at Vestel headquarters showed Martin J. Singer had worked for them for three years and Donna Schachter for two months. Each had an apartment in West Los Angeles, phone numbers, cars—the whole bag of incidental facts proving their existence. They were expensive identity shells waiting to be used. They were among the best cover identities money and forethought could create. The CIA had dozens of such covers and constantly established more, in a pipeline effect, as fake identities were "used up" by field agents.

Norris hoped Ubari intelligence had done its job of investigating through its own network of agents in the States and by querying other cooperative Moslem intelligence services. If it had, there might not be a tail when he left the brothel. Aozid was full of foreigners, and no doubt Ubari intelligence had its hands full.

Norris sauntered out into the cool desert night and climbed into the old Scout. He closed his eyes and visualized the street map of Aozid he had memorized. His objective was the road to Sabha. But first a short run to discover if he would be followed and then a short visit to the local low-grade, part-time CIA agent-in-residence, Sven Marhut, for some crucial assistance.

Five minutes later, Norris was sure he did not have a tail. He stopped on a side street and checked the Scout for attached locating transmitters. Satisfied, he drove to the home of Marhut in the old colonial residence section.

Sven answered his door warily. An overhead porch light and a heavy chain guard permitted him to safely peer out at Norris with the door opened only an inch.

John said quickly, "My company referred me to you for some special services."

"What company?"

"Vestel Films."

The Swede had received a special advertising brochure from a front publicity company about Vestel. Marhut's tanned face showed scowling apprehension. He studied Norris for a moment, then nodded. He closed the door, unhooked the chain, then opened it for Norris to enter.

Sven stood in the arch-ceilinged entranceway of his home

and didn't lead the way to the living room. He asked, "What can I do for you?"

"I need a gun and some night glasses."

Sven grimaced, scratched his scalp, and said, "Stay here." He wanted as little contact with this tall CIA man as possible. And the less he knew, the better.

Norris could divine the man's thoughts easily. He didn't blame him.

Marhut returned three minutes later with a pair of BensonTech ELNV goggles. He handed them to Norris, then took an old German Luger and three clips of bullets from his pants pockets. "I don't want these back. Throw them away or bury them."

Norris pocketed the gun and equipment. "Thank you."

"Good-bye."

John smiled wryly and left the man's house.

He had no trouble finding the road to Sabha. He drove slowly, lights on, and in thirty minutes encountered only one vehicle—a crowded old bus heading in to Aozid. After a while, he stopped, put on the awkward night-vision goggles, and proceeded without lights.

The ELNV goggles provided a strange, flat gray field of vision. It had been several years since he'd used a pair, but after a few minutes he was able to drive very fast on the twisting, ragged road. He turned on the Scout's heater. When he saw the distant, oncoming glow of headlights he steered the creaky Scout off the road far enough to avoid being seen.

Pearly predawn light had edged into the sky six hours later when Norris found the wrecked Land Rover.

He passed it and one hundred yards farther pulled off the twisting, rocky track behind a thirty-foot-high outcropping of shale. The Scout jounced and rocked to a stop.

Norris killed the engine, pulled off the goggles, stuffed them in his coat pocket, and stepped out into the cold morning air. He listened. There wasn't a sound.

He trotted to the road and followed it back to the crumpled, bullet-riddled Land Rover. It was lying on its side, the driver's door open, canted back against the body, an open wound to the sky. The passenger side was crunched inward by a small boulder. The seat had been bent sideways.

The grease-caked underside of the Rover showed a new, gaping, cutting-torch wound. The secret compartment had been reached from below. The recorder case was gone.

The quiet desert was slightly disturbed by a small metallic clinking, a small trickle of pebbles, a distant cough.

Norris froze for an instant, then slipped quickly around behind the crushed Land Rover, drawing the Luger from his belt as he moved.

The sounds of movement nearby multiplied. Abruptly, a man's voice, amplified by a loud-hailer, burst in the near silence. He spoke in French. "Come to the road. You are surrounded. You cannot escape. We have your car."

Norris considered trying to slip through the tightening cordon, but the sky was growing lighter every moment, and he sensed a large force of armed men. An escape try would incriminate him. If he tried shooting his way to the Scout or attempted to steal one of the military vehicles parked somewhere nearby out of sight, that would also blow his cover. Marty Singer, Vestel Film Corporation advance man, would not be carrying a gun or shooting Ubari soldiers.

He saw a line of soldiers in desert camouflage garb snake onto the road fifty yards away, at the curve. He heard sounds from the direction of his Scout. He heard boot-crunch sounds from behind him in the desert.

He buried the goggles, the Luger, and the two extra clips as deeply and as quickly as he could in the gritty soil between rocks. He yelled, "Who are you? Can you speak English? What's going on?" He walked around the wrecked Land Rover and pretended to see the line of advancing, heavily armed soldiers for the first time. "Hey! Hey, I'm not armed or anything!" He raised his arms.

They closed in on him. An officer appeared and stalked toward him. "An American? An American has come to sniff at our little trap?" He spoke fair English.

"What? Hey, I just saw this wreck and stopped to have a look at it. That's my job, looking at things. This would make a good— Hey!"

Two soldiers had come up behind him and pinned his arms

roughly behind his back. A third soldier searched his coat, shirt pocket, and slacks. His wallet was handed to the officer.

Norris said, "I've got government permission to be here! You check with your Ministry of Development."

The officer said to the soldiers, in Berber, which Norris did not understand, "Take him to Maradi. Bergendahl will want to question him."

CHAPTER 15

SHERIFF O'BRIEN LEANED BACK IN HIS CREAKING DESK CHAIR, folded his arms across his barrel chest, and said to the two men who had just entered his office, "Sit down, gentlemen. What can I do for you?" There was grim satisfaction in his voice. Maybe now, after two weeks, he'd get some answers.

Capt. James Ferris of the Oregon State Police grimaced sourly. "O'Brien, I'd like to introduce you to Mr. Ernest Wallace of the United States Defense Department."

Wallace said quickly, smiling, "Call me Ernie." He stepped forward to shake the sheriff's hand.

O'Brien rose, grasped the man's weak hand, noted the phony smile, and sat down again. He said, "I guess my calls to people up in Salem and to our senators in Washington brought you here."

Wallace smiled ruefully as he and Ferris took seats opposite O'Brien's big old wooden desk. "Well, yes, sheriff, your strenuous inquiries have done just that. I've been briefed on the . . . shall we say, the Kimberly Beales affair . . . and I understand your concerns and problems. I hope I can allay your official and personal worries in this matter."

"Fine. First tell me what that place is out by Wolf Creek."

Wallace chuckled. "Well . . . I'm afraid that's a question I can't answer specifically. It's a government installation. A top-secret facility. I really can't say anything more than that."

"So secret the local law enforcement people aren't allowed to know about it, huh?"

Wallace shrugged, still smiling. "I'm afraid so."

O'Brien stared hard at the man for long seconds. Ernie Wallace's strained smile broke. The sheriff finally said, "I

97

had a talk with Bob Tumbrill, manager of our branch of the Northwest Bank. At first he didn't want to tell me anything, but I wore him down and got him to do a little tap dance on his computer. I learned that Wolf Creek 'facility' is supposed to be run by something called the Greater West Development Corporation.''

"Ah, sheriff—"

"I'll finish, Mister Wallace. That was a mining company which had permission from the federal government to look for and mine rare minerals on federal land. The federal government pressured local and state agencies to grant various licenses and permits. This was back in 1975, before my time here.''

"Yes, private enterprise . . . A private contractor was used—"

"They ran in a lot of mining machinery and did a lot of digging and such, poured a huge amount of concrete, but after five years all that stopped, the payroll disappeared, and for all anyone knew, the place closed up shop.''

Captain Ferris asked, "What are you getting at?"

"There's a little more. Tumbrill's computer yielded up the fact that Greater West Development Corporation was based in Seattle, but in 1981 it went dead. It was a shell. It had no credit rating, no stock listing, no loans outstanding, no bonds. It doesn't exist.''

Ernie Wallace capitulated. "Sheriff, you're a thorough investigator. I admire you.''

"Like hell you do.''

"No, you're an excellent law enforcement man. You've caused us problems, but in a way they're good problems. I can tell you that GWDC was a government front. The DOD wanted to build a secret installation in southern Oregon, and that mining-company subterfuge was used. In the interests of national defense and security, I must ask you to keep this information totally confidential.''

"What kind of installation is it?"

"Oh, I can't tell you that.''

"Some kind of nuclear project? Biological weapons?''

"Sheriff, I simply cannot tell you. I can, however, assure

you the installation presents no present or future danger to this area. Absolutely none."

O'Brien nodded and folded his arms across his chest again. "Are those military guards out there?"

Wallace frowned and scratched his cheek nervously. "They are federal government guards. And I can tell you that the two guards who attempted to kill Miss Beales have been arrested and will be imprisoned in a federal prison for a long time. And that Miss Beales has received the finest of care in a large hospital. She will be very well compensated for her injuries by the federal government. She has been very cooperative. She's a very patriotic young lady."

"So you say." O'Brien turned to Captain Ferris. "Can you vouch for any of this?"

Ferris asked, "Would you believe me?"

O'Brien asked Wallace, "Do you have any ID?"

Wallace appeared startled and angry. Then he sighed. "Of course. You don't trust anyone, do you?" He produced a card case and handed it to the sheriff.

O'Brien looked up a minute later. "This is just a lot of plastic. Credit cards, a driver's license, a government airline credit card, and a FEMA ID card with your picture. But nothing showing you're with the Department of Defense." He tossed the card case into Wallace's lap. He waited.

Wallace flushed. "Sheriff, my superiors and I thought that if you believed the installation was defense related, you'd be more likely to be cooperative and maintain the total secrecy required. That facility must not be known to exist! If the Russians found out—"

Ferris said, "O'Brien, for God's sake! You've got to take some things on faith. The government has a secret base or whatever out there, and it has to remain a secret. What in hell do you want? What are you afraid of?"

O'Brien said, "Ferris, you were recruited from New Jersey two years ago, and you still don't understand the people around here and in Oregon in general. We've had nothing but a steady diet of lies and ripoffs from the federal government for thirty years. They lied to us about Vietnam, about Watergate, about pollution, about our money, about oil shortages and gluts and prices, and especially about that vicious 'police action' going on in southern Mexico right now. And Christ knows what else! We don't trust the government anymore, and that includes the state government! That's what used to be called the bottom line; the damned government is morally and probably financially bankrupt, and they don't have any credibility left. They've blown their so-called full faith and credit with us. Now you don't care about that because you're a well-paid asshole who follows orders and wants to be promoted at any cost. But—''

''Sheriff!''

''—we've about had it with the sacred word from on high. What I want, and what the people of this county want, is the truth for a change. I'm not going to take the word of my government because its limp-dick representative has just admitted two minutes ago that he and his superiors conspired to lie to me, and I don't know if he's still lying. He's a goddam shit-eating bureaucrat who treats citizens like dumb serfs. He thinks, you think, and his superiors think the end justifies the means: Tell the dumb hicks anything that will work.''

Ernie Wallace had risen from his chair. He trembled with anger. ''Sheriff, I've taken all I'm going to from you. I—''

''Fine! Get the fuck out of my office! And you'd better keep the hell away from Josephine County after this, too, with your precious FEMA power tripping. We'll take care of any emergency around here, including anything caused by that mysterious 'installation' of yours. If I have any more trouble from there, I'll go in with every man I've got, with a legal court order, so if you want it kept secret, you make damned sure it stays secret from your end. Don't come crying to me to get you off the hook.''

''Sheriff, if you leak anything I've told you, or anything of what you've learned about this, to a newspaper or any of the media, if you interfere with that federal facility out there—''

''I know, you'll cry.''

''I'll have you indicted and prosecuted for treason! That is the real bottom line here. And it'll happen so fast you won't know what hit you!''

O'Brien rose. "Get out of here, Wallace, and take that piece of ass-kissing shit with you."

Ferris paled. "You're a marked man. You might last out your term, but forget reelection. And after that you can forget anybody giving you a job. We're going to smear you—"

For the hell of it, O'Brien said, "I don't think so, Captain Ferris. Not while I've got a tape of our little meeting here."

Their eyes dilated. Both men glanced around the office as if to spot a hidden microphone or recorder. Wallace yelled, "Recorded or not, O'Brien, don't tell anybody about the Wolf Creek facility, and tell your men to keep quiet!"

He and Ferris stalked from the office.

CHAPTER 16

WASHINGTON, D.C.
January 7, 1992

IN THE SITUATION ROOM DEEP BENEATH THE WHITE HOUSE, twenty-two men and one woman sat at a large circular table as a fifty-inch holoscreen showed the same video tape recording for the fourth time.

A slow zoom from the secret camera once more brought the narrow face of Jebel Nukheila to screen-filling size. He was saying, "—again, gentlemen, and I do not lie, I do not, as you say, bluff, if an attempt is made by you, by America, to destroy the Sword of Allah's control base at Wau el Maradi or if an attempt is made to assassinate Abu Ben Salamat, the Sword is programed now to strike first at Sharm el Shula and then"—he read from a paper taken from a briefcase—"after four days to strike in sequence Moscow, Bombay, Bangkok, Manila, Panama City, Madrid, Cairo, Singapore, Brisbane, Honolulu, San Francisco, Minneapolis, Detroit, and New York"—he slipped the paper back into the briefcase—"unless the program is altered or canceled from Wau el Maradi by a secret coded signal. Further—"

President Barr yawned and called, "Shut the damn thing off."

The depth screen went empty.

The president turned in his chair to the highly polished walnut table and, drumming his fingers nervously, asked, "Anybody have any new thoughts?"

Vice-President Julia Waggoner, sitting by courtesy to the right of the president, asked the secretary of defense, "Mike, why can't we knock that thing down? We've lost two satellites now."

"It seems to have better missiles."

102

"Better than our Rattlesnake? Isn't that what we've got on our h-k satellites?"

"Yes."

"But we have better attack missiles than the Rattlesnake, don't we?"

Michael Rudd, the secretary of defense, grimaced and admitted, "Yes, but they're not in space yet. They're waiting to be mounted on our new generation satellites."

Julia said, "My information is they've been waiting for that new satellite series for over two years."

The secretary snapped, "Daniels, explain that for the vice-president."

Frank Daniels, Pentagon weapons analyst and coordinator, leaned forward. "Yes, sir. You see, ma'am, the new fluidic computers we want to use in the Dragon series satellites have developed a lot of programing bugs. It's taking a long time to work them out."

Julia resented Rudd's snotty, patronizing attitude toward her. She looked directly at Rudd and asked, "Michael, if the Salamat satellite has better missiles, where did they come from?"

His mouth tightened. "That's a question we've gone over in other meetings."

"Not in meetings I've attended."

"I'm sure one of my assistants can fill you in at another time."

President Barr had sipped fresh, hot coffee while waiting for this exchange to end. Now he said, "Bob, anything new from the other countries visited by Salamat's messengers?"

Robert Adams Samuelson, secretary of state, stopped whispering to an aide and replied, "Not a lot, sir. Mostly anger and frustration. They see themselves as hostages to us and to Russia, since we're the main targets of Salamat's demands."

"Anything from Russia?"

"Gronski, I'm told, is furious. We don't know what Salamat is demanding from them beyond boycotting Israel."

Harvey Mueller, head of the National Security Council, wiped his cigarette-smoked eyes as he commented, "Perhaps he was told to get out of northern Iran."

President Barr stood up and walked tiredly around the table. He stopped to look at an illuminated holographic wall map of north central Africa. "Anything from Norris, Dick?"

Richard Soble shook his head. "Not yet."

The president said to a technician, "Bring Sharm el Shula in again."

A giant depth field six feet across and six deep appeared in a silvery frame at one end of the large room. The cube was flanked by holoprojectors, and the solid image created showed an utterly real ground-level view of the abandoned Sinai settlement from a distance of half a mile.

The technician ran through the various views available. Fixed-position holocameras, some on automatic scan, some remote controlled, provided images from a drone camera plane, from inside the empty settlement, from the far side.

Julia was impressed. The marvelous technology and efficiency of the communications industry was amazing. And this closed-circuit secret satellite transmission was even more astonishing, given the extremely short notice. It was ironic that most of the equipment and workers involved in setting it up were from Israel.

She used the lull to ask the director of the CIA, "Richard, what's-his-name—Nukheila—said the Sword was equipped with a superlaser beam of some kind. And we also know it's armed with defense missiles better than anything we or the Russians have in space. The question that comes to my mind but which I've not heard raised yet is how could this mad genius in charge of it all, how could he have acquired all this advanced secret technology—missiles, lasers, computers— without our knowing about it? Where did it come from? How did he get it?"

The room fell silent except for the background murmur of a few scattered technicians talking into com nets.

Richard Soble glanced at the president. The president turned to look sardonically at Julia.

The White House chief of staff, Carl Fennley, sitting to the left of the chair vacated by the president, smiled wearily and said, "We covered those areas earlier."

Julia said icily, "I see. How convenient."

Fennley added, "A message was supposed to have been sent to you about the meeting. Ahh . . . there must have been a screw-up."

"No doubt. I received word at six A.M. When did this meeting actually start?"

President Barr came around the table and clapped her on the shoulder. "We've been at it all night, more or less. I just thought you'd want to get in as much beauty sleep as possible."

Julia held herself in rigid control. Then she shrugged the president's hand off her shoulder.

There was an uncomfortable silence.

Julia ignored the smirk on the round, stubbled face of Michael Rudd, opposite her. She returned to her prime question. She asked him, "How did Salamat acquire our most advanced missiles?"

Rudd's smirk vanished. "We don't know that he did."

The secretary of state said, "That really doesn't matter now. The question is Can the weapon do what is claimed?"

Rudd said quickly, "We'll know that in two hours. Personally, I'd bet the farm this whole affair is a bluff, a propaganda ploy. There is no way in the world that satellite could be carrying an advanced particle beam weapon. Such a device would have to weigh tons!"

Julia wondered why Rudd was sweating. Secretary of State Samuelson seemed very nervous. Even the president was ill at ease. And they all kept changing the subject away from Salamat's acquisition of secret technology. She sat back in her chair, pale blue eyes narrowed in thought.

The president said, as if to distract her, "If that thing has a weapon that can do any kind of damage to us, there will have to be a meeting of heads of state to decide on a course of action. We'll have to have world opinion with us."

Robert Samuelson rubbed his forehead. "Yes, that contingency is being arranged for. We have preliminary agreement on that. We have just gotten confirmation from Peking. Sen Yat Fung has agreed to attend a meeting in Geneva with all other heads of state from those countries which received an emissary from Salamat."

Julia asked, "Isn't that dangerous?" She looked to President Barr. "Bill, you'll all be a target. You'll only be there if a superlaser weapon exists, and Salamat could turn it on Geneva, couldn't he?"

The president replied, "The satellite's orbit can be altered to a degree but not that much. It would take days for them to shift it far enough to manage a pass over Geneva, and by then our meeting would be over. Even if he could attack Geneva, our actual meeting place will be deep inside one of the large Swiss military tunnel complexes."

"And, Julia," Samuelson said, "it wouldn't be in Salamat's interest to attempt to kill the world's leaders, who would be, he'd think, meeting to arrange compliance with his ultimatums."

The secretary of defense repeated, "The meeting won't be necessary. It's impossible for any conceivable satellite-borne laser to generate that kind of power. It's technically impossible."

Julia wondered if he was protesting too much. Did he know something? This meeting, ever since she'd joined it, had been askew, somehow. There were hints of unspoken agreements, guarded information, secret relationships. Or was she letting her resentment of their blatant sexism warp her judgment? They didn't want her there; that was obvious. But there nevertheless seemed to be something else going on.

A technical supervisor called, "All signals are good, sir."

Julia glanced at her watch: 7:14. She frowned and asked the man seated next to her, an assistant to Harvey Mueller, "What time is the satellite supposed to demonstrate its weapon?"

"Around ten o'clock, our time."

"Thank you." She saw the president in private conversation with General Foote of the air force. She picked up the fresh, piping-hot cup of tea she'd asked for and just been given and moved around the table to CIA Director Soble. "Mr. Soble, may I ask you some questions?"

He stood. He was six feet two inches and thin, with big hands. "Of course, Mrs. Vice-President."

"Over in that corner . . . do you mind? And the name is Julia, between us, informally. And I'll call you Richard." She led him away from the table, aware that many eyes were watching.

CHAPTER 17

WAU EL MARADI
January 7, 1992

"TIE HIM IN THAT CHAIR." BERGENDAHL POINTED TO A METAL swivel chair bolted to the tiled, concrete floor of the control room.

John Norris, stark naked, hurting badly from a dozen small burn craters in his chest and stomach, shoulders, neck and arms, did not resist. The past two days of questioning, torture, and lack of sleep, food, and water had weakened him.

Four big, strong Berber soldiers held him easily. They used two-inch-wide strapping tape to bind his wrists to the arms of the chair and his ankles to the seat column.

Norris feigned nearly total collapse. The soldier who bound his legs was a trifle careless. Norris managed to position his ankles so that a bit of slack could be created. There was no way he could keep his wrists from being bound flat to the arms of the chair. The strong, nylon filament tape was used lavishly.

Bergendahl inspected the bonds and told the guards to leave. He reset the electronic locks after they left.

George Napier had watched it all from one of the computer consoles. "What's all this, Calvin? Why the bloody hell do you want him in here?"

Bergendahl turned and smiled at the deep-chested, moustached Englishman and at the others of his team where they sat at consoles. "It pleases me. I want this CIA pig to watch us demolish Sharm el Shula. I want him to know he's witnessing the greatest event in the history of mankind."

Hans Lichtner glanced over his shoulder contemptuously. He continued tapping coded instructions into his computer's memory.

108

Skeletal, wild-haired Pedro de Molino had been watching from beside a floor-to-ceiling bank of telemonitoring equipment. He grinned derisively. "He is to know you are the man who caused the great event, yes?"

Bergendahl mock saluted de Molino. "Of course. I need an audience. I need ego gratification."

Jonas Andersson, the Danish mathematics wizard, always frowning, keyed in a countdown voice module from his console. A grating, robotlike voice sounded from a speaker. *"Ten minutes."*

Then Andersson turned and examined Norris. "He's not much of an audience, is he?"

Norris had slumped forward, apparently unconscious.

Bergendahl grabbed a handful of John's dark blond hair and jerked his head up. He glared down into Norris's half-open gray-green eyes. He sneered, "Stop faking! You're not that bad off."

John croaked, "Please give me some water."

George Napier said, "Give the bloke something to drink, for God's sake. He won't pay attention to you otherwise."

Bergendahl strode to a food table nearby and returned with a big mug of hot coffee. "Open your mouth." He poured Norris's mouth full, waited until it had been swallowed, then poured again. . . .

Some of the hot fluid spilled down John's heavily muscled chest. Rivulets encountered the deep, raw burns, and he arched and writhed in agony.

When the mug was empty, Bergendahl put it aside on the metal desk, also bolted to the floor, beside Norris's chair. "Feel better, Mr. Singer?"

The wall speaker intoned, *"Nine minutes."*

Pedro de Molino said, "Switching into the ITT satellite feed. Transponder channel three." He flicked switches. A large television monitor came alive. The picture was out of focus. He flipped color-coded switches. The picture sharpened. "They're using compatible holocasting."

Hans Lichtner snorted, "Nothing too good for the capitalist swine."

Bergendahl said, "Good! Good! The better the picture, the

easier to convince them.'' He yanked Norris's head around to face the monitor. "Watch! You'll see the beginning of the end of capitalist domination of the world.''

Hans called, "Calvin, we need you. You can play with him later.''

Jonas said, "The first capacitor bank is up. Plasma flow is pressured to six hundred p.s.i.''

Bergendahl left Norris to take his place at a central console. "How many solar blankets are out?''

"Six. Charge rate normal.''

"Eight minutes.''

John Norris was ignored. He watched the team closely monitor their satellite as it brought itself up to full power and perfect orbit for its pass over the Sinai.

He tested his bonds. It was almost impossible to move his wrists, but by flexing his knees open farther an inch at a time, he managed to break the seal of the nylon tape on his left ankle. He began the slow, grueling process of stretching the tape little by little. His powerful thigh and calf muscles flexed continually. He thought it possible to free his left foot, given enough time, and then his right foot. Simultaneously, he fisted his hands to bunch the muscles in his lower forearms. He tried leaning left and right to loosen and stretch the tape holding his wrists to the metal arms of the chair. He gritted his teeth with the enormous effort.

He stopped when one or another of the team in the satellite control room looked around at him.

"Four minutes.''

"Got some cryo boil-off from number-six tank.''

"How much?''

"Hard to tell. Just a minute.''

"Auto switch kicked in the auxiliary nozzle. Beautiful!''

"F-three gyroscope rotor is heating up. Coolant valve opening one percent.'' There was a tone of awe in Bergendahl's voice.

"Three minutes.''

"By the great bloody Christ! She's healing herself everywhere! Everything is green!'' George Napier was jubilant.

Breathless time passed.

Norris had the ankle tape loose enough to withdraw his feet from their noose if necessary.

"Two minutes."

Calvin Bergendahl glowed as he left the console and moved back to get a good view of the TV monitor showing Sharm el Shula. The others stared raptly at their telemonitoring. Lichtner whispered, "Everything is up. It's going to do it!"

Andersson responded to a trilling telephone. He listened, scowled, and said, "Calvin, Salamat wants to talk to you."

"That stinking toad!" But Bergendahl took the phone. "Yes, leader. . . . Yes, everything is perfect. The Sword is self-correcting small maladjustments and malfunctions. The backups are functioning beautifully. . . . Yes, sir. . . . In less than two minutes. . . . They're doomed!" He laughed, a rising inflection of wildness in his voice. "You'll be master of the world. . . . Thank you, leader. Keep watching."

"One minute."

"I must attend the instruments, sir. Fifty-two seconds from now— Yes, sir. They'll all lick your boots! . . . Thirty-one seconds. I must go." He hung up, his eyes on the monitor. He whispered fiercely, "Do it! Do it!"

Norris watched, too. He watched the changing numbers on the big digital clock and watched the TV screen. He wasn't sure what to expect.

Sharm el Shula shimmered in the afternoon sun. Its buildings glared white and deep, shadowed black. The settlement was being observed now from one of the circling drone helicopters.

De Molino said tensely, "Everything is still green!"

Three seconds . . . two . . . one . . .

Precisely on the instant, a blinding, incandescent beam of pure light lanced down into Sharm el Shula. Bergendahl howled with glee. The others yelled incoherently.

The shaft of boiling radiance was fifty yards wide. The air in and around the beam fractured into separate gases from the instant one-million-degree heat. The TV screen flared as the helicopter-borne camera burned out. A second later, another view came on, ground level, with heavy filtering.

Solidly built brick buildings and houses exploded as the

terrifying laser swept through the settlement. Whole blocks of
apartments and paved streets erupted under the searing impact.
Wooden doors, and window frames, stairs, railings—anything
that could burn—flared instantly into wildfire. In four seconds,
the town became a seething cauldron. Disintegrated brick and
stone dust rose in clouds to obscure the view.

Suddenly, the terrible white lance of light winked out.

Sharm el Shula had disappeared. In its place roiled an
impenetrable cloud that boiled higher and higher. . . .

Bergendahl, Lichtner, de Molino, Napier, and Andersson
danced and howled with joy. They clutched and hugged,
kissed and laughed. They were flushed, exalted, transported,
in the grip of monstrous success.

John Norris was stunned by what he had just seen. It was
beyond belief that this small band of terrorist scientists, even
with Salamat's billions, had in secrecy managed to put into
orbit a satellite capable of repelling U.S. and Russian hunter-
killer satellite attacks as well as carrying an immense particle
beam weapon of such power!

Norris stared at the large TV picture, which continued to
show the swirling brown and gray cloud as it erupted higher
and higher from the ruined settlement.

Bergendahl and his team broke out chilled bottles of
champagne. They toasted each other, guzzled the bubbly
wine, and couldn't stop laughing.

Calvin Bergendahl came over to Norris. "What did you
think of the Sword, hmm? More than a flashlight, hmm?
What do you think your big, hairy, macho president is doing
now, hmm?"

Norris shook his head.

"He's shitting his pants! That's what he's doing! Every
capitalist, Christian leader in the West is either shitting or
vomiting!" He poured champagne on Norris's head. "Celebrate
with us, pig! CIA pig!" He laughed wildly as the champagne
flowed into some of Norris's deep burns, causing him to jerk
and writhe in pain as the alcohol ravaged exposed nerves.

The phone rang again, and Bergendahl was called to accept
Salamat's ecstatic praises. Each team member was called to

the phone and praised in turn. Salamat promised them all enormous bonuses and privileges.

A few minutes later, on the TV monitor, the wind blew away enough of the clouds boiling up from Sharm el Shula to reveal an aerial view of glowing red pools and rivers of still-flowing lava—melted stone and brick.

Bergendahl returned to Norris. "Your CIA director is on the carpet now, isn't he? Two agents killed trying to find out about the Sword. How could we do this thing? How could the Sword exist? Why didn't he know? And in Russia the same questions. In England. In France. How could a stinking pervert, a raving homosexual, and a gang of underground terrorist scientists do this thing?" He giggled.

Norris lifted his head. Rivulets of champagne trickled from his sopping wet hair. "You tell me. How did you do it?"

George Napier heard and said, "We did it with great bloody difficulty!" He roared with laughter and swigged from a bottle.

Bergendahl smiled down at Norris. "Your name isn't Singer, is it? Why don't you tell me who you really are? It isn't going to matter one way or the other. You're still going to die."

"I told you I just stopped at that wreck to look at it. I was curious, and I thought it would make a good prop. I'm Martin James Singer. For the thousandth time, please check me out! I can't tell you anything more than I have."

"Oh, yes, you can. You were seen burying things behind the Land Rover before you gave yourself up. You buried a pair of ELNV military goggles and a fine old Luger."

"I—" Norris sighed and shook his head again. "Okay, if I'm a CIA spy, tell me how you got that satellite up."

"Such dedication! Such patriotism!" Bergendahl sat on the desk by Norris's chair. He crossed thin legs. He laughed, "All right. It took an enormous amount of preliminary computer analysis and an unprecedented number of error-loop MMFR systems. We built, in our computers, seventy-four different framework clusters for fifteen old Uranus Two rockets until we found the most reliable, most efficient configuration. We refitted those rockets, packed new solid fuel into them, installed on-board advanced computers to keep those babies

113

firing in the proper sequences, tested them on the ground near here, built frameworks, and disguised them as a bridge. . . ."

Bergendahl grinned. "It couldn't be done. It was off the wall, very ugly, very functional. And to everyone's vast surprise, the damned thing went up like a dream, balanced on five pillars of fire, then on five more, and five more."

The other team members crowded around, grinning. Hans Lichtner scratched his ragged beard and said happily, "Your fucking America will die! It will be gone—and the world will be cheering. We'll all be international heroes!"

Bergendahl's eyes glowed. He licked his sensuous lips. "The Sword carries a very large, very, very powerful plasma gun. That is no secret now. Not after what happened to Sharm el Shula. What is a secret"—he laughed, and the edge of insanity in the sound made Norris look up at him more intently—"is what happens next! What will our fire beam do next? Where will it be aimed? Hmm? Wouldn't you like to know?"

Jonas Andersson sniggered like a little boy. "Wouldn't Salamat like to know."

George Napier brought over a foot-high metal model of the Sword of Allah. "This is what we've got up there! This ugly mess of girders and tanks and control clusters is going to change the world for a thousand years." He waved the heavy model in front of Norris's face, then thudded it down on the desk. "Mankind will have a thousand years to rebuild from a capitalism-free new beginning."

Norris said, "You can't kill capitalism."

Bergendahl slapped Norris's face, hard! "Can't we? We think we can. We think we can cauterize the open social wound that is capitalism. We can burn out the core of the disease. And that core is the United States of America! That core is the heart of the bloodsucking international banking system in New York, Chicago, Los Angeles, and all those offshore, unregulated banking centers in the West Indies, Panama, Costa Rica—"

Pedro de Molino turned away. "It's time to set up the final program. Have the pig taken out and shot."

Bergendahl shook his head violently. "No! No. I want him

to know everything before he dies." He peered down into John's calm eyes. "This is no ordinary spy. He's one of the best they have. The pain he can endure is amazing. He's a true patriot, a pure, wholehearted, brainwashed servant of the capitalist ruling class. He's a prime dupe!" He laughed. "A dupe in time saves nine."

Hans Lichtner shrugged. "Play idiot games, then." He returned to his computer console. George Napier and Jonas Andersson returned to theirs, too.

Bergendahl got off the desk and paced back and forth in front of Norris. "You have no conception of what we're about to do. With a weapon like the Sword and with my knowledge of astrophysics, why waste it on mere cities?" He paused and said quietly, intensely, "Why not shoot the sun?"

Norris stared at him blankly for three seconds and then laughed.

It was like a slap in the face to Bergendahl. His white skin paled even further. His full-lipped, self-indulgent mouth twisted with hate. "You're stupid! You're like all those so-called scientists who laughed at my theories. They persecuted me. They knew I am a genius, and they were jealous. They had to protect their reputations, so they got rid of me. They knew that sooner or later I'd show them up for the small-minded, purblind idiots they are."

Norris said, "Shooting the sun does sound crazy."

"Not if you have a toroidal Theta Pinch laser! Not if you can throw a plasma stream along the sun's magnetic helixoidal field lines. The coulomb repulsion effect is countered by spiral— That's gibberish to you, isn't it? I might as well be talking to a monkey!"

Bergendahl turned away in disgust, then turned back. "In simpleminded terms, we're going to fire five long bursts of charged particles into the heart of the sun. Those impacts will cause huge sunspots." He asked sarcastically, "Does that sound possible to you?"

"Yes."

"Good! Now pay attention. The sun will compensate for these large, 'cool,' magnetically polarized areas in its photosphere by automatically diverting more boiling plasma to its

surface. Because of the immense size of the sunspots we will
have created, the need for plasma will be very great, and this
in turn will cause a very slight imbalance in the core hydrogen fusion level. A temporary buildup of helium will result.''

Lichtner called, ''Calvin, we're going to need you in a
minute.''

Bergendahl ignored him. He was enjoying himself, building up to a revelation. His lips writhed in a crazy smile, and
he locked his wild gaze to Norris's calm gray-green eyes.
''Because of the buildup in helium, the sun's automatic thermostat will kick in an extra afterburn in the inner radiative
zone layering the core. When this afterburn of helium is
completed, the sun will be back to normal. No harm done to
the sun.

''Ah, but that afterburn! To get rid of the extra internal
pressure, the sun will have to—in effect—cough! That cough
will spray outward an intense bubble of thirteen-point-six-centimeter microwave radiation. This 'cough' will occur twenty-
seven hours and thirty-seven minutes after the completion of
the final, fifth shot into the sun.''

Bergendahl waited for comprehension in Norris's eyes.

Norris said, ''So?''

''Ignorant fool! Thirteen-point-six-centimeter radiation is
not radio waves. It isn't heat or light. It is the kind of waves
created by an electron tube called a magnetron, which is used
in microwave ovens!''

Bergendahl glared down at his naked prisoner. Utter contempt contorted his face. His voice rose. ''This bubble of
microwave radiation from the sun will cook everything on the
daylight surfaces of Mercury, Venus, Earth, and Mars!''

Norris felt an icy chill in his guts. He looked quickly to the
other members of the team. George Napier had been watching
and listening. He grinned and said, ''Bloody truth. And you
can guess which side of Earth gets that dose, eh?''

Norris said, ''Even if it was possible, you couldn't time it
that close.''

Bergendahl chuckled with evil superiority. ''You believe
me now. Oh, yes, the timing is there. The pion decay rate is
known. I've studied the sun for twelve years. I've watched

116

the electromagnetic spectrums of radiation fluxes and helium imbalance dynamics. I've charted positron annihilation in solar flares. I know exactly how to produce that precise helium afterburn. It's all in the timing, and it's all in having a powerful plasma-beam weapon in space. I've planned this for six years!''

Lichtner called again, "Calvin, come check these figures.''

Bergendahl continued. "I planned this moment of sweet, sweet revenge long ago while I spent years in hiding, living like dog shit in mud hovels. But I finally got the ear of Salamat—greedy, power mad, credulous Abu Ben Salamat—a man with billions of dollars I could use. I recruited these men with superb skills and knowledge. And now . . . it's all in place. Sharm el Shula was the final test run. The accuracy was phenomenal! From 135 miles up, at forty thousand miles per hour! Every component functioned perfectly. In a few minutes, the West will be doomed.''

He observed Norris's face greedily for a few seconds, then turned away as Hans called yet again.

Norris sat stunned. He worked savagely to stretch the multi-layers of nylon tape that bound his wrists to the chair. He could pull his legs free, but the chair was bolted down! He had to free his arms, too!

He saw Bergendahl swiveling away from his computer console and ceased trying to weaken his bonds.

Bergendahl swaggered back to Norris. "You're sweating. It's really hitting you now, isn't it? Your entire Western civilization is doomed. The continents of North and South America will burn away. The radiation will last about fifty-eight minutes, give or take a few seconds. It'll follow a bell curve in intensity. Parts of eastern Siberia, northern Japan, and almost all the east coast of Australia will boil away, too.''

"You're talking about killing billions of people!''

"Well, there'll be a few survivors. Miners, maybe some engineers in deep sub-subbasements of large buildings, if there's enough metal over them, and some navy people in submarines. They will live, but their warmongering military-industrial complex masters fucking well won't! For once, the big boys will get it! Those bastards who call the tunes—they'll bake and broil with the rest of their rotten, warped civilization."

Norris said incredulously, "You think that's the final solution, don't you? The end justifies the means."

"Whatever works, Mr. 'Singer.' The poor, oppressed peoples of the world must be freed of the shackles of merciless, exploitative capitalism."

"You sound like a *Pravda* editorial. Don't you know mankind is imperfect? Final solutions never work because man cannot be perfected by man. 'Evil, exploitive capitalism' will spring up again because it's part of man's nature."

Bergendahl had tensed. He became very angry. "No! You're wrong! The human race can be improved! All that is required is the proper socialist environment and time for it to establish itself once and for all."

"That's what they've been saying in Russia for over seventy years."

"They haven't—"

"Listen! What you're trying to do is insane!"

Bergendahl cocked his head and smiled. "Of course it is. What we're doing is monstrous! Cataclysmic! We're all men who are outcasts, criminals, revolutionaries, and fanatics. By definition, we are insane. Sociopaths beyond recall." He waited for Norris's next argument. He was invulnerable and enjoying himself.

Norris took a more personal tack. "Then your insanity goes back to childhood, and all this socialist love-for-mankind talk is posturing, phony, nothing but masks to hide furious little babies who were denied love and affection and security. Now you want to teach everybody a lesson and get even. That's pathetic."

Jonas Andersson, frowning, turned from his console. "He's a psychiatrist, too. Quite a spy. Is that Freudian shit or Jungian shit?"

Bergendahl snorted. "We've heard all this psychoanalysis before. All of us. Maybe what drives us is misplaced hatred for our fathers or mothers. Maybe it's all misplaced rage at all authority figures and the superrich masters of the United States are the natural targets for our anger and hate. So what?

The reality is that we have the means to finally destroy the core, the seedbed of capitalistic power and injustice—America! —and we will do it! Whatever happens to us, we will give the surviving masses time for socialism to at last grow strong and pure, unfettered by the octopus of personal greed. Our act will create a new destiny of mutual love and cooperation by, for, and of the masses.''

''What about the billion or so poor, exploited masses in Central and South America?''

''They must sacrifice themselves for the ultimate—''

Lichtner called again. ''Calvin, we're about ready for the final programing transmission. The Sword is coming into range.''

Andersson said, ''Orbit at one eighty thousand miles. In the bow shock.''

Bergendahl nodded. ''The final deed. Watch us do it, Mr. 'Singer.' We're about to murder your world and your people. But at least you won't live to see it.''

Bergendahl returned to the banks of computers and transmitters.

John Norris now believed that Bergendahl and his crew might be able to do as they claimed. He was no astrophysicist, knew nothing of the complex internal dynamics of the sun, but he had just witnessed the terrifying destructive reality of the Sword of Allah. He knew from his CIA briefing that the best scientific advisers, the best science professors in the best universities in the United States, considered Bergendahl a crackpot theoretical physicist whose ideas were absurd. The weapon just demonstrated had been judged impossible. Norris's mouth was dry and his guts slimy with dread. He watched Bergendahl and his team cluster at Lichtner's console. The bearded German's fingers flew as final instructions for the Sword were entered in the computer.

Norris couldn't get free! Sweat popped on his skin as he strained to break his wrist bonds. During his struggle, he turned the bolted-down swivel chair toward its companion desk. He saw the heavy metal model of the Sword that Napier had shown him and left on the desk. He heard Bergendahl say gleefully, ''One more timing sequence.''

George Napier called out, ''The dish is up.''

Norris freed his left foot from the loose tape that encircled his ankles. He raised his naked leg and slid his foot along the desk top to the model of the Sword. He quickly worked the narrow stem above the wide base between his big toe and second toe.

He lifted the model—it had to weigh at least ten pounds! —and bent his leg back, holding the model high, and turned the chair by using his right foot and toes on the floor.

This was it. The only possible way to interfere with or delay the final, critical coded radio transmission of instructions to the Sword of Allah.

Norris whipped his leg forward and flung the heavy model toward Hans Lichtner's computer console.

The replica arched high and crashed down on Lichtner's head. Its sharp miniature girders and beams slashed into his scalp and neck. He screamed, and his fingers danced askew on the computer keyboard as he collapsed forward, dazed. His right hand skidded to the EXECUTE key, smashed aside the hinged, red plastic cover, and depressed the square button.

Simultaneously, the heavy, angular model fell onto the keyboard and depressed other input keys.

The other team members were thunderstruck. Their heads jerked around, astonished, to glare at Norris, then back to the console. Bergendahl howled and pulled Hans upright, off the keyboard. Andersson lifted away the Sword model. "Cancel that—"

"Wipe that sequence. We can—"

"*It was sent!* Holy Mother of God—"

Bergendahl screamed, "No! Cancel that transmission! Cancel it!" He jabbed buttons frantically.

Lichtner lolled back in his chair, forgotten, bleeding.

"Calvin, stop it! It can't be undone! The program—"

"Reprogram the on-board computers! Andersson, there has to be a way to get into them again!"

"We can't! We designed that program to keep anyone from tampering. Once that final sequence—"

"No! It can't be ruined! You— You!" Bergendahl's pale skin had become blotched with his intense anxiety and rage. He panted, and his eyes darted like frantic, captive gray mice.

His mouth contorted, and saliva sprayed as he screamed his fury. He went for Norris.

John met him with a powerful kick to the groin.

Bergendahl doubled over, staggered, and fell to his knees, moaning, hands instinctively covering his crotch. He shrieked, "Kill him! Kill him!"

George Napier grunted, "Bloody right!" He picked up the phone and ordered guards to the control room. Then he circled Norris warily as he went to unlock the steel door.

Norris began breathing fast and deep. He stared fixedly ahead. His big hands fisted and relaxed, fisted and relaxed. . . .

Twenty seconds later, three young Berber soldiers tramped into the control room, armed with MAK-18 automatic rifles.

"Take that bloody bastard out and shoot him!"

John Norris lived by making instant decisions, trusting his decisions, and acting without hesitation. His mind, from long experience and with lightning speed, assessed probabilities, strategies, tactics, moves, angles—consequences. He had survived for years, through many seemingly sure-death situations, because he could become an utterly ruthless human machine with but one supreme goal.

One of the soldiers handed his rifle to another, unsheathed a combat knife, and bent to cut the filament tape that bound Norris's wrists to the immovable chair. Perhaps because he misjudged Norris's pumping chest as a sign of abject terror, perhaps because he felt a naked man would instinctively be at a disadvantage, humiliated, shamed, perhaps because he saw the man's deep burn wounds and assumed weakness, perhaps because Norris was slumped over, and perhaps because he was accompanied by two armed fellow soldiers and considered himself and them among the best fighters in the world—he was careless.

He moved in front of Norris, slashed the tape bindings with two swift flicks of his razor-sharp knife, and began to straighten up.

John Norris erupted from the chair, tearing his wrists free of the clinging tape, clamped a viselike grip on the soldier's knife hand, and twisted and spun in a forcing, leveraged move that dislocated the soldier's arm and sent him staggering, howling, into one of the other soldiers. The eight-inch combat knife clattered to the tiled floor.

The remaining soldier was encumbered with two rifles. By the time he had dropped one and assumed a firing grip and stance, Napier was shouting, "Don't shoot in here! Don't shoot in here!"

The soldier hesitated.

In those seconds, Norris had grabbed up the heavy knife and whipped it at that soldier. The blade slammed into the youth's stomach, forcing a surprised grunt. He went down.

Norris's knife-throwing move merged into a dive for the dropped MAK-18.

The first wounded soldier was thrust aside by his fellow Berber, who fired a wild burst that tracked along the far white plastered wall toward the computer banks. The noise was deafening.

Team members dove for the floor. Everyone was shouting.

Norris snatched the MAK-18 and rolled behind the metal desk. He put a thundering burst of .33 slugs into the line of computer consoles. CRT screens imploded into glass fragments. Board lights winked out.

There was a sudden silence. The one remaining armed soldier had regained his composure and was crouched, moving slowly, seeking an angle for a killing burst at Norris.

Bergendahl lay whimpering, knees to chin, in shock.

Norris's ears were ringing. He put his head to the cool floor and peered under the desk. Its six-inch metal legs permitted more efficient vacuum cleaning and mopping. That mundane design consideration allowed him to see the soldier's position and sideways movement.

Norris floored his MAK-18 and shattered the man's legs to the knees with a roaring hail of bullets. Splinters of bone and spatters of blood joined the flying white plaster from the wall behind the shrieking, toppling youth.

Norris looked next for the soldier whose arm he had dislocated. He saw him crawling for a fallen rifle. Norris blew his head away.

The satellite team members were scattered, huddled, hands to their ears. Norris didn't bother with them. He was satisfied they could not now change that skewed final signal to the Sword of Allah, even if it might have been possible before. Their expensive top-of-the-line computers were ruined.

But the satellite might still be programed to send its fire beam into a string of cities around the world. There was no way of knowing now what the Sword of Allah might do.

He discarded his nearly empty MAK-18 and picked up one of the others. He ran to the open door of the control room. The thunderous bursts of automatic rifle fire would bring more soldiers.

He padded down a short hallway and spotted an up stairway. He dodged into the alcove and sprinted upward as far doors crashed open and soldiers entered the building.

He burst, naked, into the second-floor hallway and encountered a big, fat, unarmed, fortyish soldier just exiting a room. Norris slammed the steel-frame stock of the rifle into the man's startled face. The man's jaw shattered, and he fell back, unconscious.

Norris quickly entered the room and saw it was part of a two-room apartment. He dragged the man back inside and closed and locked the door. An upright vacuum cleaner stood in the middle of the room. There was a caddy of cleaning and dusting cans and rags in a corner. The soldier was apparently an orderly, part of the maintenance crew.

The closet revealed civilian clothes, too small for Norris to wear. Papers and envelopes on the old-fashioned wooden dresser were addressed to Pedro de Molino.

Norris returned to the unconscious soldier. The man breathed shallowly. There was no option but to take his uniform.

Boots thudded in the hall outside. The doorknob rattled. The boots moved on. Other doors were tried.

He worked swiftly. The pants were too short, the waist too big. But the shirt fit, and best of all, so did the leather boots. With the orange beret tilted rakishly, Norris would pass a quick-glance first inspection. He winced when the starched shirt cloth touched and rubbed against his burns.

He took the soldier's military digital watch, noting the time: 4:01. The sun would be down very soon. That would be an advantage.

He listened at the door, then exited the apartment and ran to the far end of the upstairs hall where he found another stairwell. A great deal of shouting in French came from below.

Holding the MAK-18 in proper alert position, he thumped down the stairs to the ground floor. He walked purposefully between two guards at the outer door and squinted as the dying sun struck his eyes.

He had been held and tortured in the base's vehicle repair garage. He had observed that all the patrol drivers received and returned their Scout's ignition keys to a sergeant in an office at the rear of the garage. He had noted fuel-pump locations and other potentially valuable information.

As he turned to trot toward the garage, a Scout roared up to the door behind him. A voice cried in French, "Attention!" He spun and came to attention.

The Scout held a driver and a Berber general. The officer bolted out of the car and into the building. Before the driver could drive away, Norris held up his hand, boldly moved across in front of the car, and leaned into the open driver's window to look at the instrument panel. The gas gauge showed the tank almost full. He opened the door and said in French, "Join the general. I'll park it for you."

The driver angrily said something in Berber and reached for his sidearm.

Norris angled his MAK-18 to the right and with one ear-shattering, sweeping burst shredded the driver's throat, blew out the Scout's left side windows, and took down the two watching entranceway guards.

He pulled the driver's body out of the Scout, leaped in, and gunned the car toward the garage.

There was an above-ground six-hundred-liter kerosene tank adjoining the rear of the ramshackle metal building. As he tore past it, he put a burst of slugs through the tank.

The bullets ripped on into the sergeant's office. They ignited the kerosene. Within seconds, the tank was a fountain of sooty yellow flames, spouting streams of fire against the corrugated sheet-metal garage walls, seeping fire into the building.

If the sergeant was dead or if his office became unapproachable, only a few Scouts would be available to pursue him.

Norris circled at high speed and riddled the two gasoline pumps at the front of the garage. They billowed into orange and black fire.

He drove away from the base on the best track he could see, into the sun, at maximum speed.

There was some automatic weapons fire behind him, and once a spattering of slugs touched the Scout, but none hit him. The glowering, blinding sun ruined the aim of those firing at him. And then he was into a long, rocky gully, out of sight.

CHAPTER 18

THERE WERE SEVEN UNOPENED BOTTLES OF CHILLED HOME-made beer remaining on the beautifully finished handmade wooden table. Five men sat, drinking and talking, in the large front room of the six-room log house.

Cold rain pelted the windows. A Fisher wood stove radiated cozy heat. A glass-front gun cabinet showed shotguns, rifles, and a rack of large-caliber handguns. Another cabinet housed battery-powered shortwave and CB radios.

Darrell Beales, owner of the house and the surrounding fifty-three forested acres, drank deeply from his bottle. He lounged in his cushioned wooden armchair, a husky, weathered young man with thick, short-cut brown hair. He said, "I'd guess they've got atomic bombs stored in that place."

Kimberly Beales sat near the big, double-paned front window. Her head was still bandaged, though not as extensively as when she'd been in San Francisco Memorial a few days ago, and she was off the IVs.

She reclined in a huge chair whose rope webbing creaked under the foam cushions when she moved. She had been reading a medical text but now listened fearfully to her brother and his survivalist friends, including the county sheriff.

The sheriff had just revealed the existence of that secret government base and what she had told the forest ranger who had found her on the highway. His words made her hit-and-run story a lie. She felt betrayed.

Sheriff Jackson O'Brien turned to her. "I guess that lawyer convinced you to tell that story."

She chewed her lower lip and couldn't answer.

126

"Did you get any clue about the function of that place while you were inside?"

She lied. She didn't know if any of the men were government spies or if the sheriff was testing her. She didn't like lying, but she frankly dreaded the possibility of losing the secret hundred thousand dollars a year she was scheduled to receive for the next ten years, and above all, she didn't dare lose the nonsecret scheduled plastic surgery on her cheek and scalp.

She said, "I don't remember being inside."

Darrell's wife, Sylvia, a skinny, early-thirtyish woman in jeans and an *Oregon Roadrunner* T-shirt, looked up from her desk near the stove. She had been tapping away on an old Royal office manual. "That was very traumatic for her. You get your skull crushed in and see how much you remember."

Sheriff O'Brien looked skeptical but didn't press. He said to Darrell, "I think you're probably right. It's got to be something deadly. Why else would they have a blockhouse and guards and enough clout to order state police from three counties just to keep me from going up that road?"

David Russell, editor and publisher of *The Survivalist Newsletter*, sat making notes on a pad. He flipped to a fresh page. "How about biological weapons?"

O'Brien nodded. "Maybe. Top secret as hell."

Another man, in worn overalls and mud-crusted logging boots, leaned forward and took another bottle. "I'll bet they've got the governor in their pocket, too. Probably paid him off. They sure as hell couldn't do that when old Tom McCall was governor. He wouldn't let the feds get away with any kind of shit in Oregon."

The fifth man, a grizzled, stinking little old man in a patched wool shirt and ragged jeans, shook his head. He spoke up for the first time. He was a recluse whom Darrell had befriended and invited to this get-together.

Now he said, "I hermited over'n Wolf Ridge for fifteen years." His eyes darted suspiciously at the other men and at the women. "I moved two years ago. I watched'm dig out that place and do all they did. Had guards then, too. Took'm years to get it dug out and built in there. Place must go down hundreds of feet, like a big building sunk into the ground.''

Russell asked, ''Yeah? What did they put in? Any equipment you could identify?''

The old man would not be hurried. ''They worked nights, too. Got a big freight elevator in first, seems, and took down what looked like generators and big tanks and musta been a mountain of supplies. I put my glasses on 'em, and they took tons of canned goods and things down into there.''

''See any communications equipment going in?'' Russell sat up straighter. He was a short man, barely five feet six inches, and whip skinny.

''Sure. Buried cables, and right today, if you look close, you can see fancy antennas high up in the firs around there. I had to move when they came up on my ridge. Put in a big satellite receiving dish. Dropped'r in with a big army helicopter.''

Sheriff O'Brien said, ''That sounds like a secret government hideout.'' He nodded grimly. It all fit. ''Those fat-ass politicians and bureaucrats are going to run out here and hide if they fuck up and start a nuclear war.''

The recluse bobbed his head. ''What I think. Took carloads'a fine-looking furniture down. Freezers'n stoves. Toilets . . .''

Darrell swore, ''Isn't that a goddam sweet deal! Tax us to build themselves a luxury hideout! We get into a war and I run out of food, they'd let me starve!''

''Betcher ass.'' The recluse cackled and took his third beer.

Russell scribbled on his pad. ''I think my subscribers will be very interested in this story next month. It'll be picked up by the wire services, I can tell you that.''

O'Brien said, ''Don't mention my name.''

''Don't worry. I'll—''

Kimberly had become very alarmed. ''Are you going to expose everything? Isn't it supposed to be a secret? Can't they put you in jail?'' She was afraid she'd lose everything if the installation's existence and location were made public. The government would blame her!

David Russell looked innocent. "I don't know it's supposed to be a secret. Nobody's told me."

"But—"

"You sticking up for those statists after what happened to you?"

"No! But—" She didn't know what to say. A terrible sinking sensation claimed the pit of her stomach. She was afraid she'd go through life with terrible misshapen scars crisscrossing her cheek and ugly bald spots on her head where her scalp was missing or damaged. Who'd go to a doctor—or even employ a nurse—who looked like one of the victims in a horror movie? Would she even be allowed back into medical school? On her own she wouldn't be able to afford the four expensive corrective operations, and Darrell was only able now to buy her books and help her meet expenses in Portland. Fifty thousand dollars' worth of plastic surgery was far beyond his means. Their parents—forget it! Dad was on social security disability from a ruined back, and her mother worked part-time as a waitress.

Sheriff O'Brien didn't give a damn if the secret retreat was exposed. It would serve the feds right! He chuckled to himself. Maybe Captain Ferris and that Ernie Wallace prick from FEMA would lose their jobs. If they zeroed in on him, he'd deny telling anybody anything. Blame it on the hermit.

O'Brien said to David Russell, "You'd better get out a quick special issue. The way the Mexican rebels are going, they could invade Texas and California by spring."

Russell said, "Naw . . . costs too much. The February deadline is only a couple days away, anyway. Don't worry about those Mexican guerrillas. If worse comes to worst, the government'll dust a twenty-mile-wide strip on the Mex side of the border. Make it so radioactive nothing could get through and live more than a day."

The overall-clad man chimed in with, "Yah, and then Cuba lobs some nukes to support their comrades . . ."

"No, they'd know we'd nuke them back. They wouldn't—"

"Russia! Russia'd tell us, 'You nuke our puppet and we drop a couple hundred megaton loads on you.'"

Darrell laughed. "And that's when the whole damned U.S. government turns tail and runs to its hidey-hole out here."

Unnoticed, Kimberly closed her eyes and silently wept.

CHAPTER 19

THE SCOUT'S TANK WAS ALMOST EMPTY WHEN NORRIS SAW the lights of Aozid from the open desert. It was two A.M., and he had been dodging, racing, playing cat and mouse with pursuers from Wau el Maradi, and anticipating government traps and interceptions from Aozid for an utterly exhausting nine and a half hours.

He slumped forward, closer and closer to the wheel, fiercely willing his bleary, leaden eyes to stay open as he drove without lights through the rough terrain. A seductive, floating weariness permeated his body. The constant jouncing and rocking of the Scout and the ever-changing growling of the engine helped him concentrate.

He needed alertness now more than ever. He was sure the entire government of Ubari had been notified of his escape. Salamat would be furious. Aozid had to be crawling with military patrols and intelligence agents.

Norris was afraid April Weaver had been picked up.

He steered the Scout past a line of dark hovels to a rutted road. Streetlights began a quarter mile ahead. He forced himself to consider options and tactics. His cover was blown now, as was that of April. After his phone call three days ago, she should have waited twenty-four hours and then flown out, if possible. She'd had several alternatives. But if the Ubari intelligence forces picked her up soon after he had been captured near Wau el Maradi . . .

He turned on the Scout's headlights and drove slowly through the unimproved streets of Aozid toward the old colonial residence sector of the capital. He guessed the highways and roads entering Aozid were swarming with military, wait-

131

ing for him. He had circled around, far out in the naked desert, and crept in from the north. He was surprised at not seeing any police or military patrols on the streets.

He parked the Scout next to a small, derelict-cluttered car-repair garage, took the MAK-18, and walked away. He expected the native owner of the garage would quickly strip the car, cut it up, and thank Allah for the miraculous gift. The appearance of the Scout would not be reported to the authorities.

He trudged wearily toward Sven Marhut's house. The curving streets were dark and empty. The owners of these once-expensive houses were upper-middle-class Ubaris, some foreign businessmen operating foreign corporate enterprises, and a few lifetime European residents who had hung on through the revolution. They had all learned to keep their cars locked in garages and to keep their windows locked and draperies closed.

When he reached Marhut's block, Norris lurched wearily down the back alleyway and climbed the back fence next to Marhut's adobe garage. The exertion nearly wiped him out. He slumped to his knees on the inside and slowly pulled himself upright. He staggered to the rear door of the house.

The overhead light clicked on in response to his loud knocking, and Marhut, wearing a robe, opened the solid door only an inch. There was a chain guard on the back door, too.

Sven exclaimed, *"Gott!"* as he recognized Norris. He looked past him to scan the shallow backyard, then closed the door, clicked off the overhead, freed the chain, and opened the door wide.

Norris sighed and almost toppled inside. He said, "I need more help. Clothes . . ." He clunked the heavy MAK-18 on the kitchen counter. He fumbled off the uniform shirt as Marhut relocked the back door. ". . . and some quick way out of this damn country."

April Weaver, wearing only a loose native shirt, entered the kitchen. She held a small automatic. She gasped when she saw Norris's burn wounds and his haggard face. "God, I thought you were dead."

Norris collapsed into a wooden chair. "I am." His head lolled. "I need some stimmers. Five or six."

Sven said, "Damn you if you've led them to me. How did you get here?"

"With great . . . difficulty." Norris slid off the chair to the oiled wooden floor. He grunted as he hit and then was asleep.

He fought to stay asleep as Sven and April dragged him into the living room and propped him on the sofa she had been using as a bed. He almost gagged as they pushed several capsules into his mouth and poured in wine to force him to swallow.

He was vaguely aware of his boots leaving his feet and his uniform pants being pulled down and off. He moaned as thick, sticky salve was applied to the dozens of deep burn craters in his flesh and as bandages were taped on.

He struggled to stay in the soft, floating darkness, but soon the stimulants from the capsules entered his bloodstream and crashed into his brain.

He opened his tired gray-green eyes and stared up at April. She was sitting on the edge of the sofa, leaning over him, buttoning a white tunic over his bandaged chest. Her long, attractive brunette hair glowed with reddish highlights from a nearby table lamp.

He looked down at himself and saw that April and Sven had managed to pull a pair of old jeans up his legs. They were tight around the hips. His feet were still bare.

He said, "I'd rather sleep."

"You asked for uppers, you got them."

"Thanks." His mind felt as if it were floating precariously in a quicksand of exhaustion. He glanced around the poorly furnished living room. The walls were crowded with superb, framed, color and black-and-white photographs of the desert, of nomads, enlarged insects, animals, ancient, crumbling ruins. He asked, "Where's Marhut?"

"In the kitchen. He has a special radio. He's been monitoring the police and military bands for days. We knew all night they were looking for you."

Sven came into the living room with a bowl of something that steamed. "I've made some cracked wheat mush with raisins, if you want it." He carried in his other hand a small radio scanner that constantly emitted scratchy voices speaking French and Berber. He placed it on the end table behind Norris's head. "They still think you're out in the desert, now probably out of gas."

Norris put both hands on his brow and slowly rubbed his aching eyes. "Thanks. I need something inside." He accepted the bowl and a tablespoon. Sven had added milk and honey to the mush.

Sven asked worriedly, "Where did you leave the Scout?"

Norris told him, and why.

The tall Swede smiled for the first time. "You're right. It'll never be seen again."

As he ate, Norris said to April, "I'm glad you didn't stay at the hotel."

"Give me some credit for cowardice. When I realized you were going to Wau el Maradi, I thought you'd be captured or killed, and I was afraid Ubari intelligence would come for me right after that. So the next morning I moved in on Sven. Much to his displeasure."

Sven folded his arms across his thin chest. "What am I supposed to do with you two? Your government doesn't pay me enough for this kind of risk."

April pouted at him. "Poor Sven. I wouldn't go to bed with him." She jerked her shoulders and waggled her full, loose breasts at him. Her shirt barely covered the tops of her bare thighs.

From his angle, Norris could see the dark, shadowed triangle of her naked crotch. It had no effect on him at all.

Sven asked Norris, "What happened to you?"

"They used the Land Rover as bait. I was caught and encouraged to give my true identity and anything else a red-hot poker could burn out of me. Later, I managed to get loose and escape in one of their new Scouts."

April asked, "Did you find out anything about their satellite?"

"No." John concentrated on eating his mush. His body was suddenly alive and famished. He asked April, "Did you bring your typewriter when you came here?"

"Yes, why?"

Norris spooned a delicious mouthful of honeyed mush and said to Sven, "Molded into the plastic rubber platen of her typewriter are ten diamonds worth fifty thousand new dollars. We'll leave three with you if you can get us out of Ubari."

April exclaimed, "I didn't know that!"

Norris smiled. "Sorry." He asked Sven, "Is there a way out?"

"Oh . . . maybe." Sven was interested. "Let me make a call." He left the living room.

April said, "He has a phone in his darkroom because he's in there working so much of the time."

Norris asked, "Do you trust him?"

"I guess so. Shouldn't we?"

"Go see if you can hear what he's saying on the phone."

When she had followed Sven out of the room, Norris groaned upright from the sofa and walked unsteadily into the kitchen. He found the MAK-18 where he had left it and carried it back into the living room. He hid it behind the sofa.

Two minutes later, April reentered the room, came to him, and whispered quickly, "I think he's bribing somebody. I—"

Norris heard Sven approaching through the bedroom. He reached up to caress April's soft, warm breasts, and he kissed her.

She tensed, then understood as she heard Sven come into the room. She giggled and responded.

Sven said sarcastically, "I see you're feeling better."

Norris eased April away. "You'd better get some pants on."

April grinned. "Oh, Marty, I was beginning to think you'd never notice." She left the sofa and took up a pair of panties, a bra, and green-striped slacks from the arm of a nearby chair.

While April dressed, Sven said, "There's a local drug runner—an Arab—who has a flight coming in just before dawn. It's a private jet. He'll send his limousine to pick you two up, in the alley, in an hour. At the airport, the drugs are off-loaded, and you are loaded. You'll go into the plane inside empty hot food containers."

"How much does he want for this service?"

135

"I negotiated thirty thousand dollars; twenty when he picks you up and ten more when he lands you in Algiers."

April paused as she stepped into her slacks. "Is that the Aozid airport?"

"Yes, the commercial side."

Norris said, "He must be high up in the government."

Sven smiled and shrugged. "That may be true."

Norris kept the MAK-18 with him every step of the way. The initial diamond payment was made when the limousine arrived. He and April rode uncomfortably in the large trunk. They could hear two Arabs in the back seat examine and value the gems.

They were let out after the big car drove into a private hangar at the airport.

The private twin engine jet, a Lear twelve-passenger Y-3, taxied to a stop before the partly open hangar doors. A crew of Arabs worked with manic speed while emptying the plane's luggage compartments. The bales of hashish, boxes of stim drugs, and cases of raw opium disappeared into three innocuous Fiat delivery vans.

Norris stood by, yawning, his mind sinking slowly back into darkness. The stims were wearing off already.

The Arabs motioned Norris and April into fake aluminum hot-food chests. The sides slid open.

That was a critical moment; they'd be most helpless in those boxes. But Norris nodded for April to comply. He cradled the MAK-18 between his legs as he folded himself into the container. If something went wrong—an attempt to murder them or simply abandon them on the tarmac—he'd blast the end panel out of his tight little coffin and anyone in the way of that hail of slugs would be shit out of luck. The drug-smuggling operation would be at risk of investigation.

But there was no problem. The boxes were lifted onto a large dolly and wheeled out to the plane. They were lifted into the galley compartment and released instantly.

The plane, empty of passengers except for Norris, April Weaver, and a watchful, armed Arab in a business suit, took off without incident ten minutes later.

Once the jet reached its twenty-five-thousand-foot cruising altitude, Norris insisted on using the radio. He took April's small, digital, CIA-issued watch from her and pressed a hidden pressure switch. A super miniaturized computer within began displaying coded information.

April said resentfully, "I'm getting the idea I'm not to be trusted. I just carry diamonds and high-tech gadgets around for you to use if needed."

Norris nodded as he made calculations. "Need to know."

She stalked back to the passenger compartments.

He waited till 6:53 A.M., fighting sleep every second. The sun was up at this height, even though the ground was still in predawn twilight. At this moment, a Defense Department satellite was supposed to be within range of a radio signal on a certain frequency that would be "honored" only once. He spoke slowly and carefully into the microphone, using code numbers that he had memorized weeks before in Langley. It was a simple language of only fifty "words," and it, too, had a one-time-only utility. He concluded with his code identity.

The satellite should have recorded his message for relay to a ground station in Rome a few minutes later. From Rome it would be beamed to CIA headquarters in Virginia.

Norris went back to sit by April. He handed her back her watch. As a tide of irresistible exhaustion crept over his mind and body, he said, "You'll have to arrange travel from Algiers. I'm going under."

She nodded and cradled his head against her shoulder.

Fifteen minutes later, the copilot of the jet tried to contact Algiers International Airport and discovered all radio bands were being hashed by massive sunspot activity.

CHAPTER 20

ERICA STONEMAN, BUNDLED IN FURS, STOOD AT THE FARM-house window and saw the headlights turn off March Road into the long driveway leading to the eighteenth-century farm. She idly picked a scab of blistered brown enamel from the window frame and said, "He's here."

Bradford Stoneman only grunted an acknowledgment. He huddled deeper into his overcoat and muffler. He snapped at the only other person in the bare, carpetless room, "Lamb, bring him in."

A pale white light filled the room from a two-mantel propane lantern.

The man said, "Yes, sir," and walked noisily on leather soles into the entrance hall and opened the door.

The late-model Pontiac crunched through the snow and stopped next to the Stonemans' Mercedes-Benz sedan. A plump man in a heavy plaid lumber jacket and stocking cap got out and trudged to the house. He was met by Lamb.

When he entered the lantern-lit room, Edward Marin, CIA covert operations section chief, stamped his feet and said, "Sorry I'm late, sir. There was a three-car pileup on the expressway. It's icing pretty badly out there now." He took off his stocking cap in deference. His pink-skinned bald head seemed a necrotic, mottled gray in the dim light.

Stoneman rasped, "I haven't waited for anyone more than five minutes in thirty years, and that was a president. And I've never gotten up at four A.M. and driven sixty miles in the dead of winter to hear a news report. This had better be damned important, Marin."

138

"It is, sir. It could be absolutely critical. I couldn't say more than that when I called."

"I know all about bugging and taps. This house is safe. Now get on with it."

Edward Marin hesitated. He glanced at the man who had escorted him into the house. "Is this—?"

"Yes, that's Professor Webster Lamb, the one you wanted to hear whatever it is you've got to say. Get on with it! I'm freezing!"

Marin nodded. "First, we received a top-secret transposition cipher report from John Norris. It was very brief, necessarily. I had left orders for the code room to call me the moment anything came in from him."

"Fine! What was the message?"

Marin took a piece of blue notepaper from his wallet. He handed it to Stoneman. Stoneman squinted at Marin's small, crabbed printing and handed it to Erica. "Read it aloud."

She knelt beside the lantern. " 'New Bergendahl Allah program. Beam sun. Cause spots? Flare? Death billions?' "

Bradford Stoneman said querulously, "What? Read it again."

Erica complied. She finished and said to Marin, "Is that it?"

Marin nodded. "That's why I asked you to bring Professor Lamb. To me that says that Calvin Bergendahl and his team have reprogramed the Sword of Allah computers to aim that plasma gun at the sun. Norris isn't sure what might follow from that, but he thought it might cause sunspots, a solar flare, and maybe the deaths of billions of people. He probably got that from Bergendahl."

The professor said, "That's absurd. There are sunspots all the time. There are solar flares all the time. As for the existence of a plasma gun powerful enough to cause sunspots—impossible!"

Stoneman said curtly, "Tell him everything."

Marin blinked rapidly. These were the most sensitive national secrets! But he had been taking Stoneman money, secretly, for ten years, and now—now it was payback time. He couldn't refuse his secret master. He knew Stoneman's power. And he had anticipated having to tell Lamb some of this information.

Marin described the international blackmail being attempted by Abu Ben Salamat by means of a terrifying plasma weapon aboard a controlled, invulnerable satellite. He told of the cataclysmic fire-beam destruction of Sharm el Shula.

The professor listened with increasing amazement. Finally, he said, "Even granting such a weapon is in orbit, it's ludicrous to think spraying the sun from this distance would have any effect at all. Calvin Bergendahl is a discredited madman."

Edward Marin was sweating in spite of the freezing temperature in the old farmhouse. His voice betrayed stress as he said, "But simultaneously, as Norris's report came in at three A.M., we received tracking-station reports on the Salamat satellite, day side. It had been in a stable orbit and had been for an hour shooting that plasma beam toward the sun."

Erica looked quickly at Stoneman. "Brad—"

The professor blurted, "Plasma—"

Stoneman held up his hand for silence. "Let him get it all out. There's more, isn't there, Marin?"

"Yes, sir. Nineteen minutes later, we received an urgent observatory report that a huge sunspot had appeared on the" —Marin closed his eyes and concentrated—"on the northeast quadrant of the sun. Satellite photo transmissions were garbled, but it is so large it's causing astronomers on the day side to go crazy with excitement. Almost all radio and satellite broadcasts, even tight beams, were hashed by that first sunspot."

Professor Lamb tensed. "There are more?"

Marin nodded and licked his lips. "As I was driving up here, I received a scrambled call on my car phone. The satellite stopped its sun shot after precisely one hour, and then its orbit took it around into the dark side. When it got to day side again, it immediately began beaming plasma toward the sun again. It's still going on now, I think."

The professor was incredulous. "I can't believe there's any connection."

Marin said, "Let me go out to my car and get an update."

Stoneman nodded. "Go. And take him with you."

When Marin and Professor Lamb had left the house, Stoneman cackled a laugh. "There goes Salamat's power. His precious weapon is wasting its fuel shooting at the sun! Bergendahl has double-crossed Salamat and is testing some fool theory."

Erica crossed to the window to watch the two men tramp through the snow to the Pontiac. She said, "But don't we have to act as if the Norris message is correct? It said the beam might cause sunspots, a flare, and the death of billions."

Stoneman burrowed his thin, cold hands deeper into his thick wool coat's pockets. He was wearing heavy gloves, but his hands were still freezing. His feet, in fleece-lined zip boots, were cold as ice. Damn his lousy circulation and creaky heart!

He considered Erica's question. His mind shrank from the implications. "We'll wait till we get Lamb's best judgment. He's the brilliant astrophysicist, after all."

Erica persisted. "All of your experts and all the government experts said it was impossible for Bergendahl to have done any of what he has already done. Why believe an 'expert' now?"

Stoneman stamped his feet. "Let's get all the information we can first. Damn, why didn't you think to bring along a heater of some kind?"

"Darling, let's go out to the car. We can all talk there as easily as in here."

Stoneman grunted agreement. He knew he should have thought of that. Why hadn't he? Why had he insisted on coming into this two-hundred-year-old icebox in the first place? The car had been swept for bugs two days ago. It was probably safe to discuss sensitive matters in it. He led the way out of the house.

Erica carried the lantern and locked the door. Then she caught up with Stoneman and helped him through the snow. He said, "A solar flare might be a good thing . . . get some heat in my bones."

Edward Marin and Professor Lamb met them as they reached the Mercedes. Marin said, his breath puffing in the frigid air,

"A second gigantic sunspot has appeared. They're reported as like giant blotches on the face of the sun."

The professor was nervous and silent.

Erica said, "Let's get inside and get warm." She slid into the driver's seat and started the engine as Stoneman, Marin, and Lamb climbed into the large rear-seat area.

Stoneman asked, "What else? Is that all?"

"John Norris and April Weaver are on a jet now from Algiers. We chartered it to get them back as soon as possible. They'll arrive about nine A.M."

Erica twisted around in the front seat to face the men. She asked Marin, "Is this Norris a good agent? Experienced? Do you believe his report about a possible killer flare?"

Marin said reluctantly, "I don't like the man, personally, but he's the best field man we have. And his report so far is correct, isn't it? The sunspots have appeared, and they're monsters."

Stoneman huddled against the velvet upholstery, grimly trying to keep body warmth. When was the car heater going to start blowing?

Then it came on—a fan of warm air. He sighed and asked Marin, "Who else knows all this, about Norris's message and the plasma gun on that satellite shooting the sun?"

"Only the director, and I presume the president in Geneva."

Stoneman poked at the professor. "Lamb, what about it? Do the sunspots mean a flare or something is coming?"

Professor Lamb's narrow face twisted with insult and anguish. "I can't tell you. All I've heard are vague reports. I don't have any hard data! There is no legitimate theoretical possibility of extraordinarily large sunspots causing a solar flare of a size that would affect the inner planets in any way. I can't even believe that plasma-gun story, much less that it's causing sunspots!" He squirmed with outrage.

Erica pinned him with a contemptuous look. "All right, but just suppose for argument the plasma gun exists and did cause the sunspots. If the giant sunspots cause or are a symptom of something going wrong with the sun, and assuming Calvin Bergendahl knows what he's doing . . . how long will it be before a killer flare occurs?"

Lamb threw up his gloved hands and rolled his eyes to the roof of the car. "I don't know!" He slapped his knees in exasperation at these stupid questions.

Erica persisted. "Make a guess. Think like Bergendahl."

"If I—" He sighed deeply, remembering the secret retainers, the consultations to Stoneman-controlled corporations. . . . Stoneman had made his career and controlled his income. "Maybe . . . maybe . . . well, if he destabilized the hydrogen balance in the radiative zone and caused a helium burn problem . . ." Lamb gritted his teeth. "It might— Oh, maybe a day or a day and a half later . . ." He shook his head. "It's all so ridiculous."

The warm air in the car was making Stoneman feel better. He positioned his feet in front of the back-seat grill. "Thank you, Professor Lamb. You've been helpful. Now, I'm not feeling too well. I want to get back home and get into bed." He shot a warning look at Erica. She had been about to speak. "I'm going to ask you to ride back to New York with Mr. Marin. And I want you to remember that everything you've heard here is extremely confidential. I trust you to keep silent. Men who have betrayed my trust have lived to regret it, if they've lived."

Lamb's eyes widened. "Of c-course I wouldn't—"

"Good. Now please go. I think I'm catching the flu."

Marin and Lamb climbed out of the warm Mercedes.

Stoneman smiled at Erica. "Now, my dear, drive us to the White Plains airport."

Erica laughed. "You don't have the flu."

"No. I'm feeling better and better." He picked up the car phone. "I'm going to have our jet meet us at White Plains. From there we fly to our retreat in Maine, just in case. A great deal of hedging is in order, and some speculation."

Erica nodded. She remembered the tour of the house near Millinocket soon after she and Brad had been married. There were six levels under the house that were, in effect, a deep, well-stocked nuclear bomb shelter, complete with private apartments, a central kitchen, supplies and food stocks for several years, and elaborate communication facilities.

She drove at speed, but carefully, as Stoneman made calls to important people and made massive shifts of assets in Asian and just-opened markets and exchanges.

CHAPTER 21

Edward Marin, haggard, unshaven, met the chartered jet when it landed at cold, rain-swept Kennedy International. He sat in a CIA limousine, and he was alone except for the driver.

John Norris came down the wet ramp steps wearing a borrowed crew jacket. He bowed his head against stinging sleet in the rain. He had slept three hours on the plane and had eaten and shaved in Algiers, but he still felt drained.

April Weaver followed him. She had managed to buy a decent blouse and a cuddly shorty imitation fur coat for an exorbitant price at an Algiers airport shop.

John paused at the bottom of the ramp when he saw the round face of Edward Marin peering at him through a side window of the black limousine 150 feet away. He muttered, "Shit!"

April said, "Now, now, be nice. Don't screw up my promotion."

They walked through slushy snow to the car. Marin opened the door and said, "Good to see you two again. Oh, April, will you sit up front with Jack? I need to talk with John in private."

She shrugged and went around the front of the car.

Norris climbed in past Marin and settled into the luxurious rear seat.

Marin shut the door and said to the driver as April got in next to him, "New York, for now." Then he pressed the control that raised a soundproof wall of glass.

Norris noticed an open white pastry sack next to Marin on

145

the seat. But the section chief seemed oddly nervous and anxious. Norris asked, "Are you all out of goodies?"

"What? Oh, no— Do you want a jelly doughnut?" Marin offered the sack.

"No, thanks. You look worse than I do."

"I've been up all night. Your message kept a lot of people up." Marin dipped a hand into the sack and took out a fat, oozing doughnut. But he didn't take a bite. He asked, "Does Weaver know much about what may have caused the sunspots and the . . . ah . . . the possibility of a flare?"

"No. She knows I went to Wau el Maradi, was captured, interrogated, and that I escaped. That's all Marhut knows."

"Fine. Then we won't need her." Marin pressed a speaker control. "Jack, stop at the United terminal. Miss Weaver, we'll drop you there. Jack has a voucher for you and your ID. You're free to fly to Washington. You have earned a seven-day vacation. But keep in touch with my office. We may want a debriefing tomorrow or the day after." He switched off the microphone-speaker and leaned back. He took a messy bite from the rich doughnut and fumbled in the sack for a napkin. He said indistinctly as he chewed and swallowed, "We're going to the Fiftieth Street office."

Norris knew the address to be a secret CIA office-bedroom-communications center disguised as an import firm.

Five minutes later, April was let out at the United Airlines terminal. She came around the car for a last word with John.

Marin grudgingly unlocked and opened the limousine door. She leaned in, kissed John on the lips, and urged, "Get those awful burns taken care of. They could be infected."

He nodded and touched her neck affectionately. "I will. Take it easy."

"You, too, hero." She backed out and turned away. At the last instant, she waved to John and then passed quickly through the big glass sliding doors.

Thirty minutes after that, Norris and Marin entered the suite on the thirty-sixth floor of the Travis Building. As they passed through the anteroom of the fake Cholb & Sieg Traders, Inc., a field agent, Conrad Obert, emerged from a rear office,

saw them, and called, "Mr. Marin, hot news on the wire."
He nodded to Norris. "Hi, John."

Norris smiled and waved. He followed Marin down a hall
to a door that required palm-ID and eye-scan confirmation
before opening.

The inner room hummed with radio transmission and receiving equipment, line printers, and computers. AP, UPI, INS,
CNN, Reuters, and AIS machines chattered constantly. Agents
sat at desks complete with computers and phones.

Marin headed for an empty desk and punched up the latest
compilation of Sword information. Black word lines tracked
upward on the green screen.

8:46:22 76 USSR SIBERIA TRACKING STATION LOCKED
ON SWORD. NO ACTIVITY. SHARED. 206-MILE
ORBIT.

9:17:57 77 WHITEHORSE STATION LOCKED ON SWORD.
NO ACTIVITY. SHARED. 221-MILE ORBIT.

9:21:02 78 NO ACTIVITY DAY SIDE.

9:23:18 79 GENEVA. BARR ORDER EIGHT STEALTH BOMB-
ERS AIRBORNE ATLANTIC COMMAND. ARMED
PIRANHA MISSILES. ATTACK SOONEST ORBIT
APPROACH SWORD.

10:02:29 80 GUAYAQUIL STATION LOCKED ON SWORD.
ORBIT NOW 260 MILES. SHARED.

10:36:41 81 LIBREVILLE STATION LOCKED ON SWORD.
260 MILES. NO ORBIT CHANGE. NO ACTIVITY.

That was the latest entry.

Norris had learned on the jet of the sunspot activity and of
the worldwide communications interruptions. He was relieved
that the Sword had apparently stopped shooting the sun.
Bergendahl had said five consecutive orbit shots of one hour
each were required to trigger the sun into the reaction he wanted.

John asked, "How many times has the Sword shot its beam
at the sun?"

"Three times, so far. Why?"

"And it isn't doing it this time?"

"No. It'll be dark side again in twenty minutes."

"How much time does the Sword take for a complete
orbit?"

Marin punched up the information. "Three hours and fifty-two minutes, now, in its present very high orbit. Why?"

"I'll tell you in the safe room."

Marin grunted softly from the exertion of standing up from the computer station. He led the way into a specially shielded, swept, electronically and mechanically spy-proofed room. He switched on a holotape recorder. "Take the throne."

Norris sat in the chair and looked into the cameras. He identified himself and began to relate his experiences in Ubari.

Marin interrupted at one point to say, "Show the burns."

Norris gingerly stripped off his shirt and jacket. The large doses of painkillers he'd taken aboard the chartered jet were wearing off now. He set his jaw as he peeled off the bandages.

Marin winced at the sight of the deep, crusted wounds. He adjusted the holocameras for some close-ups. He said, "We'll get you to a doctor in a few minutes. Finish your report, now."

When John had completed his statement, Marin began asking questions to clear up several points. The recording continued. "You're sure that final coded transmission to the Sword was skewed at the end?"

"They sure as hell acted like it was."

"Bergendahl and his team weren't sure what the effect would be on the Sword."

"That's right."

Marin smiled and took a deep breath. "And we know the satellite didn't fire at the sun all during its last day-side pass. The sequence must be scrambled now."

"I sure as hell hope so. And I hope those Piranhas can reach the Sword next time it comes around."

Marin sucked at a tooth. "Did Bergendahl say anything about a radical orbit change during the sun-shot sequence?"

"No."

"Then its move up to two hundred and sixty miles might be because of that scrambled feed."

"Yes, but who knows? Bergendahl might—if he's still alive. Salamat must know by now that his prize weapon is out of control."

Marin pursed his lips. "Anything more to add to this report?"

"No."

Marin switched off the holorecorder. "Let me say, John, you did an excellent job on this assignment. I'm sure the director will agree with my recommendation for a special bonus and a departmental commendation." Marin offered his hand. It was ignored.

Norris stood up slowly and carefully reattached his bandages before slipping on his shirt. "Is there a coat around here I can use? This flight jacket belongs to the copilot on that 727."

"Get something from the sleeping-room closets. Tell Jarvis to see about that jacket." Marin moved to the door. "You can get over to the Angus Clinic alone, can't you? You have an unlimited expense card now, by the way."

"I'll manage."

Marin said, "You know, your heroics make me look good. I appreciate that. Take two weeks off if you like. But keep in touch." He opened the door and went out into the noise of the communications room.

Norris followed and asked, "What about the Sword?"

"That's over. You may have saved the world. If only you could brag about it, hmm?" Marin leaned over a computer desk and said to the agent at work, "Call up the latest on the Salamat satellite."

The man punched keys—the screen wiped, and entries marched up the green field. The latest showed the Sword's orbit at 287 miles. No attack had been made upon it on the dark side. There was no apparent reason for the orbit change to an even higher altitude. There had been no plasma-beam activity.

Marin walked away. "It's out of control. It'll probably fling itself into outer space."

CHAPTER 22

THROUGH THE RISING, WAVERING HEAT WAVES FROM THE desert, the orange globe seemed to carry dark blotches on its face. Was it an illusion? Was he hallucinating? Could the sunspots be that huge?

For a moment more, Calvin Bergendahl contemplated the setting sun from the driver's seat of the heavily loaded Scout. He had lost everything in the past few hours, but at least he had his sweet Fari.

He ruffled the black hair of the boy, who sat fearfully on the seat next to him and turned to observe the distant, noisy landing of four of Abu Ben Salamat's largest American helicopters.

His rosebud mouth writhed into a smile. General Djabo hadn't wasted any time once that incredible CIA man had escaped. The news of the ruined control room must have reached the leader very quickly. Then, when the surviving radio monitors had reported the Sword was discharging its beam toward the sun . . .

Salamat must have gone mad with rage, as only an Arab can. His international blackmail, his megalomaniacal dreams of supreme world power—gone!

Bergendahl started the engine. He took one last look at mile-distant Wau el Maradi and drove down the rocky slope of the ridge. Salamat and his soldiers would find only the corpses of guards, of Lichtner, Andersson, Napier, and de Molino, who had suicided.

Soon after that agent's escape, Djabo had virtually emptied the base of soldiers and vehicles to recapture the man. And Calvin had fully realized the extent and consequences of his blunder in bringing that "Singer" into the control room in order to boast and gloat . . .

Bergendahl braked to a stop and screamed with anguish at the top of his voice. Fari cringed. Calvin huddled against the wheel and wept.

He took Fari into his arms. "I still have you, darling. We have lots of food and water and gas. I have a radio. We'll go south and west . . . to Niger. I have gold. . . ."

And he had a heavy revolver. If Salamat's soldiers found him, he'd shoot himself.

His thoughts turned to the Sword. It was still up there, on automatic, obeying its instructions. But what had been in that final, scrambled set of instructions? How much of the program had been altered? Was there a chance that all of the sun shots would be carried out in the exact, preplanned, timed sequence?

He had to know! He had to stay alive long enough to know!

CHAPTER 23

"There's nothing like a gentle, loving sponge bath given by a beautiful, half-naked young woman, is there?" Sandra Timmons carefully eased the damp, soft sponge around a particularly deep, red-crusted burn on John's tightly muscled lower belly.

They were lying on his bed after she had thrown an old blanket over it to protect the expensive quilted spread from water stains.

The FM band of the clock radio on the night table played softly. A classics station was doing an evening of Vivaldi. The lamp glowed at its lowest setting. The time read 11:29 P.M.

John smiled. "Nothing like it in the world." He ran a big, strong hand along the velvety white skin of her right thigh, down the slim calf. "But—"

"I know, not tonight. I wasn't hinting." Her blue eyes shaded with anger. "I couldn't bear to make love with you this way . . . hurting and tired. I'm not sure I can forgive you for coming back this way."

"You're lucky I got back at all."

She bit her lip to restrain a scathing, sarcastic rejoiner. Finally, she said, "I don't think you really want to go on living. You just pretend. You're using the CIA as a way to commit suicide."

"There may be an element of truth in that. Maybe I do have a kill-me-if-you-can life script. Or maybe it's an I'm-a-great-hero script. Or a mother-didn't-want-me-so-I-don't-deserve-to-live script."

152

Sandra shook her head in irritation. "You know so much about everything. Why do I keep on seeing you?"

"Look thee at thine own script."

She sighed and continued to carefully bathe his big, scarred, burn-pocked chest and belly. To change the subject, she said, "I'm tired, too. We were up to our eyeballs in work today, in spite of those giant sunspots messing up most com links."

"The life of a CIA analyst is a hard one." He grinned and stroked her silvery blond hair. He gently urged her head lower for a kiss. The kiss was slow and tender, a soft melding of warm lips.

Sandra held the sponge away from his body as they kissed. After a moment, their mouths parted, and they smiled at each other. John asked, "A drink?"

"Okay. Don't move. What may I concoct for you?"

"Just pour a few ounces of scotch, no ice."

She put the warm, wet sponge in the small stainless steel bowl she'd placed at the foot of the bed near her folded skirt and blouse. She walked lithely, gracefully into the living room to the paneled bar.

Norris emerged from the bedroom a few seconds later, naked, and slowly began a series of twisting, bending exercises. He stopped when she handed him the drink.

Sandra sank into a yellow corduroy club chair and sipped from a glass of white wine. "I don't know what it is about unusual events in the sky. The cults and the financial markets go crazy. To quote the high priest of something or other, 'The mottled sun is a sign of coming doom! Repent and—' "

Norris finished for her, "Give all your money to the church."

She laughed. "No, not so explicitly. They usually talk a lot about defying God's Word, living in sin, retribution, Armageddon, and roasting in hell. All the smart money went into gold, silver, and commodities."

"Anything on the nets about a beam of fire sent down from heaven to warn mankind to be good—or else?"

She looked at him sharply as he stood sipping his scotch. "Not quite that. Reuters and AP almost broke the Sword of Allah story . . . about a new satellite put up by Abu Ben Salamat which carries a super particle beam weapon which was demonstrated on an abandoned settlement in the Sinai yesterday. All the powers that be in Geneva got them to sit on it for a while. Were you involved in that?''

"In a way." He came over and sat on the wide arm of her chair. "Tell me again how much clearance you have."

"I'm C-1. I work with everything but the ultrasecret files, and only God and Marin and the director have access to those." She couldn't resist touching his rock-hard thigh. His magnificent male body sent chills up her spine. She let her slim fingers drift toward his genitals. "I could do something nice for you, if you'd like."

"Maybe . . ." A thought came to him. "Do you know if that attack on the Sword did any good today?"

Sandra laughed. Her hand slipped from his thigh. "You mean there's something I know that you don't?"

"I'm afraid that's possible. I was at a clinic having those burns looked at, and then I spent the rest of the day getting home."

"The answer is yes. It was ambushed this afternoon over the South Atlantic by Stealth bombers carrying every Piranha missile they could be rigged to carry. They overwhelmed its defenses. At least one of the missiles got through, and the Sword broke up. Pieces of it will be burning up in the atmosphere for the next few months and years."

"That's good news!" He smiled and tossed down the rest of his warm scotch.

"For you, but when I get to work in the morning, I hope those damn sunspots are gone." Sandra became pensive.

"They will be." Norris felt a vast sense of relief. "You were saying something about doing something nice—"

"John, could those three crazy plasma-beam shots the Sword threw away into space . . . could those have caused the sunspots?"

"I'm not expert on astrophysics." He stood up to get more scotch. He stopped. "There were three shots at the sun?"

Sandra looked surprised. "Were they deliberately aimed at the sun? The tracking stations all said—"

"There were *three*?"

"Yes. The last one was during the Sword's final orbit. It lasted over three times as long as the other two."

"Three hours? How could it last that long? You mean it shot the sun for three solid hours?"

"Yes. It stopped only minutes before the Piranha missiles got through its defenses."

"But its orbit was too quick to let it be in daylight that long!"

"Not the last one. It was clear out to 362 miles—and climbing. I think a complete orbit for it at that height would have been over seven hours. That's partly why the Piranhas could reach—"

Norris had thrown his glass across the room.

He stood transfixed. The Sword had managed at least five hours of shooting the sun! Would it matter that the sequence was different and the timing different? Could the sun still have been destabilized enough to cause that deadly flair of radiation Bergendahl had planned on?

When had that madman said it would occur?

Norri closed his eyes and tried to remember that bragging, insane monologue. Something about a "cough" after the final hour-long shot— Twenty . . . twenty-seven and a half hours!

Norris snapped, "Get dressed! We've got to get to the director!"

CHAPTER 24

CALVIN BERGENDAHL AWAKENED WHEN THE FIRST DIRECT rays of the sun speared over a ridgeline to the east and angled through the Scout's windshield to his face.

The shortwave radio continued to whisper news from the powerful twenty-four-hour English station in Gibraltar.

Fari still slept, his head resting in Calvin's lap.

Calvin listened to the news for a few minutes. Nothing more about the sunspots. The major news was about the extraordinary gathering of heads of state in Geneva. Rumors now being reported told by "reliable sources" revealed the international blackmail attempt by Abu Ben Salamat by means of the fire beam of the Sword of Allah! Other stories leaked spoke of the Sword's destruction by massed American missiles.

Bergendahl cursed under his breath. He'd have to assume a new identity when he reached Niger. For years, Salamat's assassination teams would be seeking him.

He eased Fari's head off his lap and got out of the car. He walked a few feet away to urinate. He squinted into the rising sun, trying to see any mottling or other changes.

And—the sun did seem odd. The light suddenly appeared more . . . intense! He blinked and lowered his watering eyes. His skin began to prickle. He was abruptly very warm. What was happening? What—

Then he knew! The radiation flare was occurring! His theories had been correct. But it was too soon! America was still in the dark. The wrong side of the planet was going to be destroyed!

He screamed and lunged back into the Scout. His head was hurting. He was suddenly sweating. He ducked low and scrabbled in the map compartment for his revolver. He thumbed off the safety, cocked the heavy pistol, and pressed the muzzle to Fari's head.

The boy's eyelids fluttered. He was opening his large dark eyes when Calvin pulled the trigger. The shot was impossibly loud in the enclosed cab.

Calvin sobbed with fear and remorse. He cocked the gun again and poked the barrel into his mouth. The cold metal tasted brassy. There was a bitter taste of powder from the muzzle.

His body was cooking! He was sweating heavily, panting through his nose. His head ached terribly.

He had caused the greatest disaster in the history of mankind! They'd remember him! His name would be known for thousands of years!

He pulled the trigger.

CHAPTER 25

RICHARD SOBLE CINCHED TIGHT THE BELT OF HIS PAISLEY robe for the third time. He stalked across his wide living room, spun, and returned. He sourly regarded John Norris and Sandra Timmons. His thin gray hair was uncombed, and he was grumpy. It was 1:30 A.M., and he did not like having been ripped from a rare sound sleep. As he grew older, he valued a good night's sleep more than a fine meal or good lovemaking.

He said, "All right, John, I believe you. There may be a chance those plasma-beam shots into the sun did cause those monstrous sunspots yesterday and may cause some kind of internal solar adjustment which might result in a bubble of radiation."

He lit a cigarette, with one of the new sensor lighters. "But I can't do anything. You've presented me with a string of maybes and mights. I can't pick up that phone and call Geneva and say maybe this and maybe that to the president of the United States before he's gotten out of bed."

Norris said, "But everything Bergendahl predicted is coming true. And the satellite did get off five hours—more than five hours—of that beam into the sun."

Soble nodded patiently. "So Sandra has confirmed. But you just told me he said it all depended on the timing of those shots. And that timing sequence was altered by your actions. Therefore, the effect of those mistimed shots cannot be known. The sun may not be impelled to react at all, or it may react in an entirely different manner. I cannot—" He continued over Norris's attempted interruption. "I cannot cry wolf. If I surfaced this maybe-might disaster—even to the president's staff—and nothing happened—which is what the odds are—my position as director of the CIA would be in extreme jeopardy. And my voice in this administration, as far as Near East and Mexican policy is concerned, is too important to risk—''

His hot-line phone rang.

Soble and Norris looked at each other. Soble picked up the phone. "Yes?" His eyes narrowed, then widened. He glanced at Norris. He reached down and punched a speaker button.

". . . cable from Berlin saying people are literally roasting in the streets!" The male voice was almost hysterical. "Every com link with Asia, Africa, and Eastern Europe is out. We're getting burnouts from robot observatories, and almost all day-side com satellites are dead. It isn't sunspots, sir. Before the robots went dead, they recorded and transmitted a sudden solar flare of microwave radiation."

Soble said, "Franklin! Franklin, activate all the crisis-alert com nets. Feed everything you have immediately to the president in Geneva, to the vice-president, the speaker of the house, all of the Cabinet, FEMA, the joint chiefs, all sector commanders."

"I've done that, sir. I took that initiative a few seconds before I called you. All hell is breaking loose here."

"Good. Now get everyone back to headquarters. Crisis recall. I'm leaving now." Soble lowered the receiver.

Franklin blurted, "Sir! We can't get to Vice-President Waggoner. She's not— Hold on a second, sir. . . . Sir, she's not home, and no one knows where she is. She avoided her Secret Service guards."

Soble said into the receiver, "All right, keep trying on that. Everything else goes forward."

"Sir, the news nets are putting everything on the air. There'll be panic."

"All right. I'll be there as soon as possible." He cradled the phone and clicked off the speaker. He lifted shocked eyes to John and Sandra. "My God . . ."

John said, "I hope the president is warned in time. It might be dawn in Geneva about now. If Berlin is getting it . . ."

Soble grimaced. "If the president dies . . ." He picked up the hot-line phone again and punched a sequence of numbers, waited, then carefully punched four more. He listened and scribbled an address on a note pad beside the hot-line phone console. He cradled the phone, tore off the small sheet of paper, and handed it to John. "She's probably there. I want you to get her if she's still there and bring her to CIA headquarters as quickly as you can. Can you find that address?"

John nodded. Soble turned to Sandra. "You come with me, Miss Timmons."

CHAPTER 26

TOKYO, JAPAN 2:00 P.M.
January 9, 1992

OFFICE WORKERS IN THE HIGH-RISE ALUMINUM-CLAD MITAKA Building, shielded temporarily from the intense microwave radiation, watched in astonishment and horror as cars and buses in the crowded street below crashed into each other, people ran wildly, collapsed, sought shelter in buildings.

"Is it an attack?"

"What is happening?"

"The cars are exploding!"

Their building rumbled from small explosions. Below, a propane-fueled bus became a blowtorch and careened into a storefront.

Opposite, a building of imported stone and glass, receiving the full blaze of suddenly lethal sunlight, began popping thin slabs of stone facing above the shadow line. And down the street people were clawing at their steaming flesh as they jumped blindly from shattered windows.

Then the frightened onlookers felt strange, horrible internal heat as the radiation, pouring through the windows on the opposite side of their building, penetrating wood, plaster, and plastic, bouncing off pipes and conduits, suffused their offices, too.

WAU EL MARADI, 6:40 A.M.

Abu Ben Salamat bolted from his bed moments after the screams and explosions began outside. His whip-slender, copper-skinned body was naked. By long habit—some said instinct—he slept with a *kris* under his flat pillow and a Colt .44 in his hand.

The air was hot in the normally cool room. Sweat popped on his forehead and trickled into his fierce black eyes.

What was happening? An American attack? Why would the infidels bother? They had destroyed his Sword!

Gripping his Colt in a sweat-slippery hand, he ran to the closed metal venetian blinds, which had kept the full force of the radiation from him for perhaps thirty seconds.

He yanked the blinds open and had a split second to see what was occurring. Several of his brave Berber soldiers writhed on the ground, howling like tortured women. Before his eyes, a water tank ruptured with steam and spewed boiling water. A palm tree boomed, split asunder, and toppled, shattering itself into kindling.

Salamat staggered back from the invisible impact of radiation. He knew with his last coherent thought that the Western dogs were using a death ray on him and his men. They were destroying him and his government as a lesson to discourage others from rebellion against the filthy Christian capitalist plot to control the entire world. He shouted, "There is no God but Allah! Allah be—"

He stood until his eyes ripped and burst, until his brain swelled, until his blood boiled. He stood on rigid, quivering legs until his lungs and stomach swelled and squeezed his madly pumping heart.

THE AMERICAN SPACE SHUTTLE IN ORBIT OVER NEWFOUNDLAND

Frank Kincaid radioed, "Roger, Alexandria, we understand. Rotating Challenger now to twenty-six degrees. Will keep sunlight from entering windows. Loading all cameras and recorders. Do you read? Do you read?"

"Transmis—eaking up, Chall—you are—day side—luck—"

Frank snapped off the speaker. "That's it."

Joseph Marcussa settled his space-suit helmet over his head and spoke through the suit radio. "I hope to hell the metal between us and the sun is enough."

Ken Pryor finished adjusting a robot camera. "Some mission this is turning out to be. Watching Earth die."

Frank said doggedly, "We'll do our duty as long as we live. Get your helmet on."

Marcussa twisted to look at a robot camera view of the white-glowing underside of the shuttle. "We've been in sunlight for two minutes. Anybody feel anything?"

Frank said, "The danger is the fuel tanks and hydraulic lines. Watch those temperature gauges. We may have to tilt up to protect those tanks."

"And expose ourselves to the radiation."

"We can hide in the shower."

"One of us can hide in the shower. Hey, we're losing tiles."

"All cameras on. All recorders on."

PRINCESS MARTHA LAND, ANTARCTICA, 6:15 A.M.

Kurt Warmbad, flying a Kroonstad R-3 helicopter, five minutes west of the secret ice shelf base of the Union of South Africa, noticed first the sudden disappearance of the low cloud ceiling. Then an amazing phenomenon presented itself.

Ahead and below, the tips of huge icebergs were exploding and melting.

He couldn't believe his eyes. What could cause that? Then he made a connection: When the beams from the newly risen sun touched them—the ice couldn't melt fast enough! It was melting faster on the inside. Boiling! Exploding!

He swooped lower, unaware that the helicopter mainframe and engine were protecting him from powerful radiation.

Ahead he could now see ice floes being riven and shattered. Great cracks appeared in the bergs nearest him. The mountains of ice were melting at an extraordinary rate in the strangely brilliant light.

He took up his radio pod. "Zebra. Zebra. This is K.W. The ice is melting! All the ice is melting! Are you all right? I'm flying on to the mother ship. Zebra? Come in, Zebra." The speaker popped and hissed with white noise.

The helicopter engine began to cough. Kurt began to sweat. His belly felt full of gas. He was confused and suddenly terrified. He sought ahead in the sparkling blue and green and white horizon for the U.S. ship *Karoo*.

The engine spluttered to a stop.

TANZANIA, 8:35 A.M.

Itigi Makubako placed his hard hat and headlight in their proper compartments near the entrance of the Kitunda ruby mine and moved into the white room. He went to his cubicle and stripped off his single-piece denim overall for the usual physical search. The fluorescent lights overhead flickered. But they often flickered in the mine. The guerrillas.

His mind was full of the time he was going to have with Consi. He had a two-day off, and after a bath—

A commotion caught his attention. A clerk was jabbering into a phone. Those around the clerk were agitated. He called, "What is the matter? Get back to your jobs so I can go."

Instead, to his mystification, they ran out of the white-room exit toward the mine exit. He frowned and stepped into his pants. To allow the possibility of ruby theft would lose those men their jobs. What magnificent event could cause this to occur?

He followed them and met a man coming back, his face unnaturally pale, his eyes staring, unable to speak more than gobbling sounds of terror.

Itigi cautiously approached the steps to the gaping outer doorway. Other men cringed back. They cried, "The sky is a diamond! The sun is death!"

He peered over the top step at the outside. His eyes widened. There the pond was seething. The sky was a sparkling, intense blue he had never seen before. The bare ground, wet from an early-morning rain, was steaming—and on the caking ground he saw a grotesque, impossible thing, a man sizzling and roasting. A horse lay burst open, its legs stiff in horrible death, its great open belly spilling steaming organs.

Itigi shrank back, down, and ran back into the mine, deep into the mine.

LONDON, 6:20 A.M.

Jock Newton called from the bedroom, "Can I have an extra ten in the kip, Bridget?"

Bridget was hunched over the radio in the kitchen, listening intently to a news broadcast. She called urgently, "Jock, get in here! Have a listen to this!"

"What? Turn it up, then!" He grumbled his way out of bed. He knew Bridget wouldn't have said listen in that frightened tone unless it was bloody important.

The news broadcaster's voice came loud. ". . . Minister Hambly is likely beyond help in Geneva, as are all the heads of states gathered there. No further reports have come from any part of Europe east of Lyon. The line of breakdown and—we'll have to call it death, won't we—is advancing with the dawn, and very unreliable last-second reports from the afflicted areas tell of people by the hundreds and thousands, inside buildings and out, dying of a kind of internal heat generated in some way by the rising sun."

Jock came into the kitchen in his shorts and top. "What the bloody hell?"

"Listen!"

"—with Chester Winsford, a full professor of physics at Havering Institute who has been hastily advised of the events and reports of the past ten minutes. Dave, are you on?"

Another newsman came on, his voice tinier, as from a telephone link. "Yes, Philip. I have Professor Winsford here

166

in his home. He has very kindly agreed to make a few remarks. Professor, could something have gone wrong with the sun?''

"Well, of course, without seeing instrument readings—''

"But all reports tell of clouds evaporating miraculously as soon as the sun touches them, and other reports speak of water and other fluids actually coming to a boil.''

"Yes, so you've said. But lacking—''

"Professor, apparently millions of people on the continent are being killed by this manifestation. You owe the people of Great Britain some informed guess as to what is happening and how they can protect themselves.''

"My dear man, I have no idea. The only explanation I can conceive would be some kind of burst of radiation from the sun.''

"The sun is going nova?''

"No, no. A flare . . . a shift up the spectrum from mostly heat and light to a more deadly area . . . into somewhere in the two-thousand- to three-thousand-megahertz area. That would perhaps explain what you tell me is happening.''

"But, sir, why are the rays of the sun so deadly in that part of the spectrum?''

"Well, you see, if that is what is happening, anyplace now in daylight has in effect become a giant microwave oven.''

There was a stunned silence. Then the newsman asked, "What protection is there from that?''

"Going deep underground, I'd say. Perhaps keeping thick metal between yourself and the sun. It would have to be—''

He was cut off. Slow, soothing music came on. A smooth male voice said, "We regret the interruption of normal broadcasting. Her Majesty's government has put in place the Emergency Information Service. There is no need for alarm. Correct and legitimate news will be forthcoming soon. Please stay in your homes. Please wait for further information.'' The music returned.

Jock was outraged. "Stay in our bloody homes? Stay in our bloody ovens, he means!''

Bridget whispered, "What are we going to do?''

Jock looked around the kitchen. "Get everything out of the

fridge. Damned oven isn't big enough . . ." He peered out of the window at the predawn sky. "Bloody hell!"

The eastern winter clouds were melting.

A strong wind began to blow.

THE KREMLIN, 8:06 A.M.

The emergency power generators had been on for over forty minutes. There was enough power in this second sub-basement of the Kremlin, but there had been no responses to his desperate pleas for human contact along the intercom network.

He sat at his broadcasting console in the soundproof, metal-shielded room and tried again and again, pressing buttons for the library, the restaurant, the intelligence offices, the engineering section, even the maintenance staff office.

He sat at the first broadcast station. There were seven stations, but all the others were empty. The reports had started coming in, and one by one the other announcers had left the room to discover what was really going on . . . and they had not come back.

He was afraid to leave the room.

He pressed the button for security. "This is Boris Komi in broadcasting. Comrades? I require instructions. I must know what to say. Comrades?"

There was no reply.

He looked at the heavy metal door. There were no windows showing the offices, the desks, the people who should be gathering news, writing commentary, scheduling programs.

He had been broadcasting a tape of a Shostakovich symphony for twelve minutes. He paced the long room and always turned away from the unlocked metal door. His mouth was dry. His stomach roiled with fear. Why hadn't anyone come back? Had the Americans really created a terrible death ray and used it on Moscow? Had the Abu Ben Salamat affair actually been a diversion, a trick?

Was everyone outside—dead?

He sat at his microphone and switched off the symphony. He took up the last sheet of copy he had been given to read. His hands shook. He licked his lips and began to read it over the air for the twenty-fourth time.

"Comrades. Be brave. Mother Russia is being attacked. The capitalist swine seek to impose their typical 'final solution' on the Socialist world. We must survive to counterattack! The leadership calls upon you to defend . . ." His voice trailed off. He cradled his face in his hands and sobbed helplessly.

The deadly solar radiation had bounced down the elevator shaft to the operations center. It had permeated the basements. It was waiting for him beyond the door.

CHAPTER 27

NORRIS KEPT HIS RADIO ON AS HE DROVE. HIS GRAY-GREEN eyes flicked left and right as the Shelby snarled down Greenleaf Boulevard. He switched on the heater even though he wore gloves and a parka. Warm air purred into the sports car to offset the rivulets of cold from the custom-made convertible top.

". . . we're giving all news bulletins to you as they come in over our wires. A world crisis—a world disaster—seems to have occurred. WKKY News will stay on the air as long as necessary. This just handed to me. Associated News reports a total blackout of all telephone, wire, radio, and satellite transmissions from Asia. All of Asia. A tremendous solar storm seems to have wiped out communications from the entire daylight side of the world. No reception is possible.

"Universal Cable News reported a few minutes ago garbled messages from Damascus about a death ray from the sky. But now that link is gone.

The unusual sunspot activity of the past day is suspected to have caused this massive communications breakdown. Wayne Blankenship, a professor of astrophysics at Princeton University, said a few minutes ago when we contacted him by phone that any disruption of this magnitude would not last long. He said the peak of such a broadband inter—

"This just off the cable! UNI bulletin! Cuba is charging the United States with an unprovoked attack on the U.S.S.R. Moments ago, Radio Havana broke into a music program to announce continent-wide destruction and death in Asia and Russia and charged that the United States had fired a huge missile into the sun to create sunspots large enough to inter-

170

fere with worldwide communication. Under cover of that interference, Havana charges, the United States launched an all-out preemptive attack against the U.S.S.R. with new death-ray weapons of terrible killing power. A U.S. government response has not yet been—"

Norris switched off the radio.

He turned left at Verney Terrace and roared up a gently curving road that served estates of million-dollar homes. His headlight smeared across wide, deep lawns.

He noticed that every one of the big houses was alive with lights. The phone company must be logging a record load of calls as the news spread and friends awakened friends, as relatives called relatives.

An ornate, stone-mounted mailbox by twin driveway light posts marked the address he wanted; 522 Verney Terrace was a low-slung ranch of brick, stone, and glass. The wide driveway was crowded by eight expensive cars. The blue Audi belonged to the vice-president.

But the house was dark. What was going on? What was Julia Waggoner into?

Norris skidded to a slewing stop. He left the engine running but snapped on a hidden alarm system. He slammed shut the driver's door and ran across the flat, well-groomed lawn to the ranch's porch. His Benelli-heavy holster thudded against his chest.

He rang the chiming doorbell and pounded on the intricately paneled mahogany-veneered door. After a moment, a light came on in the porch roof and a small, round inspection panel opened at eye level behind ornamental iron grillwork.

Norris saw an eye and heard a male voice ask, "What do you—"

He held up his open CIA ID case. "John Norris. I must speak to Vice-President Julia Waggoner right away!"

"I'm—I'm sorry. There's no one— She isn't here."

"This is a matter of extreme national emergency!"

"Let me see that ID again."

Norris held it up, close to the grill.

The man asked, "What does the CIA want with the vice-president?"

"I'm here as a guard and as a driver. She's needed. There is a national emergency!"

"Well, we'll have to make a few calls. . . ." The inspection door closed.

John Norris took three deep breaths. In the distance, he heard the wail of an ambulance. It was joined by the hooting, scree-scraw sound of a police car moving on a code-three call. From the far left distance came the boom of a shotgun.

Norris pounded on the door again.

The protected little round inspection panel opened again. The man said angrily, "I'm sorry, but we can't get through. The lines are all tied up. You'll just have to—"

"Turn on your radio or TV! And get the vice-president out here!"

"Well, don't get arrogant with me, Mister CIA Agent! Besides, I never said she was here at all! For all we know, you're some kind of terrorist with forged credentials. As soon as—"

"Jesus Christ!" Norris took three steps backward to the wrought-iron railing, leaped forward, twisting, legs drawn up, and kicked with savage power at precisely the correct instant. His 190 pounds, multiplied by the striking force of his straightening legs, concentrated in his closely placed leather heels, burst loose the two dead-bolt locks in the hollow-core door.

The shattered door flailed inward, striking the man behind it. He cried out and fell.

Norris landed in a crouch, spun around, and pushed into the house. His 9-mm. Benelli—a replacement for the one he'd had to ditch in London—was in his big hand. His burn wounds hurt fiercely again.

He ignored the fallen man, who was in his fifties and whose clothes subtly suggested servant.

Norris walked quickly down a dark hallway toward a closed door with light showing under it. The wall-to-wall deep-cushioned carpet muffled his approach. He paused at the door and listened.

A familiar, syrupy male voice was saying, "If the CIA knows this place, then—"

The voice of Julia Waggoner interrupted. "It was ridiculous to think you could keep meetings like this a secret. What is going on tonight? I can't get through to the White House!"

Norris holstered his automatic and straightened his parka. He opened the door.

The room was a windowless library with books solid in floor-to-ceiling shelves. Middle-aged men, dressed informally in sweaters and blazers, sat in armchairs or at a conference table. One tall man, Daniel Drucker, honey-voiced TV spokesman for the progressive National Manufacturers' Group, stood at a bar pouring a drink.

Julia Waggoner, trim in gray slacks and an alpine pullover sweater, stood by a small oval table, phone in hand, irritably stabbing out a number.

Three minutes later, she buckled her seat and shoulder harness as Norris gunned the Shelby away from the house.

She said, "I would not have gotten into this car if I didn't know who you are. I've seen your name and picture in top-secret CIA reports."

"Yeah. I really appreciate Marin putting in my picture."

She laughed, then sobered. "All right, now tell me what's happening."

"Did you read my report?"

"On what? The possible funding sources for the Salamat satellite? Yes. But what—"

"You didn't—or you didn't get a copy."

"What are you talking about? What is the national emergency?"

He took the gentle Verney Terrace curves at ninety-five miles an hour. The Shelby GT 500 KR growled like a black panther as it raced through the new urban jungle.

Norris said, "Bergendahl and his team double-crossed everybody. They pointed the Sword of Allah at the sun and pulled the trigger. That caused all those sunspots. It also screwed up the sun's internal temperature control, and that in turn has caused the sun to throw out a wave of microwave radiation that is roasting the hell out of the day side of the planet."

"What?"

Norris whipped the car onto Greenleaf. "Bergendahl said the radiation will only last about an hour, as the sun regains its internal equilibrium. But I managed to foul up the timing of the satellite's shots into the sun, and the timing of the radiation surge was off. He and his crew had it planned that we'd get roasted, and instead they got it right in the face!"

The vice-president rubbed her forehead. "Just a minute. Just a minute. You're saying the sun has begun to radiate killing microwaves because it was triggered to do so by the plasma gun in Salamat's satellite . . . and that you ruined the timing somehow. . . . You were there?"

"Yes. And I managed to get away. It's all in my report."

"And because of your action—the other side of the world is dying now instead of our side."

Aware of her stare, he nodded.

There was a moment of silence. Julia Waggoner was stunned. Finally, she said in outrage, "But doing that to the sun—making it do this—it's insane!"

"That's what I told Bergendahl. He agreed with me."

"But they went ahead—"

"With full, rational premeditation. They planned it all years ago and tricked Salamat and his backers into funding it. Surprise!"

"He knew he was insane?"

"Oh, yes. Paranoid schizophrenia powered by a world-class IQ."

Julia Waggoner slumped lower in the red leather bucket seat. She said nothing as she absorbed what Norris had said. Then she blurted, "But the president is in Geneva! That's in daylight now, isn't it?"

Norris swerved skillfully to pass an old station wagon. There was more traffic than normal for 1:30 A.M. on Greenleaf. He nodded and said, "The odds are you'll be sworn in as president in a couple hours."

"Oh, God!" She huddled in her short fur coat.

He burned through a red light at 215th and made a power turn onto Lombard Way at seventy-five miles an hour. He said, "Bad night to run off without your Secret Service boys."

She turned suddenly frosty brown eyes on him. "The identities of the men you saw in Daniel Drucker's library—will they be in your report of this little adventure?"

"Maybe. I do discretionary editing, sometimes, in the national interest."

"No need. I'm not ashamed of anything. Those men want me to be available for the Democratic nomination if the front-runners run out of gas. They have to know in advance."

"That's all out the window now. There probably won't be elections."

She was shocked. "What do you mean?"

"Mrs. Vice-President, half the world is cooking in a planet-wide radar oven. Right now! Billions of people are dead, now! Whole continents are on fire! The odds are the president is dead. You're going to have to declare a national emergency and rule by executive order—like a dictator—for the foreseeable future."

"But if the radiation stops—"

"No, you don't understand yet! There are enormous environmental consequences to what is going on now, day side. The weather will go crazy! The economy will be paralyzed. The—"

He saw a roadblock two blocks ahead as they rounded a curve. Several overturned cars were burning, and there were dozens of scurrying figures in the area. He shifted down as he finished his sentence. "—natives will get out of control."

Several cars had been stopped by the burning cars' blockade, and their passengers were obviously being robbed at gunpoint.

"What's going on? What are you doing?" Julia Waggoner used both hands to grab the dash hand-hold bar as Norris swerved off the street into a driveway and then across a lawn and into a gap between two old Queen Anne-style houses.

He plunged the big sports car across a narrow backyard, through a line of rose bushes, and into the adjoining backyard. The tires chewed up rain-sodden lawn and then thumped and rattled on redwood as he lurched the heavy car across a patio. A second later, he was onto a driveway and dipping into the next street.

The Shelby fishtailed as he turned right and snarled the

powerful classic car to the nearest corner. A left turn . . . The way was clear.

He turned on the radio for Julia Waggoner's benefit. WKKY was still giving the latest bulletins. ". . . seems to have disappeared from the earth. UNI reports a total absence of communication with Africa since one-fifteen. Now another self-defense bulletin. Before private satellite relay channels were cut off by the British government a few minutes ago, we played reports that told us metal can be used as shielding against the deadly radiation from the sun. The thicker the shield, the better. Remember the microwaves will deflect off metal and also bounce off a metal floor at an angle. It is best to get below any other metal in your area. We have reports of office-building janitors building themselves small ratholes by using dozens of stacked metal file cabinets in subbasements.

"At last report, London was erupting into riots and pitched battles as desperate people fought over metal hideaways or containers large enough for at least one person.

"Gunfights are breaking out here in the Washington area. The police are overwhelmed by reports of looting, armed robbery, rape, and murder. This just in: The railroad yard has become a battleground as armed families fight and kill to gain control of metal freight and tank cars. Ten people are reported dead, six from breathing chemical fumes as they tried to stay in a recently emptied tank car.

"Garbage trucks have become a prime—"

The broadcast was cut off. The radio hissed.

Norris turned onto Columbia Pike and said, "We'll be at CIA headquarters in a few minutes."

Julia Waggoner scowled and twisted the tuner knob to find another station.

They passed a hardware store with shattered doors and windows. Boys and young men were looting it, emerging with digging and metal-cutting tools.

She found a station. ". . . special broadcast by the Federal Emergency Management Agency. We urge all citizens to remain calm. Do not panic. We strongly advise you to stay in your home or apartment and stay tuned to this channel. Your government is investigating the strange stories from overseas and will report as soon as verified information is available. We repeat. The preliminary stories of disaster and mass deaths caused by the sun on the daylight side of the earth have not been confirmed. There is no immediate need for alarm. Stay tuned to this channel. All nongovernment radio and TV channels have been asked to leave the airwaves. We will report to you again in a few minutes.''

Quiet orchestral music came on.

Julia searched the dial for another news voice but found only two other stations on the air, one very faint, and all played the same music.

She asked, "Who is doing that? Who has the authority?"

Norris didn't answer. He kept his gray-green eyes on the pike lanes ahead. There were more and more cars on the streets. Everyone was driving like a maniac. His feet danced on the brake, clutch, and gas pedal as he maneuvered at high speed. Cold winter air whistled past the car's black canvas top.

Julia Waggoner was silent for a few moments. She kept rubbing her high forehead and brushing aside her unruly, graying blond hair. Finally, she asked, "Who decided not to send me a copy of your report?"

"It would have reached you this morning at the latest."

"If I was considered important enough to receive a copy."

Norris smiled grimly. "You are now." He skillfully changed lanes. Carlyle Boulevard was coming up.

Julia screamed, "Look! Stop!"

Ahead, a skinny, shallow-breasted girl, naked to the waist, had run out into the street. She screamed and waved frantically at passing cars, which blared horns and swerved past.

Five young men emerged from the shattered display windows of a furniture store.

Norris said quickly, "We can't! You've got to get to the Situation Room before—"

Julia Waggoner's thin, refined features contorted. "Stop them! Save her!"

"You have a higher priority!"

"*No!* Stop, damn you!" Her brown eyes glittered with outrage.

"Jesus Christ!" Norris swerved toward the curb and skidded to a squealing stop, positioning the car between the girl and the men running toward her. He didn't kill the engine.

Julia Waggoner's side was nearest the girl. He said, "Get her in the car, quick!" He unzipped his parka halfway as he opened his door and got out to face the yelling pack. He held up his hands in a placating motion. They were too close.

Julia urged the weeping, terrified girl into the small rear-seat compartment, then flipped her bucket seat down and got in. She snicked the door lock down as the men arrived and blocked the car.

The pack was led by an older man in his thirties wearing a flannel shirt, a quilted vest jacket, and dirty green slacks. He stopped and confronted Norris. He laughed wildly. "Gonna be a fucking hero, huh, man?" He produced a big switchblade stiletto and flicked it open. "Give her over, dumb shit, or I'll spill your guts all over this pretty old car!" He trembled the knife point inches from Norris's face.

The four younger men circled close, interested. One called, "Hey, we can fuck the old lady, too!"

The man with the stiletto nodded too quickly. "Yeah, yeah, yeah! Give her one last thrill before the fucking world ends!"

Norris said calmly, "The world isn't going to end. Why don't you go find another girl? I'll give you my wallet." He slid his left hand into his ski coat. He gripped the 9-mm. Benelli and slipped off the safety. He said, half turning to the left, "Honey, hand out your purse. We'll have to give them—"

He shot through his parka. The big man with the stiletto shrieked with agony and realization as he dropped the knife and fluttered his hands to his groin. He sagged to his knees, staring down at the blood rapidly staining his pants.

In that frozen instant, Norris pulled the automatic free of its holster. A tall youth on the other side of the car began awkwardly hauling a pistol from the waistband of his tight jeans. Norris shot him. The kid grunted, doubled over, and lurched away.

The other youths scattered.

Breathing fast, Norris took a slow look around, got back

into his car, and drove away. He took the turn at Carlyle Boulevard going seventy miles an hour.

The young girl was sobbing, huddled over, on the narrow rear seat. Julia Waggoner had wriggled out of her fur coat and was straining sideways to cover the girl. "You're safe now."

Norris said, "Buckle up. We're not there yet."

Julia obeyed, but she was angry. "Did you have to shoot?"

"In my judgment, yes. I stay alive by trusting my judgment."

"You tricked them!"

Norris's jaw muscles worked. "Mrs. Vice-President, we are not in the middle of a national-crisis test exercise. This is real. Half of the planet has been cooking to death for at least half an hour. There is a chance the sun will not go back to normal. In that event, that rapist back there was right—this is the end of the world, and all bets are off. No more laws, no more punishment. A few hours of total freedom—for those with weapons and lusts they want to satisfy."

"That doesn't justify what you—"

"Listen! I'm an expert in these matters. I know the look he had in his eyes. I know that funny edge in the voice. He was going to cut me open and rape this girl and let the others do what they wanted with you. And if you'd said, 'Stop! I am the vice-president of the United States!' they might have recognized you and given you some very special attention before killing you. Do you realize that?"

The girl had stopped sobbing. She had been listening. She said in a broken, watery little voice, "I do. Oh, God, I do!"

Norris continued. "The tall kid with the gun was too stupid to know he couldn't get off a shot. Too stupid and too stubborn."

Julia Waggoner had paled. She kept silent.

They passed a burning house. Three bodies lay in the yard, one a young woman in a torn nightgown.

The radio continued to play soft, soothing music.

Julia Waggoner began to tremble. She whispered, "You're right, Mr. Norris. I thank you for saving our lives."

When he didn't respond, she studied his face and watched the sure, skilled moves of his driving.

In a way, he reminded her of her dead husband, who had

been so competent in so many things, who had been so fit, so active . . . so terribly, suddenly dead from the massive heart attack. It had happened seven months ago, and the emptiness, the awful ache of sadness and loss, still plagued her every day.

After a moment, she faced forward and composed herself for the ordeal ahead.

CHAPTER 28

THE SITUATION ROOM IN THE SECRET NINTH SUBBASEMENT
level of the CIA complex was a madhouse.

The walls were huge multicolored hologram depth pictures
of the earth as seen from satellites. There were relief maps of
the world with overlays of national boundaries, cities, railroads,
highways, airfields, military bases. Two men sat at computer
consoles constantly updating the maps and conditions on the
earth as reports and feeds reached them.

The maps of Eurasia, Africa, and the Middle East were
frozen, with no input from day-side satellites. There were
many changes at the westward-creeping dawn line.

A planetary weather map showed strange cloud vortexes
forming in the Pacific and Atlantic, everywhere on the fringes
of the sunset, sunrise lines.

A large circle of U-shaped desks occupied most of the
floor of the room. Each desk was occupied by a harried department head who constantly consulted a computer screen
and whose assistants and aides constantly fed him or her
additional printouts, notes, memos, reports, studies, voice
messages. . . .

The room was filled with shouts, the buzz of talk, the
sounds of machines. Men and women rushed from place to
place.

The cluster of aides and advisers was greatest at the desk of
Vice-President Julia Waggoner. Sitting before her, on the
outside curve of the wide, U-shaped oak desk, at her specific
request, were Richard Soble and John Norris. Next to them,
standing behind them, were science advisers, analysts, and
military liaison people.

181

Julia was acutely aware of the men with mobile, hand-held recording holocameras who hovered around her desk. "For the historical record," Soble had said. But they made her self-conscious.

She had been there only four minutes, and it seemed an hour. People talked to her all at once and kept raising their voices to get her attention and to be heard.

A four-star general strode to her desk. He was in full uniform and announced, "General Webster Bolger reporting, ma'am. Joint chiefs of staff. I was at a party nearby." He scowled at the crowd of seated men around the perimeter of her desk. There was no room for him. He recognized John Norris as a lower-level CIA man. He tapped Norris on the shoulder. "Move it out."

Julia said quickly, "Thank you for coming as soon as you could, general, but that man stays at my desk. He is a special adviser and assistant. I would appreciate your taking over another desk and organizing high-level liaison with the Pentagon. That will be crucial in the next few hours. Richard, will you place him?"

Soble and the general walked away.

The other VIPs at Julia's desk glanced at each other. They looked at Norris with new interest and respect.

Then the voices rose again to command her attention.

Julia held up both hands for silence. "Stop! Do not speak until I point to you! Put your hand forward if you have new information or a vital linkage of facts. Be brief. Now— somebody update me on the president."

A political analyst named Yorxa put his hand forward. Julia pointed. He said, "Nothing new. He may be alive in the basement of the hotel. Those mountains are probably shielding hundreds of thousands of people."

The vice-president pointed to an agitated former newsman, now CIA analyst. He said, "President Barr is in the Jusse Grande, tenth floor, suite D. It has a large balcony facing the morning sun."

Julia took a deep breath and pointed again. A young woman said, "The White House Situation Room has been informed you are here. The staff there—mainly Carl Fennley—has been issuing orders in the name of the president. Fennley wants a video conference right away.''

Julia nodded. ''Set it up.'' She pointed to John Norris.

He said, ''The country is going crazy.'' He pointed to her computer screen.

1:49:56	165	NEW YORK SUBWAY GRIDLOCKED. CROWDS FIGHTING FOR SPACE IN LOWEST LEVELS.
1:50:03	166	BASCOMB C & W ROCK CONCERT CENTRAL PARK DISASTER. EIGHTY-ONE DEAD. HUNDREDS INJURED.
1:50:15	167	HAM RADIOS, CB NETS SPREADING DISASTER, END OF WORLD STORIES.
1:50:22	168	L.A. FREEWAY INTERCHANGES GRIDLOCKED. SHOOTING.

Norris said, ''You'll have to go on an all-net hookup—TV, cable, radio, shortwave—and act in the name of the president. You'll have to tell the people what to do. They need an anchor.''

She resented his bluntness, his ''telling her what to do,'' and his arrogant lack of respect. She snapped, ''And what do I say? The truth? The sun has gone nova, and the day side of our planet is broiling alive? Do I tell them nobody can guarantee that damned radiation will stop before it broils *them?*''

''No. You tell them it *will* stop. If you're wrong, it won't matter. If the radiation flare does stop soon, you'll have saved maybe a million lives.''

Julia flushed. She covered her face with her hands and hated him for an instant. But she had to admit he was correct. She took her hands away and avoided his eyes. She nodded and said, ''Somebody get started on setting up for a broadcast on the FEMA network.''

Two men left her desk.

She asked, ''Anyone, assuming the radiation does *not* stop in time, what will be the actual consequences?'' She pointed to a young man who had just arrived and whose hand shot up.

He said hurriedly, ''We have one radiation reading from a

new research satellite before it went dead. The radiation is wandering or pulsing in the 2,460- to 2,500-megahertz range, and the intensity is high enough to''— he wiped his mouth—''to kill anyone exposed to it within two minutes. Shallow lakes and rivers, ponds, tanks of liquids, anything that will form steam or gases if heated—they will all boil and explode if in tight containers—tanks. Water to a depth of ten feet will boil after about fifteen minutes. The earth will be baked and sterilized to a depth of five feet after fifteen minutes. Nine feet after an hour. All the moisture in the air will instantly break down into gases. Thin metal, that is, less than half an inch thick, will not protect anyone after an hour. The thinner the metal, the sooner the radiation will penetrate and also heat the metal.''

Julia's eye was caught by a new entry on her computer screen.

1:51:37   173   PARIS GONE. SEINE STEAMING. RADIATION
                CONTINUES.

The young man had more to say, but she cut him off. Richard Soble had returned. She told him, ''I'm going to mobilize the armed forces.''

The CIA director agreed. ''You have the power. In the event of the president's incapacitation or inability to act as chief executive and commander in chief, the vice-president has full constitutional authority to act in his behalf until he is able to resume his duties or if it is determined that he is permanently unable to perform his duties.''

Julia ran thin fingers through her graying hair. She nodded. ''I'm also going to declare a national emergency.''

Soble said, ''There are forms to sign. There are sets of them here and at the White House.''

An aide came by with a large trayful of cups of hot coffee, plates of small, trimmed cheese sandwiches, and peeled, sectioned oranges.

Everyone waited until Julia Waggoner had served herself. She gingerly sipped very hot coffee and asked, ''Are there any reasons for waiting before acting in Bill's absence?''

No one responded. John Norris moved his hand forward. When Julia nodded, he said, "None. Until the radiation ends, there'll be absolutely no communication with Europe. If it does end soon, the Swiss will come on the air with army transmitters from their deep mountain forts and would be able to tell us if the president is alive or dead. But all the planes will by unflyable, the airports will be messes, and the weather will make flying in or out impossible. Even if the president is alive, you'll have to act here in his place."

The young science adviser shot his hand up and began talking. "He's right. Look at the map. See those tremendous storm fronts forming? It's incredible! All that superheated air will produce superhurricanes, tornadoes, cyclones—you name it."

Julia looked up at the new, visibly moving lows on the weather holomap of the world. She turned to a colonel sitting at the end of her desk. "Tell General Bolger to inform the joint chiefs that I'm ordering a full mobilization as acting president. Call up the reserves . . . everybody."

She turned back to Richard Soble. "There are sets of contingency plans that fit this situation, aren't there?"

Soble nodded. "They're in the top-secret computer memories if you'd like to review them. Under the heading Nuclear Attack. Access code is—"

"I'd like to, but we don't have time. Advise all state governors to activate their national guards if they haven't already. Is there a FEMA man here?"

Soble said, "He just got here five minutes ago. Three desks to the left. Press the red override and then key in sixteen D."

She did so. She said into a small computer intercom mike, "This is the vice-president. Come to my desk immediately."

A short, pudgy man in a rumpled brown suit rose from his already crowded U desk and approached. His large-lensed glasses glittered with trifocal surfaces. "Daniel E. P. Meeker at your service."

Julia looked up at him, instantly didn't like him, but realized she had to use him. "What's your position?"

"I'm national coordinator. President Barr appointed me last year when Harry Tewes retired. The White House called me at home, but I knew after a few minutes on the road I couldn't get to the district. So I came here. There are actually better communication facilities here than in the White House Situation Room.''

"Fine. I'm declaring a national emergency. It'll be official in a few minutes. In the meantime, start coordinating. Adapt the nuclear attack plans to the present situations.''

Meeker nodded happily. "I'm familiar with them. There are at least fifty queries from governors, mayors, and local FEMA persons whom I can now advise. May I say, Mrs. Vice-President, this is the wisest move. This is what FEMA was created for.''

"Just do it!''

Julia lifted her gaze to the maps on the high walls. She glanced at the never-ending record of local, national, and foreign disasters that marched up her computer screen.

She wanted to crawl away. Everybody was watching her! Those damned ever-present hand-held cameras hovering near . . . Everybody wanted her to make earthshaking decisions and take on the weight of the dying world.

She found herself beginning to tremble and used both hands to grip the seat of her swivel chair. *I don't want this! I do not want this! Dear God!* Her shaking became worse. Cold sweat appeared on her high forehead.

John Norris saw what was happening and said loudly to the people at the desk, "My dad used to say the imminence of death did three things: concentrated the mind, loosened the bowels, and proved beyond doubt the existence of God.''

There was laughter and grinning. Julia laughed loudest. Her trembling stopped. The terrible weight of fear and dread and despair shifted aside enough for her to continue.

She leaned back in her chair. The springs creaked. She closed her eyes for a moment. She said, "If I'm going to make a speech—somebody find my purse. Is it still in your car, Norris? I'll have to fix my face for the cameras. And my hair! And somebody had better write something for me to say.''

One of Richard Soble's aides came to the U desk. "Mrs. Vice-President, the teleconference link with the White House is ready now. This way.''

She was led out of the Situation Room, down a side hall, and into a small, boxlike room. The door was very thick. In the center of the room was a computer console, a TV depth screen and, mounted at each side of the screen, two holocameras. Holotape recorders were running.

In the screen were the head and shoulders of Carl Fennley. His shirt was open and his red tie askew. He looked in despair. He straightened as Julia came within the twin cameras' range and sat before the screen. "Mrs. Vice-President, it's good to see you're safe."

"Thank you, Carl. Any late word on Bill?"

"I'm afraid not. We hope—"

She felt a terrible sense of urgency. And she felt sick to her stomach. She interrupted. "Carl, we have to settle the matter of command. I'm going to declare a state of national emergency and act in Bill's stead until we know if he's alive and can get back home."

"Ah, Mrs. Vice—"

"For God's sake, call me Julia. Carl, are you getting all the data we're getting?"

"Yes, there's a cable link. We're capable of making decisions here just as easily as you there. We're acting in accordance with clear presidential policy provisions. We—"

"When did Bill Barr make policy on the end of the world? We cannot just keep on playing soothing music on the emergency network while we keep everyone else off the air. The country is falling apart!"

"Julia, it's only forty minutes or so since the first reports came in. Don't you think we should wait? Your taking power so soon would appear—"

"I'm not 'taking power'! I don't want to do this! I want to be home in my cozy bed reading a dull report and sipping hot wine. But people all over the country are being killed because everyone thinks the world is coming to an end! And their government is sitting paralyzed behind Muzak! I'm getting urgent questions from governors, big-city mayors, bureau heads, cabinet officers, representatives, senators—all asking what the hell is going on and what are they supposed to do.

187

Somebody has to make decisions, and God help me, Carl—I'm going to start making them.''

"Of course, Julia. We took it upon ourselves to order all the commercial stations and nets off the air. We're bending every effort to contact the president. In the meantime, Julia, I think your place is here in the White House. A helicopter—''

"Carl, this teleconference is being recorded here. I presume also at your end. I understand your position. But I am not going to waste an hour doing nothing until a helicopter arrives and ferries me to you. I'm going to act, from here, in President Barr's place. The moment he returns to the United States and is capable of assuming his office, I will happily, gratefully, eagerly, step aside and resume my role and my office as vice-president. But in a few minutes I'm going on the nets and declare a state of national emergency. I'll make it clear I am acting as chief executive only in the absence of the president.''

"The procedures for that do not allow—''

"Please inform everyone there of my decision. Something has to be done, and I'm the only one in a position and with the constitutional authority to do it.''

"Julia—''

"I won't argue with you any longer, Carl. Neither you nor anyone else in the White House is to issue any orders, directives, or guidelines in the name of President Barr. Everything must be approved and directed from here. I will not have a jurisdictional fight or a power struggle going on between us, Carl. You're an excellent White House chief of staff. I'll need your skills and abilities in this terrible period we face. Please help and support me.''

Fennley turned his head to say to someone off camera, "She's going to take over!"

Julia stepped away from the screen and left the small, soundproof conference room. The myriad sounds of the frantic Situation Room filled the hallway.

She felt exhilarated from her confrontation with Carl Fennley. But then the responsibility she'd assumed crushed down on her, and she wanted to hide—run—escape to other floors, other rooms in the labyrinthine underground CIA complex.

The young woman aide who had been waiting stepped close and said, "Mrs. Vice-President, my name is Debra Wiley, and if you have the need, the executive restrooms are down this hall and to the left. Director Soble has assigned me to assist you in any way. If there's anything you want—"

Julia said, "Thank you. Call me Mrs. Waggoner." She noted that Debra was her size and wearing a conservative blue skirt and jacket. "May I try on your jacket? I may need to wear something better than this sweater when I face the cameras in a few minutes."

"Of course!"

They discovered Debra's jacket fit perfectly. Julia handed it back, smiling. "Thank you. Stay close."

Julia returned to the Situation Room madhouse and took her center seat at the crowded U desk. She noted that John Norris was conferring with a naval officer at a nearby desk. She told Richard Soble, "Get those emergency proclamation papers ready. I'll make my statement to the nation from this desk. What should I say?"

"A list of must says is being prepared." Soble gestured. "And we have a makeup man."

Julia turned her chair and was quickly draped with a large white towel. A slim professional beautician bent to prepare her for the holo-TV cameras.

As the man cleaned her face and applied base, color, shadow, and lipstick, she said, "Somebody bring me up to the minute. Has the solar flare ended?"

The science man said, "Strictly speaking, it isn't a flare. It's a burst . . . a bubble. It shouldn't last much longer."

"Give me a guesstimate on how much longer."

"Well . . . I can't. There's no known precedent for this phenomenon. It all depends on how much internal imbalance was created by the plasma beam and how much internal radiation pressure the sun must release."

Julia gestured to Richard Soble. "Norris told me about his report of what happened at that place in the desert—something or other Maradi—which I did not receive a copy of, by the way." Her voice turned icy. "I want a copy now!"

She signaled the young science man. "Is it possible that

the type of radiation the sun is emitting will change as its internal pressure diminishes?''

"Yes. Well, it's been radiating a spectrum all this time, with the main blast of radiation in the two to three thousand megahertz range. We might see a shift to extreme heat and light, or down into the radio waves. Or maybe not.''

Julia glanced contemptuously at the man. He flushed.

She couldn't reach her computer keyboard. The makeup man had tilted her head back. She said, "Update on mobilization.''

Soble said, "Debra, get General Bolger over here.''

When the general strode over a few seconds later, he said, "We've contacted a majority of the chiefs. The Pentagon is up to red-alert staffing. We've had a quick conference on policy and ordered all bases and all units to a war footing.''

Julia said, "Fine. Here's the big question: Who will the armed forces obey—me or Carl Fennley in the White House?''

Bolger didn't hesitate. "You, Mrs. Vice-President. We know the odds against ever seeing President Barr alive. You have our full constitutional loyalty. The country needs strong leadership *now!*''

"Thank you, general. Express my thanks to the joint chiefs. If you aren't already, please coordinate fully with FEMA. Thank you.''

As the general turned away, Julia said, "Mr. Soble, how long before I have to face the cameras?''

"As soon as you're ready, I think. The areas you must discuss are going onto a teleprompter now. You'll have to elaborate from the outline. There's no time to have someone write a speech. A copy of Norris's Wau el Maradi report is available to you now in the computer. The code is Zxc3468.''

The makeup man stepped back. He gave her hair a final shot of hair spray and whipped the white towel off her shoulders. He handed her a mirror.

Julia examined her face and nodded. "I haven't looked this good in years! Thank you. Debra—need your jacket now!''

Julia leaned forward to her computer. "Is my speech outline available on this?''

In the seconds it took Soble to answer, as he consulted a notebook, she took in several of the new reports on the screen.

```
1:59:03  201  FORCE 19 HURRICANE SWEEPING EAST OVER
              IRELAND, ENGLAND, SCOTLAND. SOUTH
              FROM NORTH POLE. FORCE INCREASING.
              RECORD HIGH TIDES IRISH, SCOT, ENGLISH
              COASTS. TOWNS FLOODED, BLOWN AWAY.
1:59:18  202  WHITES AND BLACKS FIGHTING OVER POS-
              SESSION OF COAL MINES. SHOOTING AT
              COKELAKE, KY.
```

Soble said, ''Your speech outline is at code FourA.''

Julia punched up the code and scanned the short topic lines as they marched up her screen. She nodded now and then, frowned several times.

Debra handed Julia her jacket. Julia smiled thanks and put it on.

A swarm of camera crews and technicians rolled equipment and lights into the area before her desk. A teleprompter was set up. Cables snaked everywhere.

A director said, ''About three minutes, Mrs. Vice-President.''

Julia nodded. Her throat was closing up. She beckoned to Debra, who came close. ''Can you get me a drink? A real drink.''

The girl smiled, nodded, and moved quickly away.

An aide arrived with a document folder, which he handed to Richard Soble. He checked the contents and handed them across the desk to Julia.

A terrible feeling of dread had been continually sliming her stomach. This made it worse. The documents were three copies of a declaration of national emergency. They had been printed on heavy linen-weave paper.

She scanned the dense legal language. She couldn't concentrate.

Soble handed her a pen. ''At the bottom of each copy, your signature, your official title, and the date.''

She chewed her lower lip as she signed.

A technician said, ''We're ready to broadcast.''

Julia handed the signed declaration copies to Soble, closed her eyes against a sudden glare of floodlights, and took a slow, deep breath.

There was a touch on her shoulder. Debra handed her a small glass of orange juice. Julia sipped and discovered it to be half gin. She smiled her thanks. She drained the glass.

The director asked, "Are you ready, Mrs. Vice-President?" Julia nodded.

An amplified male voice commanded, "Quiet! Quiet! Broadcasting in thirty seconds. Everyone away from the desk."

The makeup man did a last-second blotting of Julia's perspiration and applied a final touch of lipstick. "Don't nibble!"

She had to smile. She composed herself, lifted her chin, and looked directly into the terrifying, unblinking holocamera lenses. She was all alone. The big room was unnaturally quiet.

"Ten seconds. Broadcasting when the red light goes on."

Julia waited, frozen, staring now at the teleprompter, which displayed her opening topic.

The red light blinked on.

An announcer said, startling her, "The vice-president of the United States, Julia Fielding Waggoner."

She met the reptilian gaze of the camera. She let three seconds pass, then began.

"My fellow citizens. An unprecedented disaster has struck our world. We have reports that approximately fifty minutes ago the sun began emitting a very deadly type of radiation.

"Only the daylight side of the world is suffering this radiation. We are safe. And we are assured by our leading scientists that the period of radiation will be very short and that the radiation will have ended before daylight arrives here in the United States.

"The end of the world has not come! We will all be safe in the morning if we do not panic and if we cooperate fully with local, state, regional, and national authorities.

"Our greatest danger now is from ourselves if we yield to animal fear.

"I am speaking to you in place of President Barr, who is, we have every reason to believe, safe in a deep, underground

Swiss army mountain base just outside Geneva. Solar interference makes communication with President Barr impossible at this time.

"Because he is not immediately available to make decisions and because some emergency measures must prudently be taken, I am acting in his place.

"I have just signed a declaration of national emergency. This means the nation is technically now under martial law, and I have become, temporarily, this nation's commander in chief.

"Let me repeat again the assurances we have received from our nation's best scientists that the sun flare of radiation which is causing so much injury and destruction on the daylight side of earth will not last and will not directly affect our country.

"I urge you again to stay in your homes. Do not go out. There is, unfortunately, some panic, looting, and other criminal activity occurring in some places.

"That crime will stop! The army, the marines, the navy, and their reserves are all being mobilized, as are all state national guard units, reserve police, reserve deputies, and private security personnel.

"I am declaring a nationwide curfew until ten A.M. tomorrow morning, eastern standard time. I will repeat that. I am declaring a nationwide curfew until ten A.M. tomorrow morning, eastern standard time.

"This is a declaration of war upon those few rioters, looters, thieves, rapists, murderers—all those criminals who have thought to take advantage of the terrible events happening on the other side of the world. These criminals are subject to being shot on the spot! I repeat: Anyone on the streets or caught committing a crime is subject to martial law and may be shot!

"My fellow citizens, if you are not at home, go to your homes and stay in your homes.

"I am sorry to have to take such a drastic step. But I am determined that this great country of ours will not dissolve into blind panic, crime, and anarchy. Law will prevail! Order will prevail!"

Julia paused. She took a slow, controlled breath. She was desperately determined to convince everyone listening or viewing. "My friends, we must join together. We must cooperate as never before. We must become one large family. Because the danger we face is not radiation from the sun. Our greatest danger is chaos and anarchy, letting a few greedy, lustful people panic us all into senseless mob action. 'Every man for himself' and 'the law of the jungle' cannot be permitted to rule in America.

"After the radiation has stopped—and that will happen in a few minutes—we face violent and unpredictable changes in weather patterns which will have been caused by the heating of the air and the ground on the day side of our world.

"We face huge storms and cloudburst rains. We face great blizzards and, later, flooding. We face extraordinarily high winds.

"But we can face these hazards together! We are one people! We are a great people! And we will survive!"

Julia paused again. A painful tension had developed in her shoulders and neck. Her head was beginning to throb.

She continued, "Please stay tuned to this channel. I will speak to you again soon! In the meantime, this first address will be repeated, and there will be national and international news. In addition, local authorities will be on the air to advise you about preparing for the bad weather, to tell of local conditions and upcoming public service requirements."

She smiled into the lenses. "I know I can count on you to be cool and calm and civilized in this time of crisis. We are human beings, under God, and we must show our courage, our faith, and our love. God bless you."

Julia held her gaze resolutely until the red light went off. Then she slumped, exhausted.

The silence in the huge Situation Room continued for two beats; then someone began to applaud. Cheers sounded, and in an instant everyone in the room was standing, applauding, shouting approval and gratitude.

Julia was stunned. Tears filled her eyes, and she blinked them down her cheeks. "Thank you," she whispered. "Thank you."

PART TWO

CHAPTER 29

"BRING HER ABOUT, ANDREW! BRING HER ABOUT!" SEAN Owenmore shouted into the darkness, into lancing, bulletlike rain and freezing, howling northwest winds. Mother of God, he'd never known such a storm! Where had it come from so suddenly? His small fishing boat, the *Kathy-O*, yawed wildly in a cavernous trough between hurtling mountains of black water.

He fought to gain the pilothouse deck. He could feel the engine pounding in the stern, running at full throttle. He could barely see Andrew Nolan, his mate, spread legged at the wheel, fighting to turn the trawler to meet an onrushing crest.

The boat slewed to port as the sea moved under it, hurtling it up a terrifying slope to the ragged, spewing crest.

In that second, Sean gained the small wheelhouse and added his strength to battling the wheel. The rudder seemed in the grip of a giant.

The *Kathy-O* was almost lifted from the sea at the crest as enormous winds buffeted the momentarily exposed bow and forehull. The icy, shrieking wind tore the wave top away from under the boat, atomizing the water to white tatters that streamed away to the southeast.

Andrew Nolan yelled in Sean's ear and was only barely heard over the terrible wind. "It's our death! We're being driven to the coast!"

The *Kathy-O* quivered and shuddered for a frozen instant in the teeth of the sudden hurricane, then plunged down a dizzying black slope into seeming oblivion.

Sean laughed and shouted back, "Then pray for a miracle,

197

you Donegal bastard!'' If it was to be death, then it would
from the most terrible storm in history!

The wind rapidly increased beyond belief, becoming
solid thing that struck the boat like a great iron fist at the ne
crest. The boat heeled over. The screw spun fruitlessly. Se
was thrown against the binnacle.

A greater sound penetrated their minds, a reverberation
deep it was felt through bone and wood. Surf! More than su
as the vast wind piled the ocean into Donegal and Sligo bay
in a killer tide so high it drowned Bundoran and Kinloug
towns.

All the west coasts of Ireland, Scotland, Wales, and E
gland were drowned in those awful moments. The vast, boi
ing cauldron that was Europe and Asia was ruthlessly suckin
cooler air from thousands of miles away, creating hurrican
winds in excess of two hundred miles per hour.

Atop a gargantuan wave, poised in froth and ear-shatterin
wind, the *Kathy-O* rode over Bundoran to an impossibl
swollen Lake Melvin . . . and onward up the valley on th
dying monster wave to Lake Macrean, awash now with sa
water, where it foundered, splintering, on the slope of Culeag
Mountain. The vicious wind scoured the pieces away as Sea
was rolled, half conscious, into a pocket formed by rocks an
deformed earth.

Sean Owenmore was stone deaf, at peace with the over
whelming sounds of the disaster. But he could see, in th
crashing near darkness of near dawn, as Andrew Nolan sprea
his arms to cling to the mountain and could not. He sav
Andrew lifted and flung away into the pale darkness.

TWA FLIGHT 468, 9:00 P.M.

Capt. Haris Green tapped the ground-speed gauge as he asked his copilot, Gerald Vicha, "Can that be right?" It showed 730 miles per hour. Too high! He called to his flight engineer, "Mike, check our true ground speed, will you?"

Gerry Vicha said, "We're losing air speed. It just fell below three fifty. Three forty . . ."

"What?" Green checked the gauges. He scowled and eased the throttles forward. Now the ground-speed gauge showed their absolute speed rising: 800 miles per hour . . . 850 . . .

Mike Bleiler called forward, "We've suddenly picked up some incredible tail winds. Christ! Two hundred and fifty . . . sixty . . ."

"Air speed stable at four fifty . . . now falling a little."

Captain Green refused to push his triple-jet 797 any harder. He had a bad feeling about this sudden tail wind. The northeast trades weren't this strong at any time, and especially not at this time of the year. If they were this strong at twenty-six thousand feet, he couldn't imagine the typhoon raging below at the surface of the Pacific.

He watched the ground-speed gauge hover at nine hundred miles an hour. "We'll reach Oahu in record time if this keeps up." He switched on the radio to l.d. com. band 6. "Oahu, this is TWA 468 from San Francisco. Picking up two-seven-zero tail winds. Repeat two-seven-zero tail winds. Request revised ETA. Need local weather. Over."

Gerry Vicha suggested to Bleiler, "Mike, maybe you should tune a news channel. That must be the great granddaddy of storms under us."

While waiting with greater and greater impatience and

alarm for Oahu to reply, Captain Green said, "I don't think any ship ever built could survive—"

The speaker crackled, and a frantic air controller at Oahu International Airport said hurriedly, "Four-six-eight, we have a force-sixteen hurricane here. You cannot land. You cannot land. Return to San Francisco. Repeat, advise return to San Francisco!"

Vicha blurted, "Since when? There wasn't anything in the weather charts—"

A clammy chill settled into Captain Green's guts. His eyes flicked at the fuel gauges, at the chronometer. The big jet was well past the point of no return. There wasn't a snowball's chance in hell they could fight headwinds of 250 miles an hour and reach San Francisco before the tanks ran dry. He had a full load—343 passengers and crew.

He said urgently into his microphone, "Oahu, this is TWA four-six-eight. We cannot return to San Francisco. We are past PONR. How big is the storm? Could we land at Midway? Over."

"Four-six-eight, there is a disaster day side. The sun is roasting everything day side. The entire Pacific air basin is moving west at tremendous speeds. We are being destroyed by this wind. Planes are tumbling like leaves. Tides—Tower going down! God have—"

The transmission ended. White noise hissed from the speaker.

Before Green could react, Mike said, "Got something!" He flicked a switch. A news broadcast blared into the big cockpit. ". . . to high ground! Get to high ground if you can! Our building is swaying. It's terrifying. The windows are bulging. We have reports of palm trees uprooted, rolling into houses, cars rolling everywhere; houses are being blown apart, roofs going everywhere. The hotels—the big resort hotels are going down! The east coasts are wiped out, flooded. The waves are gigantic! The Kahana strip—all those hotels—gone! We're on emergency power. This is Joe Kamalo reporting on KHWI, Honolulu. The islands are dying, drowning! The world is coming to an end! Our building—a window just blew. The wind—can't talk—power—"

The carrier wave died. There remained only static.

Gerry Vicha cried, "What are we going to do?"

Captain Green said grimly, "We'll stay up as long as we can. Maybe something will change." He studied the gauges. They were flying west at a true ground speed of over a thousand miles per hour. Fuel for six hours, maximum. They were trapped in an irresistible mass of air, and there was no point in fighting it. There was no way they could land in this kind of wind and surface turbulence, even if there was within reach a landing strip large enough for a jumbo 797.

They faced six thousand miles of empty, raging ocean.

CHAPTER 30

VICE-PRESIDENT JULIA WAGGONER SPOKE URGENTLY INTO the still-terrifying holocamera lenses. She knew she'd never get used to them. Her eyes ached and burned, her stomach clenched on acid, but she held her gaze steady and her voice resolute as she completed her fourth all-net speech of the new day.

"I am very happy to repeat the good news. The intense solar radiation which had been destroying the day side of our planet stopped after one hour, at two oh-six A.M.

"We are all safe from that danger. That terrible event cannot be resumed or repeated. The solar flare has ended, but our danger from its consequences has not. Already, extremely destructive fires and hurricane winds are inflicting awful damage to those countries near the flare-afflicted areas. Even now vast storms are beginning to hit our nation.

"Soon it is possible you may not be able to hear me or hear your local emergency stations because of power outages. Please do not panic. Stay in your homes or apartments. Emergency crews will restore power as soon as possible. Do not go out unless you possess skills and equipment which may be of immediate value to your local authorities.

"We face the greatest struggle and the greatest challenge of our lives. We must be ready to adjust our lives if necessary during the coming period of enormous change forced upon us by the catastrophe our world has suffered.

"We will survive this huge challenge, and we will come through this period of testing triumphant, with new strength, new vision, and a new, bold future!"

She held on until the red broadcasting light blinked off.

Then she lowered her head to her arms on the desk. She closed her eyes and wanted only to be left alone.

But a hand touched her shoulder gently, insistently. She heard once more the applause and cheers of the hundreds of people in the deep CIA Situation Room.

She was almost beyond acknowledging their sincere approval and admiration. She lifted her head, brushed back her hair, waved, and smiled.

Her advisers rushed like locusts to claim their places on the outer perimeter of her large, U-shaped executive desk.

The hand on her shoulder belonged to Richard Soble. He bent to whisper in her ear, "We're beginning to get radio contact with Swiss army units in their mountain forts. They're sending search parties into Geneva. They'll report on VIP survivors or dead as soon as possible."

Julia nodded tiredly. She turned to face the horrifying reports marching up her computer screen, and the hands put forward demanding recognition.

```
12:54:46  789  BUENOS AIRES FORCE SEVENTEEN HUR-
               RICANE. SHACK TOWNS SCOURED AWAY.
               HIGH-RISES DOWN.
12:54:59  790  POWER GONE: BOSTON, NEW YORK, PHIL-
               ADELPHIA, WASHINGTON, ATLANTA, SA-
               VANNAH, MIAMI.
```

Julia pointed to the young scientist who seemed to know so much. "How strong is a force-seventeen hurricane?"

He said, after a split-second pause, "Winds of about 130 miles per hour."

"Could they blow down modern high-rise buildings?"

"They don't blow them down; they mostly suck them down by a near vacuum created behind the building. They drag them down. A force-seventeen hurricane would have gusts up to 170 miles per hour, and they could take down anything over twenty stories."

Julia turned away from him. The screen continued its relentless listing of disaster.

12:56:22	795	CHICAGO FIRE SPREADING TO FOREST PARK, MAYWOOD. LAKE MICHIGAN FLOODING SOUTH CHICAGO. POWER GONE.
12:56:31	796	DETROIT/WINDSOR FIRE STORM SPREADING SOUTHWEST. NO CONTROL. WINDS 115 MPH, RISING. POWER GONE.
12:56:44	797	LOS ANGELES SANTA ANA WINDS 150 MPH, STEADY. FIRES RACING TO OCEAN. MARINA DEL REY SHAMBLES. POWER GONE.

She lifted her eyes to the huge, multicolored holograph pictures of the earth as seen from the remaining spy and weather satellites that were orbiting repeatedly now over the nightmare of Eurasia and Africa, peering down through clouds and smoke and darkness with infrared eyes.

Those continents were spotted with leprous sores—fire storms—roiling, spreading, consuming whole cities, forests, entire regions of farmland. The vast fire lines were being driven to ever-wider gluttony by hurricane winds.

She could see monstrous, terrifyingly swift air masses rushing to the awful heat and equally massive convection currents of heated air rising, surging, seeking to relieve their torment by high-altitude return to the oceans, to cooler lands, where they dove to suck seas of moisture into themselves. The planet's air masses were like a body's circulatory system rushing heated blood to the skin for cooling during exercise or heavy exertion.

She knew that soon the lows, the violent storm fronts forming in the oceans, would sweep the Western continents, dumping vast torrents of rain and blizzards of snow. It was only a matter of hours. The winds afflicting America now were only preliminaries.

She lowered her tortured gaze to the semicircle of men watching her, waiting. She said, "We're going to have a deluge everywhere before long. There'll be floods, worse floods than we've ever seen." She began issuing orders. She pointed to this man, that man . . . "Arrange emergency evacuation of all flood plains and low-lying coastal areas. Coordinate with weather experts on this and with local authorities. . . . Order the armed forces—all kinds—and fire fighters everywhere to concentrate on saving food stocks. Supermarkets, warehouses, loaded boxcars, grain silos. We're going to need every scrap of food. . . . Rationing! Coordinate with FEMA. The entire population will have to be mobilized. We can't do this on a formal hire-fire basis. National conscription and volunteering. Everybody will have to work.''

Men scurried to obey.

CHAPTER 31

BRADFORD COLLIER STONEMAN'S GOLDEN BROWN EYES FLICK-ered with pain as Lane McDermott read to him a list of losses suffered worldwide and their consequences. He felt sick to his stomach.

McDermott noted the subtle flinching in Stoneman's face, the squinting of the eyes, but he had to complete the assessment.

Erica Stoneman sat next to Bradford on the colonial-style sofa. She held his spotted, clawlike left hand in hers and squeezed gently to comfort him. She could feel his heavy, rapid pulse and hated to think of his blood pressure. He had become like a willful child the way he refused to take his pills. The senility he feared was claiming him.

She was also aware of Lane McDermott's glances at her long blond hair, at her scoop-neck red satin top, at her long, slim legs in fashion-fitted jeans. She appreciated his appreciation. And that, she thought, is all there is to that tune.

They were in the deep, multileveled nuclear bomb shelter under the Stoneman summer retreat, a large wooded estate close to Mt. Katahdin.

The apartment was lavish and roomy, a re-creation of the main floor of the house above, with computer-programed forest holoviews projected behind fake windows, further en-hancing the illusion of living above ground.

McDermott said, "We have to consider the oil and gaso-line distribution companies in France and Germany gone. The surface tanks would have all ruptured and probably burned. All of Europe is one huge fire storm now. All of our factories will be burning, and probably all of the real estate—buildings in cities."

Stoneman pressed a quivering right hand to his eyes. "Why are there fires? How do you know there are so many fires?"

"It's a certainty gas lines ruptured, and any kind of spark—Without fire fighting—without people—there would be no stopping such fires. And the hurricane winds . . ."

"But it's winter! The rain—" Stoneman's voice pitched higher into querulous petulance.

Erica went to the core reality. "It doesn't matter if this or that factory is gone or that distribution systems are gone. There are no people alive over there! Isn't that right, Lane? If all the people are dead, there are no workers, and there are no customers."

"Yes, that's essentially correct. The estimates are of virtually one hundred percent death rates. And I expect the same situation extends throughout Asia and Africa."

Bradford Stoneman asked, "But the banks—the banks are all right, aren't they? They have deep vaults. The money—"

"Sir, there may be some cash in the vaults, but most of the assets are in loans. It's all in the computers over there, and they're probably—"

Erica said, "We could reconstruct most of the ownership links from bank records here in the States, couldn't we? And from the offshore and Central American branches?"

"Most of it," McDermott agreed. "Some we wouldn't want to admit to."

She smiled. "There are layers of control and ownership I'm unaware of, of course. If you have—"

Bradford Stoneman complained, "I have a terrible headache!" He pressed both hands to his head.

Erica said, "Lane, call the doctor."

Stoneman said, "No, no! It'll pass. I've had these before."

Erica watched him for a few seconds, then turned to Lane. "How much do we have left. About a third?"

"Approximately."

She said, "It's an opportunity, in a way. The flare has passed, and so much of our competition has been wiped out. The core of the Rothschild empire is gone. The Ludwig conglomerates are gone. The entire Middle East is empty, the sheiks are dead . . . and it all sits there now, burning, but waiting to be taken. Even if every oil well in Arabia is on fire, they can be quenched. Even if they burn for years, the reserves will be immense."

His head pounding with pain, Stoneman nevertheless said admiringly, "Listen to her, McDermott! That's what I would have said five years ago. One year ago! She's got the vision. My wife—I married a bitch queen!" He managed a laugh. But then his head lolled against the high back of the sofa. "Damn . . . dizzy . . ." He seemed to drift off to sleep.

Erica and McDermott exchanged looks. She said softly, "I'm worried—"

The phone rang. Erica answered it.

The caller was Tracy Benjamin, the top science writer they'd picked up in Boston on the flight to Maine two days before. He had been chosen and contracted for a possible sudden term of service in a Stoneman retreat. He knew a great deal about most fields of science; he kept an overview of current basic research and technology. He was a walking science encyclopedia and always up to date.

He was camped in the communications room, monitoring every possible channel to the outside world: TV, cable, news wires, radio, including shortwave, satellites, phones . . . There was even a secret tap into the ultrasecret NSA Geo-77 deep-earth link to the sixty-three U.S. nuclear, missile-armed submarines on station around the world.

He said, "The vice-president is setting up a universal service program. All food stocks will be confiscated and reserved for distribution by strict rationing. FEMA is sending out working papers now to all federal districts."

Erica asked, "Anything else?"

"Everybody who ever carried a gun is being called up for guard duty. It's a total mobilization."

"Thank you, Tracy. Make printouts of everything you can. Bring it all down here in two hours."

She hung up and turned to McDermott and her husband. She reported what Benjamin had said.

Stoneman didn't seem to hear. He was breathing loudly, shallowly.

McDermott took off his glasses and rubbed his eyes. It had

been an exhausting, nearly sleepless two days. But he thoroughly enjoyed working with Erica; her mind was first-rate.

He said, "Well, it's the only thing Waggoner can do. I'd still bet on anarchy when the big storms hit. It'll be chaos. I don't think the authorities can hold it together more than a few days."

Erica frowned in thought. Her finger idly traced the edge of her scoop-neck satin top. She was curiously excited. She felt sexy. Her nipples had grown erect against the slick material.

She wondered aloud, "Don't we control the UniMart chain? Shouldn't we organize our own guard forces . . . and . . . set up an alternate, secret distribution system?"

McDermott chuckled. "A black market?"

"It'll only be 'black' if the government can enforce its edicts against private enterprise. We can offer luxuries and critical necessities—" She snapped her fingers. "We own Tucker Medicals, don't we? We can loot our warehouses and sell those items at huge markups."

"Yes. And we have the gold coin and junk silver to buy all the guards and enforcers we need." McDermott put his glasses back on. He delved in his briefcase for certain papers. "I can use Barrow Protection Services as a nucleus, nationwide. We'll have to move enormous amounts of goods to secret storage. The pharmaceuticals especially will be valuable."

"And food?" Erica was breathing faster. Her face felt warm. She was exhilarated.

"UniMart and V-High Health Centers. The frozen foods and refrigerated items have to be sold first. Electricity is going out everywhere. It'll be gone . . . all the power grids will be down in a few days at most."

"What about tools? Spare parts?" She was too excited to stay seated. She rose gracefully and paced the room.

McDermott nodded and began making notes. "The Tool Box chain, a division of FME."

She pointed at McDermott. "A vertical organization? No. We have to be protected. . . ."

McDermott said, "An alliance with the Mafia. We've had working arrangements with them before. They've done things for us; we've helped them . . . This situation is perfect for both of us. They have the organization, the soldiers, and we have the product, the merchandise. I'll set up a primary guard system for our goods, move it, and then negotiate with the families for distribution and paybacks.''

Eyes glowing, Erica went to the sofa and hugged the silent Bradford Stoneman. "Darling, did you hear?"

"Yes, yes, yes!" He seemed irritated. "You're cutting off the blood in my arm. It feels so weak . . .''

"No, darling, I—"

"I can't lift my arm!" Stoneman struggled away from her.

McDermott leaped from his armchair and picked up the phone. He punched three numbers. He watched Stoneman collapse to the floor. A voice answered. He said quickly, "Send the doctor down here immediately. I think Mr. Stoneman is having a stroke.''

Bradford Stoneman lay, surprised, staring at his left arm as if it had betrayed him. His headache was a piercing agony.

Erica knelt beside him, "Brad—"

His right hand went to his mouth. He convulsed, twisting, gagging, as his luncheon of bean soup and weak tea spewed between his fingers.

McDermott said urgently to Erica, who was cradling Stoneman's head in her lap, "Don't let him strangle on his vomit!''

It was a messy, stinking death.

Bradford Collier Stoneman's stroke was massive, occurring deep in his brain. A major artery ballooned and ruptured when blocked by a large blood clot.

Parts of his brain died of oxygen starvation, and parts were squeezed to death by an ever-expanding pool of blood.

Before the doctor arrived, Stoneman's body voided its wastes in a series of terrifying convulsions. In spite of Erica's weeping attempts to blow air into his lungs, his heart stopped beating three minutes later.

CHAPTER 32

JULIA WANTED TO HIT THE MAN. "NO! WE CAN'T TAKE THE time to do all that paper work! My declaration of a national emergency and of national conscription for both sexes is being broadcast continually. But we can't reach millions of people because of power losses and downed phone lines. We'll have to use force if necessary. Explain, then demand able-bodied men and women work to get the power nets up. This nation will die without power and communications. We'll disintegrate into howling, looting mobs and a hundred thousand tiny enclaves—dictatorships."

The men at her desk were visibly impressed. Julia Waggoner was demonstrating amazing insight, knowledge, and decisiveness. She was driving herself—and them—to the limit.

The bureaucrat she had just instructed turned away, shaken, to carry out her orders.

But all the while the horrible reality of what was happening on the surface kept intruding on her consciousness—a quick, horrified glance at the computer screen, an appalled look at the holoviews overhead . . .

Julia turned away from a small group of treasury officials to drink some coffee and eat a sandwich.

John Norris slipped into his seat at her desk and put his hand forward, asking to speak.

She grimaced. "Why do I dread what you have to say?"

He smiled. "Why do I dread having to say it?"

"What is it, then?" She washed down a barely chewed bite of ham and cheese sandwich with a swallow of tepid coffee.

"There is a strong possibility that there are Russian submarines out there, armed with dozens of nuclear missiles, that

211

don't know what's happened. Since the Riga and the Kiev mutinies last year, their commanders have been under orders not to listen to Western broadcasts for fear of 'contaminating' themselves or their crews.''

"So?" Julia felt an ominous dread in her belly.

"They will not have any contact with Russia for days and may have had a last-second alert of some kind or a set of war orders if the Russian high command misinterpreted the cause of the solar flare."

"Are you saying a Russian nuclear-armed sub might start launching missiles at us?"

"I'm afraid so. One or more of those submarine commanders might think we have used a secret weapon on their motherland or made a massive first strike. They might decide to seek revenge."

"That's all we need!" Julia keyed a top-priority call to General Bolger's desk. When he responded, she said, "General, do we know which radio frequencies are used by the Russian submarine fleet?"

"Yes, Mrs. Vice-President, approximately. They shift every day, often every hour, and their transmissions are always in code."

"What are the chances of any of those Russian missile-armed subs deciding to attack the United States?"

"My God! Why didn't we think of that? It's possible! They might think—"

"General, round up some Russian-speaking people and flood all the likely frequencies—in fact, all the maritime bands—with the true story—the whole true story—of what has happened to the world and offer all foreign ships, all foreign submarines, sanctuary and assistance. Coordinate with Soble. I believe the CIA has manpower and facilities for that here." She clicked off.

Daniel E. P. Meeker, the head of FEMA, appeared at her desk.

She snapped, "Yes?"

"Mrs. Vice-President, I believe that you should think of moving the seat of the government somewhere out of this area."

She glanced suspiciously at Norris, then glared at Meeker. Why did she resent Meeker's sleek, smug, well-fed manner so much? "You, too? Do you think Russian subs are going to attack?"

"Of course, that is one of the prime dangers."

Julia began nervously fingering a stray lock of her hair. She felt overwhelmed. She needed a shower, a few minutes alone. She asked Meeker, "Aren't we safe down here?"

"From the blast of a nearby ten-megaton hydrogen bomb strike, maybe. Residual radiation might penetrate. We might also be safe from surface radiation but be trapped here by that radiation."

Julia yielded again to her feeling of rage at what had happened in the past two days. She asked sarcastically, "Where would we go?" She jerked her head at the overhead holoview screens. "Look at that!" The spy satellites were sweeping over the burning day-side continents. Europe seemed a solid maelstrom of fire. Central Africa had yielded its jungle moisture to the heat-inducing radiation of the solar flare and now was crawling with crisscrossing walls of fire hundreds of miles long.

She pointed a shaking hand at the continuing lists of crises and disasters on her computer screen. "And look at that! Where could the government go and still have communications?"

"If I may speak with you in private?"

Julia waved him to the end of her desk where John Norris sat.

Meeker moved to the indicated corner, glanced nervously at Norris, remembered that the man had the total confidence of the new commander in chief, and said as quietly as he could, "There is a secret underground crisis control center in Oregon. We built it a decade ago in anticipation of a possible nuclear war."

Julia flared. "And I wasn't told about it? Did— Does the president know about it?"

"Ah, I believe the president does, yes. You must understand the secrecy . . . The facility had to remain invisible, unknown to all but a very, very few people. Its only value is—"

"I understand!" Her hands clenched. "Go on!"

"Well, it's quite large, far larger than this installation. As I remember, it has twenty-four levels, provisions for hundreds of people for several years, its own power supply, and is totally self-contained. It has been equipped with the latest communications. Every link imaginable. And it has very comfortable apartments for—"

Julia said, "What this planet has just endured and will endure is worse than an all-out nuclear war."

"Oh, yes. Quite right." Meeker seemed happy. "It's quite probable mankind will now plunge into a new Dark Age."

Julia's eyes had wandered with a kind of sick fascination to the overhead holoview screens. Her gaze jerked back to Meeker. "Get back to your desk! Put through a call for me to the supervisor or whoever is in charge of that place. Is that possible?"

"Oh, yes. That's Stephen Schweitzer. I've been in touch with him frequently tonight. They are receiving everything we are. They're preparing the facility for us."

"Get him for me."

Meeker departed. John Norris smiled sympathy to Julia. She said, "That bastard is enjoying this!"

Norris said, "FEMA attracts that type of personality."

She sighed tiredly. She rubbed her aching eyes. She noticed her blouse had pulled almost free of her pants. She tucked it in. "John, would you look up the young woman who lent me her coat for my first broadcast?"

When Norris had left, Julia turned back to the treasury men. "Now . . . I can see why we had to put a freeze on all the stock and bond markets, but why keep all the banks closed?"

A gray-haired elderly man in a three-piece suit said patiently, "To prevent runs on the banks that are able to open and to prevent instant inflation. You'll have a manufacturing and transport system virtually dead in their tracks and a panic-stricken population trying to buy everything in sight. You have to deny people access to their savings and checking

214

accounts. Across-the-board rationing of *everything* will be absolutely necessary.''

A younger man said, ''Bartering should be encouraged. There is a wealth of old, extra, duplicate pieces of furniture, kitchen goods, pots, pans, sheets, and so on packed away in attics and basements and garages which must be mobilized. Much of that will emerge into the open markets to be traded. A lot of it will be donated to help the millions who will be homeless. We must encourage access to that material.''

A third man, bald and lined, with gnarled hands, said, ''Mrs. Vice-President, this disaster allows us to return to a hard-money economy after the immediate emergency has passed. A gold standard is absolutely—''

Richard Soble came up behind Julia's chair. ''Mrs. Vice-President . . .''

She turned and saw something in his face. She stood and walked away from the desk with Soble. ''Is he dead?''

''We just received a transmission from the Swiss army in Geneva. The president's hotel took the full blast of radiation. It burned and later collapsed in hurricane winds. The bodies that can be found are impossible to identify.''

Julia covered her face with trembling hands. ''Oh, God. Oh, God . . .'' She lowered her head and turned away from him.

Soble added, ''All of the heads of state are dead except Veigt of Germany and Kochu of Japan. Geneva itself is burning out of control.''

She whispered, ''Oh, God, leave me alone.'' She saw Debra Wiley approaching with John Norris. She almost ran to them. ''Debra, take me somewhere. I need some minutes by myself.''

''Of course. This way.''

Julia turned to Richard Soble. ''Take over, Richard. You make the decisions for a while.'' She passed John Norris without seeing him. Her eyes were filling with tears.

Soble and Norris watched Julia leave. Soble said, ''Barr is presumed dead.''

''So we have a new president. We live in interesting times.''

"In spades. I've got to get things organized for the official changeover. Will you go up to 5E-14 and bring the chief justice down here? He'll have to swear her in on camera for rebroadcast and for the official record. He may have to swear in a new vice-president, too."

"How did the chief justice get here?"

"After I sent you to get Julia, I dispatched a team from here to get him. I couldn't get to Roland Lewis, though. He made it to the White House."

John said admiringly, "You anticipated all this from those first reports."

"It's called covering as many bases as you can."

"Do we have any good news?"

"There are a lot of survivors in Gibraltar. We're getting radio contact with survivors in Yugoslavia. The mountainous regions day side weren't hit too hard, except for forest fires they can't handle. Israel came on the air with only an estimated fifty percent dead. A hell of a large number of their people managed to get down into their extensive bomb-shelter system before the radiation did too much damage to their bodies."

Soble led the way back to Julia's command desk. "But there can't be anybody alive in Egypt or the rest of the Middle East. India is empty of life. China—three billion people roasted alive."

Soble sat in Julia's chair and paused before keying on the public address system. He said to Norris, "Get the chief justice."

John nodded and moved toward the elevators.

Richard Soble's voice boomed in the big room. "Hear this! Hear this! This is the director. We've just heard from the Swiss army in Geneva. President Barr is dead. I repeat, President Barr is dead. Ladies and gentlemen, in a few moments, we will witness the swearing in of the new president of the United States of America, Julia Fielding Waggoner."

CHAPTER 33

GRANTS PASS, OREGON
January 13, 1992

With morning, the unbelievable blizzard of the night slacked off to winds of forty miles an hour, with gusts to fifty or slightly higher.

Frigid air masses still poured down from the Arctic, down the West Coast of the United States before turning west into the Pacific to replace the masses of air being sucked into the fiery hell of China and the Indo-Chinese peninsula.

Sheriff Jackson O'Brien fought the wind and snowdrifts as he gunned his old Yamaha dirt bike up the shoulder of a road blocked by a three-foot-thick Douglas fir. The naked, white, gnarled roots clawed helplessly in the wind six feet over his head as he went around the iced crater.

He estimated at least one-third of the fir trees were down, maybe one-tenth of the pine. A few spruce were standing, too. All the trees swayed and rustled from the hard, moaning, cold air whipping through their remaining branches.

A few driven flakes of snow slashed at his visor and melted on his leather jacket. He kept his booted feet wide as he jockeyed downslope to the littered, snow-swept blacktop.

It had taken him five days to get out into the country and make a survey of the farmers, ranchers, survivalists, and retired folk in the area. Shit, at this rate, it would take him weeks!

But he was glad to do it. He was just plain fucking glad to be alive! He would never in his life forget that first midnight-to-dawn terror of huddling in the lightless basement of city hall and knowing if the 150-mile-an-hour winds didn't get him, the goddamned sun would the next day!

He had been half deafened from that awful shrieking,

screaming, roaring, bellowing wind. It had shaken the old building to its foundations. Cracks had spread through the structure, brick had been torn from it, and the roof had been badly fractured and half blown away.

But at least they'd received that precious, wonderful news on the shortwave receiver that the sun was back to normal, though he doubted he'd ever try for a suntan again. He'd never feel safe in open sunlight again, not after hearing those news reports about billions of people being roasted to death from the inside out. Christ! What a way to die. But maybe they'd been the lucky ones.

He clattered and bucked up a side road, detouring left and right around downed trees and thick, broken limbs. The snow was deeper here in Gull Junction.

He emerged into a small clearing and saw with relief that Darrell Beales's log house was intact. The gale winds whipped away woodsmoke from its stone and cement chimney.

Darrell stood near his Dodge pickup, sawing fallen tree limbs. He waved.

O'Brien snarled his bike through foot-deep snow that hid unseen debris. When he switched off, he sat and grinned at Darrell. "You know what's been going on?"

"Sure do. We've had the shortwave and CB going almost all the time."

The front door of the log house opened, and David Russell, the editor-publisher of *The Survivalist Newsletter*, emerged. "Hey, Jackson! Good to see you made it."

O'Brien said, "I had some doubts." He got off his bike.

Darrell put down his large crossbow saw. "Let's get inside and do some talking. There's a lot brewing around here."

As they entered the big front room, O'Brien saw Kimberly Beales kneeling at the open stove, inserting a fresh piece of wood. He called, "Hi, there. You're looking a lot better." And she was. Her head was still bandaged, but she wore a stocking cap, and only her cheek bandages were noticeable.

Kimberly smiled over her shoulder. She closed the wood-stove door and stood. "I'm feeling better." She asked Darrell, "Want me to bring in some hot coffee?"

"Yeah, sis, thanks."

As the men settled into chairs, Russell asked O'Brien, "What's Grants Pass like now?"

"Goddam mess. Half the windows and roofs are gone. The people are all out working, though, patching and making do. But the whole Tall Fir mobile home park blew away and burned. Nothing but kindling and ashes out there now. Gotta be a couple hundred dead and missing there alone."

Darrell clucked. "Mostly old retired folks there, I suppose."

"Yeah. The hospital's full up. You heard of anybody around here dead or needing help?"

Darrell's wife, Sylvia, entered from the kitchen with a big pot of steaming coffee. Kimberly followed with mugs, sugar, cream, and a loaf of homemade bread with a crock of butter on a large wooden tray.

Darrell said, "Jud Harper's henhouse took a tree. I told him to clear his land far enough so a falling tree couldn't touch any of his buildings, but he was lazy."

Sylvia said as she poured coffee, "Martha Trojan had a heart attack, and Norman Bester broke his arm trying to nail things down. A flying tree limb hit him."

Darrell said proudly, "Kimberly went over on her own and set Norm's arm."

When they looked at her in surprise, Kimberly said, "Well, I am a third-year medical student. Or was. It was a simple fracture. I couldn't do anything for old Mrs. Trojan, though. She was out of digitalis. I think she'll die in a few more days."

O'Brien said, "I didn't think you'd be able to get out and around so quickly."

"I'm all right as long as I keep my head warm and stay on antibiotics."

"Do you have enough of those?"

"Yes. Darrell insisted the visiting nurse leave enough, just in case. He's smart." She bent over and kissed the top of Darrell's head.

Sylvia sat and buttered herself a thick, warm slice of bread. "We're lucky to have Kimberly. She's a very important person now."

Kimberly turned away. She thought: a very important ugly person. She felt herself destroyed. There was no way now she would get the plastic surgery on her cheek. The hospitals would be too busy with higher-priority cases—for years! Decades! And she was sure the government would forget all about her million-dollar settlement now. She seethed with anger.

David Russell had taken out a note pad and pen. It was habit. Even if he could run off an issue of his newsletter on a mimeograph, the postal service was dead. Nevertheless, he asked, "How are the highways?"

O'Brien laughed. "Blocked to hell and gone. Must be a thousand trees down on 199, and I-5 is the same. It'll take the state crews months to open them up, if they ever try."

Russell said, "Some of the CB talk is for a few of us to hike on up to Sexton Mountain Pass and make sure I-5 stays closed."

Darrell said, "Fifty, a hundred pounds of dynamite in the right places'll bring down enough rock and dirt to seal us off from the north for years."

Russell's eyes shone. "And south of here, too, there are places where a good slide would block the highway till dooms-day. Ten men in the heights with good rifles could stop an army, to say nothing of any highway crews with bulldozers and backhoes."

O'Brien took a near-scalding mouthful of black coffee. He struggled for a few seconds, then said, "That'd really be a shame."

Russell said fervently, "We knew something like this would happen. We figured a nuke war, but we got something just as bad. Same difference. We were prepared for it. Now we've got to protect ourselves. We've got a chance to be a free state here. The whole damned country is in chaos. There'll be millions of people starving to death in a couple more weeks, and they'll be desperate as hell! When the supermarkets and warehouses go empty, there's going to be a hell of a lot of scavenging at the point of a gun."

Darrell nodded. "Yeah. We've got to block the interstate north and south."

Russell turned to O'Brien. "We've got to know who you're going to be with, Jackson. Those establishment types in Grants

Pass are going to want to play by the old rules. They won't have the vision to see the real situation. The United States is dead. The federal government is going to be powerless. Hell, it already is; it just hasn't sunk into people's heads yet. What government there is will have its hands full with riots and looting in the East and Midwest, in the South, and in that sewer they call L.A. It won't have any money! How in hell are they going to collect taxes? Before you know it, every town, every county, every state, will be going its own way. This country is going to break down into little kingdoms, each ruled by a police force or militia or national guard unit. Shit, half the United States army is in Mexico, and most of the other half was sitting on its ass smoking dope when it got roasted in Europe! The federal government doesn't have the armed men to make its orders stick."

O'Brien said firmly, "Hell, I've been with you people from the beginning. You have plans beyond blocking the interstate?"

Darrell rubbed his chin. He glanced around the room, meeting eyes. "Yes, we do. Something has to be done about that federal emergency center out by Wolf Ridge. We've got to take that place."

O'Brien looked surprised, then thoughtful.

Russell leaped in. "That place is the key! They're going to want to move in there! They'll send in fleets of helicopters and bring in all the damned politicians and bureaucrats who've fucked over this country for decades. They're going to come in here and squat in that place for years, safe and fat and sassy with all that food and equipment, and play God. At least they think they're going to do it."

Darrell said, "We've worked out a plan to take that place."

O'Brien snorted. "That'll be a neat trick. Who's ever been up there? Who knows the layout? Who knows the defenses?"

Kimberly spoke up. "I do. I was inside, and I remember everything I saw."

He smiled. "Got your memory back, eh?"

She stiffened, then relaxed. "I don't have anything to lose now. If I'm going to be scarred and ugly for the rest of my life, I want them to suffer, too!"

221

He nodded. "Fair enough." He looked to Darrell. "What's the plan?"

Russell pressed, "Are you with us on this, sheriff?"

"If I think you've got a chance of pulling it off, yes. But I have to know more. Do you have a time picked?"

Darrell hesitated, then said, "Two days from now."

"Why so soon?"

Russell blurted, "It has to be soon! Before the politicians and security forces begin to arrive. I'll bet you our new lady president will drop in on us in less than a week, just as soon as it's safe to fly out here. We've got to get in there first."

Darrell grinned. "Once we have the place, they have no place to go. Kimberly saw the defense control room. She got enough of a look to give us some clues as to avoiding detection. And whoever controls that place will be able to survive for years and wait out the death time. It'll be our underground castle. We move in all our families, and we live there till the outside population is thinned down by all the starvation and disease that's coming. It'll be a new beginning for America."

Russell added, "We'll be the core of New America. We'll take in a few people from around here—the best people from Grants Pass, maybe. And after a few years we come out and establish a free country. Gold money. No income taxes. No damned welfare. No subsidies. No damned two million laws, rules, and regulations. No draft."

Darrell continued the theme. "And no big banks. No debts. No huge multinational corporations owning everything and controlling everything in sight. No Rothschilds or Stonemans or Al Rashids. Keep it small, keep it simple, and keep it democratic."

O'Brien sighed. "Okay. Your ideals are great. But how many men do you have lined up for the attack? How are you going to get to Wolf Ridge in this weather, without passable roads? Even the trails are more trouble than they're worth. It's a good twenty miles, and there's more snow and wind and freezing rain coming."

Darrell answered, "Snowshoes, sleds, a few snowcats, a few bikes like yours, four-wheel drives . . . and we'll have close to a hundred survivalist-trained men who know how to shoot. Plus enough dynamite if our first plan fails.''

Kimberly said, ''The worse the weather is, the better. It'll make it easier for us when we get there.''

O'Brien was surprised. ''You're going along?''

''Yes! I know the road and the layout. A good snow or sleet storm will mess up their cameras and other detection equipment. And you can't set off mines from the top of two or three feet of snow. I'm going!'' She crossed her arms adamantly.

Darrell said, ''I think she's strong enough.''

O'Brien took another mouthful of very hot coffee, set the mug down, and stood up. ''Got to get going. Oh, if you haven't heard yet, orders are coming down to conscript every able-bodied man and woman and child over ten years of age for cleanup and reconstruction.''

Russell grunted. ''It figures. Now we're supposed to be government slaves.''

Darrell asked O'Brien, ''Are you going to enforce that?''

''I'll have to, in the towns. Out here . . .'' He smiled.

''Yeah. You'd need an army to press our group into road gangs.''

Russell asked as O'Brien moved toward the door, ''Are you going to join us on the fifteenth?''

''I might. I do have an obligation to the county, though. I was elected to do a job. They need me now with all these Mickey Mouse FEMA rules and regulations coming in. But I wish you people well. I won't stop you.'' He picked up his helmet and left the solid, warm log house.

CHAPTER 34

PRESIDENT WAGGONER WAS BLEARY-EYED FROM LACK OF sleep. Her rump was numb from sitting in the command chair at her desk. Her graying blond hair, she was positive, had surely turned fully gray during the past few days.

Yet nothing but words and pictures and numbers seemed to have changed in the deep CIA Situation Room. The lights overhead shed the same colorless light; the aides and assistants and officers and agents and officials and bureaucrats all sat or walked or rushed and talked and whispered and shouted as before. It was like living in an endless film loop.

Except for the horrible entries on her computer screen and the sweep of storms and fires on the overhead holoviews. She knew the surface of the earth was raging, burning, and that thousands of people were still dying every minute. Every minute! After six endless days!

She sighed with weariness as she listened to experts tell of the latest crisis, and she blankly studied the stitching of her sweater sleeve. She knew she had slept several times—that windowless apartment on an upper level—and had lost count of the times she had gone before the cameras. . . .

"Mrs. President, you should get some rest."

Julia looked vaguely to her left. Richard Soble. The stain of utter weariness was in his face, too. Wrinkled suit, open collar, tie askew. Tall and gaunt.

She said to him, "Get me—get me an upper. A stim bomb. Coffee isn't enough anymore."

He nodded. "As you wish. I came to tell you the surface winds are down to helicopter capability. Three long-range attack HE-26s are on the way here to take you and key personnel to the carrier *John Paul Jones* off Norfolk. At the carrier, you'll transfer to navy bombers for a flight to an air force base in Texas.''

''Why all the zigzag?''

''The airport runways are littered with small planes, parts of houses, trees . . . There isn't a runway that can be used. There are Stealth air force bombers in Texas which were protected in underground hangars, and they have a clear runway. From there you'll be flown to Portland. They're clearing the main runway there now.''

''How many people can I take?''

''The core people from here. Your personal staff, aides, whoever you want.''

''I want John Norris and you, to begin with.''

Soble advised, ''I think I can serve you and the nation best if I stay here.''

Julia grimaced. ''I suppose so. I'll hate to be without you.''

''We can have holoconferences anytime.''

''Of course. Do you have a list prepared—the most valuable, necessary people from here?''

''Yes. And I've sent several expeditions out to get your wardrobe from your home and to bring in your staff aides. I presumed—''

''Thank you, Richard. You're marvelous.'' She squeezed his arm in appreciation.

Soble went away. Julia slumped in her chair, then desperately struggled to her feet. She looked at the faces of the men who had been reviewing the crises for her. God, they all looked alike. She couldn't remember any of their names. She pointed at random. ''You . . . and you. Walk with me. I can't sit any longer.'' She walked slowly away. The two men rose and walked beside her as she circled the huge room. She rubbed the back of her aching neck. ''Who was saying something about the underground?''

The man on her left, young, crew cut, said, ''Lanier was, Mrs. President. He just left. But we can capsulate his report. The underworld—the organized part, the Mafia—has begun to operate an extensive black market. It's springing up everywhere.''

Richard Elliott

The man on her right, fiftyish, bald, a fringe of black hair, said, "Huge stocks of food and goods are disappearing. They're being diverted to the black market. There's a pattern developing. UniMart stores and distribution centers are almost all empty. The Tucker Medicals group is wiped out. All those vital hospital supplies are missing. A chain of hardware stores—"

Julia asked, "Who owns all those? Is there a link?"

"Yes . . . VMY Action Group, the Granite Foundation . . . all owned or controlled by the Stoneman empire."

Julia slumped back in her chair. "I should have guessed."

Debra Wiley came up behind her. "Mrs. President? The director asked me to give you this." She offered two paper cups, one containing a red and green capsule, the other water.

Julia sighed, smiled, and accepted them. "Thank you . . . I'm sorry, I've forgotten your name."

"Debra Wiley."

"Yes. Debra, I like you. Please tell Director Soble that I want you to look after me, to be on my personal staff, and you're to accompany me. Would that be all right with you?"

"Yes, Mrs. President! Thank you."

"Fine. Tell Soble I want you, and then stay close." Julia washed down the stim capsule, handed the cups to Debra, and turned to the two advisers. "What do you suggest we do about the black market? What are we capable of doing?"

The bald man said, "Our armed forces are spread too thin as it is. Even with our extensive volunteer militias, we can't cope with the experienced criminal groups involved. I think we should form an elite strike force, a melding of FBI and SWAT teams in each city. And we'll need an extensive undercover network of spies and informers."

Julia bridled at that. "Secret police? That smacks too much of dictatorship."

The crew-cut young man said, brashly, "Those are just words! You did declare a national emergency."

The other adviser said, "We must have an executive order for the strike force immediately, Mrs. President. We abso-

226

lutely must control the food supply to ensure confidence in the rationing system. The people are not fools. They know the transport systems are a mess. They're getting scared and desperate. They know there is normally only a three-day supply of food in the cities."

Julia nodded, still utterly weary. When was that upper going to start working? She said, "You're both from FEMA, right? You go ahead with that plan. Have an executive order drawn up for me to sign."

"Thank you, Mrs. President!" They ran to their desks.

Julia was alone for a moment on the far side of the Situation Room.

A middle-aged woman came up to Julia. Her security badge identified her as *Helen Wilhelm—Ecology*. "Mrs. President, may I talk to you for just a moment? It's vital!"

"Everything is vital. Go ahead, Helen." Julia was just beginning to feel better, perkier, sharper.

The woman seemed startled that the president would know and use her first name. Then she said quickly, "The solar flare had to have sterilized the entire Indian Ocean, as well as the eastern fringe of the Atlantic, the Mediterranean Sea, the western end of the Pacific. All life must have been killed down to about twenty feet."

Julia saw the woman's intellectual and emotional agony. "What does that mean?"

"The phytoplankton, the small zooplankton, the large zooplankton are gone. All the marine life on the continental shelves. The food chain is broken. It'll take a thousand years for the Indian Ocean and for the Mediterranean to recover."

"I'm sorry, but I still don't see—"

Helen Wilhelm blurted angrily, unthinkingly, "The consequences! The fish—the large fish below twenty feet will starve. They don't eat each other; they eat smaller, surface fish that eat the plankton. Billions of large fish will starve to death. And those in the fringe areas will migrate into the undamaged seas and compete with the native fish for the existing food supply."

"But how can we do anything about that?"

"Mrs. President, all those starving fish will go to waste!

227

You've got to greatly expand the fishing fleets. Convert every possible yacht, every big pleasure boat, to fishing. Send them out to catch as many of the large fish as possible. Tell all the Central and South American countries about it. Every fish caught frees up food for the emigrating fish from the dead oceans. And it has to be done right away!''

"Of course. Thank you, Helen. Every bit of extra food will be needed. Come with me!'' Julia led her to the FEMA desks and said to a harried Daniel Meeker, "Listen to this woman and do as much as possible to follow her advice. Divert everybody in the draft with commercial fishing experience to the coasts and expropriate all boats which can be quickly converted for fishing.''

Julia turned away as Helen Wilhelm said to Meeker, "And the fish-processing industry will have to be . . .''

And, Julia thought to herself, the transport system will have to be quickly patched back into operation to get canned and frozen seafood inland. That will call for more decrees, more force. . . .

She realized with a shock, My God! I am a dictator!

She walked briskly back to her command desk. The stim bomb was really working in her now!

She worked for two hours: issued orders, signed official executive orders, listened, questioned, judged.

The rains were still falling! They would be torrential for weeks, the weather people thought, and would cause huge accumulations of snow in the mountains, ensuring savage floods in the spring as well as ruinous floods now in every river of any significance. It didn't really matter if the rivers of Eurasia and Africa flooded. In the United States, the Mississippi, the Missouri, the Ohio, the Tennessee, the Arkansas, the Columbia, the Willamette, the Snake—all these and many more would sweep away whole towns, even inundate small cities with millions of tons of mud and debris. The loss of precious topsoil would be enormous. Vital crops in the lush interior valleys of California would be drowned.

The traditional, roughly predictable weather patterns would not return to anything approaching normal for generations.

Freak storms would be the norm. Growing seasons would be games of chance. Crop yields would decline drastically.

The stimulant she had taken wore off abruptly, leaving her a drooping, heavy-lidded zombie. She lurched away from her desk.

Debra Wiley came to her. "Shall I take you to your apartment now, Mrs. President?"

"Yes. I can't— Wait." Julia saw John Norris sitting alone at a small table in an alcove, drinking coffee. He sat like a king. He saw her and smiled. She said to Debra, "Wait for me. Stay here." She joined Norris at the small table. He rose as she approached. She waved him down.

She slumped into a plastic chair. "Want a job?"

"I thought I had one."

"You can have mine." She carefully braced her elbows on the table and cradled her face in her hands.

John asked, "Want some coffee?"

"I'm afraid I'm too tired for that to work anymore. And I think I'm going to have to be drugged to get to sleep." She rubbed her eyes. "I feel like I'm presiding over the end of civilization. Rear-guard actions all the way."

He said, "You do your best. Keep the guilt, the sense of responsibility, and the ego at the lowest possible levels."

"I'm not enjoying this."

"You have near-absolute power over hundreds of millions of people. That can be a heady brew."

"Mr. Norris, I—"

Daniel E. P. Meeker, the head of FEMA, approached the table. He was alone, a rumpled, pudgy man wearing smudged trifocal glasses. His eyes were puffed and red. "Mrs. President? May I speak to you for a moment privately? There is an extremely sensitive major policy matter which must be addressed."

John Norris stood up to leave. Julia still didn't like Meeker. She sensed Norris's gut dislike, too. She was so tired she didn't trust herself to think straight, and in her soul she did trust John Norris.

She said, "Stay." She motioned Meeker to take the third chair at the small plastic table.

Meeker obeyed. He took off his glasses and peered at her myopically. "President Waggoner, I have been taking in so much tragic information that I'm what you might call punch drunk."

Julia leaned back and crossed her arms across her chest. "Aren't we all."

"The latest is—the seas are rising. Apparently, the flare melted considerably more polar ice than we had initially estimated. The sea level is up eighteen inches! With hot winds sweeping from the superheated day side over the poles, and that likely to continue, the icecaps are being melted. They won't be completely melted, but we now think the mean sea level could rise over three feet."

Julia said, "Thereby wiping out Florida." She didn't seem to care anymore. Burnout. Overload.

"And numerous other low-level coastal regions, especially in the South."

"What major policy decision is involved, Mr. Meeker? Shall I order the seas not to rise?"

"Ahhh . . . ." He chuckled. "I've acquired an overview of the entire national and international situation, and I can see clearly that the food supply will not be adequate to feed our existing population until summer when we can expect a minimal harvest."

"Go on."

He smiled nervously. "It's a bit difficult to say, but I would be remiss in my duties if I didn't suggest you consider, once we get out to safety in Oregon, a policy of rather severe . . . triage."

"Triage?" Julia looked to Norris. Her mind was like glue. She couldn't come up with the word's meaning.

John said tightly, "Culling. Preserving or choosing the best and letting the rest rot—or die."

Julia blinked. A coldness formed in her guts. She turned to Meeker. "Are you talking about people?"

"Mrs. President, we are in the worst disaster mankind has ever faced. And really, the worst is yet to come. The projections are just horrible. I know it sounds ruthless and heartless, but if choices are not made, even more people will die than f— You see, we must keep the quality people alive, the productive people, the most intelligent, the young. To attempt to save everyone in this country now alive, to give them all an equal chance at survival, would only doom to starvation some of the best, the ones we need!''

Julia stared at him. He squirmed. He continued. "If you will sign an executive order giving us more discrete power to allocate food, shelter, and fuel on a more rational basis—"

John asked him, "What would be the age cutoff?"

Meeker licked his lips. "We think fifty-five would be—"

John continued. "And those with low IQs and the physically and mentally disabled?"

"Generally, but of course some highly intelligent, highly skilled people are physically handicapped, and they would qualify for—"

"What about emotional stability? What about people in mental hospitals? In the prisons and jails?"

"Well, we'd have to decide on an individual basis . . ."

There was a silence.

Julia felt a loathing for the man she had never felt for anyone in her life. He made her want to vomit. She began to tremble with the intensity of her revulsion. She asked, "Mr. Meeker, how old are you?"

He frowned in puzzlement. "Why . . . fifty-two."

She reached out and snatched his name badge from his coat. "You're fired. You no longer work for the United States government. You are no longer authorized to be here."

She said to John, "See that he is put out." She rose from the table and walked toward the waiting Debra Wiley.

Behind her, Meeker spluttered, "B-but I'm the head of FEMA! I have rights! I—" When Julia showed no sign of hearing him or turning to countermand her order, he shouted, in a terrified, squalling voice, "You can 't do this to me! Oh, God, please! Mrs. President! I beg you! I had to offer the plan! You don't understand! Please! Mrs. President! You can't just send me out to die!"

Julia froze her mind until she was in the elevator. Daniel E. P. Meeker would now have the same chance as any citizen.

She clung to Debra and began to weep.

CHAPTER 35

WOLF RIDGE, OREGON
January 15, 1992

THE FIVE-YEAR-OLD GIRL CRIED, "I'M COLD!" SHE WAS COMforted by her mother, who looked for her husband nearby in the frigid, howling night. The arctic wind drove snow at them like crystalline white bullets. The wind had increased since midafternoon and now, at seven P.M., was strong enough to knock some of the children down as it tore through the forest.

David Russell trudged along with the small group of women and children. He was a small man, barely five feet six inches and wore a woman's coat and wig. He had the coat hood up, zipped and drawstringed tight against the cold and whipping snow.

He had to shout to be heard over the shattering wind. He estimated the winds were up to sixty or seventy miles an hour now and maybe getting worse. That was all to the good.

The guards in the blockhouselike concrete structure a few hundred yards farther up the hill wouldn't be paying much attention to their high-tech cameras and other detection devices. They wouldn't believe anyone could organize an attack on this installation so soon after the world disaster, in this weather, and probably wouldn't believe any reading their instruments gave.

On the way up the hill, the band of women and children, guided by Kimberly Beales, had kept carefully to the all-but-invisible rutted tracks. They'd spotted three cameras crusted over with ice and snow. The designers had blundered.

On their flanks, moving among the trees and bushes, were sixteen armed men on snowshoes. If there were land mines in the ground, the deep, cushioning snow made them useless. The men were led by Darrell Beales.

Kimberly grabbed a nine-year-old boy who flailed backward in the teeth of a terrifying gust of snow-laden wind. A woman holding a carefully wrapped baby bundle went down on her rump.

Kimberly's head throbbed painfully in the area where her skull had been crushed. She was exhausted from the climb; she hadn't realized how out of condition she was. She was driven on by cold rage and bitter hatred.

Nearby, David Russell shouted. "Only a little way more!" He was both sweating and freezing. The pistol under his belt dug into his belly and groin.

The little girl began crying. Her mother tugged her along, leaning far forward against the numbing blast of icy, snow-pelting wind.

At last, the clearing loomed ahead in the white-on-white darkness. And there, to the right, was the concrete bunker.

They found the gray steel door. The women pounded on it with fists and sticks. They pressed endlessly at the inset orange ID plate. They screamed to be let in. The children howled and yelled, too, as they had been instructed. David Russell went to his knees among them and pounded. He kept his head down.

He knew the attack force was close by. He was scared and began hyperventilating, gasping cold air deep into his lungs. He wormed his ungloved right hand under his heavy coat and grasped the cold, metallic butt of the gun. A refrain ran through the back of his mind: *Liberty cannot be given, it must be taken . . . Liberty cannot be given, it must be taken . . .*

There was no response from inside. The steel door was unyielding. But the tiny, shielded overhead TV camera was alive. It moved slightly to the left and right.

The women and children begged. The cold was really getting to them now; they weren't acting. The young woman with the baby bundle kept screaming and sobbing, "My baby! My baby! She'll freeze!"

Another pleaded, "Let us in, let us in, let us in, please, please, for God's sake, let us in . . ."

David Russell shook with tension. He could barely keep from yelling. All the chips were on the table now. He doubted most of the women and children could make the trek back to their homes. Not in this weather!

Five minutes had gone by. The women and children were quieting from exhaustion and despair. Yet they kept to their mission. They stayed crowded and huddled by the steel door. The crowded together, against each other, against Russell, for warmth and solidarity. David realized with a kind of awe that they believed in this attempt more than he and were more committed to survivalism and freedom than he.

Another few minutes and the men would have to try to blast their way into the blockhouse.

Suddenly, the icy metal door clicked and swung inward to show a small concrete anteroom lit by a caged overhead bulb. A young man in a heavy gray military parka shouted against the howling blizzard, "You can come in, but only this far! This little room here!"

They surged in past him, Russell among them on his hands and knees, and they begged for food and warmth. The women besieged the youth. He was unarmed. He backed toward the blue steel inner door. "I'm only authorized to let you stay in here. I can't do anything more." He groped for the yellow button in the blue steel doorjamb. "Close the outer door, please."

David Russell had quickly gotten to his feet and examined the inside of the outer door. It had a manual handle and locking mechanism, necessary in case of electronics malfunction or power failure.

He swung the door almost closed and pulled his gun with his back to the young guard. He couldn't hear much over the begging and pleading of the women and children, but he noted the change of light when the inner door opened to admit the guard.

Russell turned and lunged for the inner door. This was it! He was tremendously excited. Movement was slow motion and hyperfast at the same time. Two parts of his brain were completely involved.

The young soldier had made a terrible mistake in signaling for admittance to the inner rooms. Russell and the strong young women chosen for this part of the atttack wrenched the blue door wide open and shoved the soldier backward, inside, off balance, and plunged into the instrument monitoring room after him.

There were three soldiers in the room, one a lieutenant. Only the lieutenant was armed. He fumbled at the flap of his sidearm holster.

Russell pointed his big .44 pistol and jerked the heavy-pull trigger. The gun leaped and boomed. The lieutenant went down, clutching his shoulder. Russell had aimed at his chest. The sound of the shot echoed and reverberated. In the sudden, shocked moment that followed, Russell shrilled, "Put your hands up!" He swung the gun toward the nearest soldier. "Don't move!" He was ashamed at how he sounded, like a hysterical girl. He pointed to the soldier at the control console. "Get away from there!" The heavy gun shook in his hand. He was breathing as if he'd run a mile! He didn't realize how wild were his eyes. "You gutless pukes! You bleeding hearts! You let us in!"

The soldiers obeyed, white-faced.

The women cheered. One of them dashed back into the anteroom and swung the outer door wide open. She shouted, "We did it!"

Armed survivalists poured into the blockhouse. Darrell Beales clapped Russell on the back. "Fantastic! Great work, David! Great! Great!" He checked to see if Kimberly was okay, then quickly detailed preplanned squads of men to the elevator and to the discovered narrow, spiraling metal staircase.

Russell suddenly snapped into strategic awareness. "Darrell, we've got to get to the communications room right away. We've got to surprise them. They can't send out an alarm!"

"Yeah!" Darrell rushed to one of the soldiers who was being tied up. "Where is the radio room? Communications with the outside!"

The soldier started to answer, then snapped his mouth shut.

Russell pushed the still-smoking, acrid-smelling barrel of his pistol cruelly hard under the young man's chin. "Tell us!"

The boy rolled wide brown eyes toward his wounded, heavily bleeding lieutenant and croaked, "Ten East."

Darrell asked, "How many guards are there?"

"I can't—"

Russell pressed the end of the gun barrel harder into the boy's upper throat, causing a choking, gagging reflex. When he backed off the pressure to allow the youth to talk, the boy rasped, "Twelve."

"Where are the others now?"

"Two—two are in the ridge bunker, and four are probably sleeping. I don't know where the others are. They're off duty . . . in the rec rooms . . . maybe the bar."

Darrell laughed incredulously. "They've got a bar? Shit!"

Russell asked, "Where are the weapons? Who has weapons?"

The soldier said, "Nobody has weapons on duty. Only the lieutenant has a gun."

"One fucking automatic? Come on, boy! Where are the guns!"

"L-locked up. Th-there's an armory. Twenty-one North."

Darrell called, "Rinzuski! Find out from this shithead coward where the other guards sleep and eat and drink. Round them up and put them somewhere safe." He asked the soldier, "Is there a jail in this place?"

"Yes."

"Great. They thought of everything. That's where you're going, kid."

Darrell and Russell ran to the elevator where ten men were waiting for the cage. Darrell said, "We've got to get to the communications room first. David and I'll get off on level ten first. Grant, you and Frank come with us."

The elevator door sighed open. It was empty. They crowded it. Darrell punched 10.

They eventually discovered that the facility below ground was configured like a round, twenty-four-layer cake, with a huge center freight elevator that reached the surface higher up the hill where it opened to a large, disguised helicopter landing pad.

The two blockhouse elevators rose from opposite edges of the "cake."

When the elevator doors opened at level 10, the survivalists rushed out and found themselves facing a long, tile-floored hallway running to the center and on either side a long, curving hallway that apparently ran around the outer edge of this level.

Darrell spotted a sign on the wall near the now-closed elevator doors. The cage was rising to bring down another load of survivalists. The sign said: 10 West.

The communications room had to be somewhere straight ahead, beyond the center shaft.

They sprinted, their boots loud in the echoing hall, but they were afraid to take the time to walk quietly. The doors they passed were solid, paneled, marked 10W-15, 10W-14, 10W-13. Odd numbers were on their left. The center was a huge elevator column; a nearby cafeteria was empty, the food line unlighted, stainless steel trays empty.

Russell dashed ahead around the freight elevator to the 10 East hallway. A metal flag sign ahead proclaimed: *Communications*. He burst into the big room and saw five men and one woman at consoles, desks, one with headphones, amid chattering printers, glowing holoscreens, computers . . . A man in a corner glass-walled office looked up, and his jaw dropped as he saw unshaven, roughly dressed strangers enter on the run.

Russell fired his big pistol into the acoustic-tiled ceiling. The earsplitting boom caused every head to jerk around, every eye to widen. He said loudly, "Stop what you are doing! Don't move!"

Darrell ordered, "Everybody out! Move!"

Russell said, "No, wait!" He turned to argue, "We have to have continuity. We have to send fake messages."

Darrell nodded. He called, "Who does the sending?"

A short, plump blond woman hesitantly raised her hand.

A distinguished man in a dark suit emerged from the corner office. He said angrily, "Who the hell are you people?"

David Russell grinned, flushed with success. "We are the survivors. We're the army of New America. And you—you just lost your cushy government job." He gestured with his gun. "Get down on the floor, face down. Frank, watch him. You—" He indicated the plump blond woman. "Were you sending anything?"

"No."

"Who do you send to?"

"The CIA Situation Room. The White House."

"Okay, send this message to both of them." He thought for a moment, then said, "Send this: An underground stream has broken through the walls of the twenty-second level, West. Uncontrolled flooding is in progress. Main electrical power has failed. You're broadcasting on emergency power. The storerooms are being flooded."

Darrell laughed. "Brilliant!"

Russell glowed. He asked, "Who's in charge of this whole place?"

The woman said faintly, "Mr. Schweitzer." She pointed to the man who had been forced to lie on the orange-carpeted floor.

Russell grinned. "Okay. After you send that the storerooms are being flooded, tell them that Mr. Schweitzer advises that the entire place will have to be abandoned."

"But the president is coming!"

"Not anymore, she isn't! Go ahead!" He watched the woman closely as she typed out the message on her computer screen. She finished and waited.

Russell scratched his stubbly chin. He studied the message. "Okay, send it."

She pressed some buttons. The message vanished from her screen. A line printer chattered.

He stared at the printed message—the one he had ordered sent to the CIA Situation Room and the War Room of the White House. "What is this shit? I told you—"

She said hastily, "That's just a printout for the records. We have it on disc, too.

He examined her nervous, anxious face. He read the previous transmission and reception printouts and relaxed. "Good enough! Darrell, we can move these people out now. There'll be no more messages going out of here. We're officially flooded. This place has been abandoned."

CHAPTER 36

T RACY BENJAMIN, THIRTY-FIVE, TALL, NORMALLY SELF-CON-
fident, entertained an erotic fantasy involving Erica Stoneman
and himself whenever he was in her presence.

He was fairly good-looking, he knew, and the only intelligent young man in the underground Stoneman shelter who
could conceivably have a chance at Erica's affections now
that old man Stoneman was dead. He had not been able to
understand her obviously genuine love for that ancient bastard.

Tracy's hands always trembled at first when she came close
to him for any reason. She wore devilishly effective perfume.
And her body— His guts twisted when he looked at her.

They were sitting at the table in the Stoneman apartment
dining room, Erica, Lane McDermott, and himself. He had to
concentrate very hard to keep his thinking on track.

He said, "The national com nets are coming back as power
grids come on line in New York, Boston, Los Angeles, and
Chicago. Frisco is still out. Dallas and Houston will be up to
normal by tomorrow."

Lane McDermott asked, "What about the transport system?"

"Air travel is out. The armed forces are using some VTO
and helicopters, but the airlines are dead. Most of their jets
were wrecked. The railroads are in much better shape. Crews
are clearing track very quickly. From the Rockies west, though,
the trains are hampered by fallen trees and slides. Thousands
of trucks and especially the big box trailers were blown over
and damaged. Not seriously, usually. The main problem is
clearing the highways, again especially in the Far West."

Erica asked, "You mean electricity has been restored everywhere in those cities?"

"No, not to most of the houses and neighborhoods. Just to the downtown business areas where there aren't many trees and the lines were protected from the hurricanes. It's reported at least ten percent of the houses sustained some damage, and the floods are doing more damage."

Erica caught Tracy Benjamin's haunted look at her breasts. She said, "Thank you, Mr. Benjamin. Go on back to your monitoring."

He was puzzled by her quick dismissal of him but knew better than to object or resist.

When Benjamin had left via the elevator, Erica said, "I want him out of here as soon as possible."

Lane smiled. "He is a bit obviously attracted to you."

"It makes me angry. I'm not available, but the basic young male ego and instinct cannot accept that."

Lane said, "Realistically, Erica, you will be available soon. After the funeral, you'll be the richest, most powerful woman in the world."

"I'm not interested. I will not be 'available' to prime males looking for a prime female. I'll be known as a cold-blooded, ball-busting bitch, the mirror image of your average hot-blooded, dominating bastard." She regarded McDermott with amused eyes. "But I'll take lovers who know my needs. Later."

He inclined his head. They understood one another.

Erica flipped through a sheaf of computer printouts Benjamin had brought down. "FEMA, FEMA, FEMA. The country is being ruled by that damned Federal Emergency Management Agency. They're even using grade-school children."

"Yes, in the name of President Waggoner. She is proving to be a powerful, motherly, charismatic leader. She's laid it on the line to the people, and they're all working like hell to rebuild and to keep from starving."

"But when is that woman going to let the banks open and allow trading again? How long can she keep the debt markets closed?"

"Maybe months. That's the power of a government which has most of the people—and the guns—on its side. Mr.

Stoneman acted very wisely before the flare in buying all those commodities, the coin gold and the junk silver. Our black markets are thriving everywhere. Our Mafia partners are making nine hundred and a thousand percent profits for us—and themselves.''

Erica nodded. She toyed with her long blond hair. "But we can't make any real money until we are free to make big loans and leverage buy outs."

"Quite right. Preflare equity and ownership must be returned and honored. Property rights must be preeminent."

She slapped the table. "Damn her! Can't we pressure her? What about Roland Lewis, my dad, and all the others in Congress we're supposed to have in our pockets?"

McDermott checked off items on a list before him. "We're getting some big radio stations on the air now, and a few newspapers are on the streets. The cable nets are linking up again via satellites. The line going out is that President Waggoner must reconvene Congress for advice and consent. She's ruling by decree now, like a common despot, and the emergency isn't all that severe. We're accusing her of lying to keep herself in a position of supreme power."

Erica smiled. "And we spread stories of FEMA injustice, mistakes, and corruption. Right?"

"Yes. That's the current attack. It should work if—"

"I don't want to wait! I want Congress to convene and impeach her. I want Speaker of the House Roland Lewis to be the next president. We own him body and soul. Brad showed me the file we have on him."

The extension phone on the table rang. Erica answered. "Yes? . . . Thank you, Mr. Benjamin." As she put down the phone, she said to McDermott, "The government is moving to Oregon! The president is in Portland right now."

McDermott asked, "Congress and the Supreme Court or just the executive branch?"

"He just said, 'The president and her closest advisers, plus the top FEMA and military people.' " Erica smiled. "I think she just played right into our hands. We can have that woman impeached in a week!"

CHAPTER 37

THE WIND WHIP FLEXED THE CANVAS ROOF OF THE JEEP TILL the loud slapping sounds made it difficult for Sheriff O'Brien to think. He nevertheless drove at high speed down Crater Street toward the Safeway store on Twenty-third.

Sleet added to his difficulties. The particles of iced rain shotgunned against the windshield, sticking, bouncing away, dancing on the hood, making the snowy street extra slippery.

As he drove, he picked up his pack set as it blared on with Margaret Fine's scratchy voice. "Sheriff? Sheriff?"

"O'Brien."

"Sheriff, a U.S. government man with FEMA—he said F-E-M-A—is coming in at the airport to see you. He said it was very, capital V important. He wants you to meet him there. He'll be in an army helicopter, and his ETA is ten-thirty. Over."

"Margaret, he'll have to wait. I've got a riot going on at the Safeway." He glanced at his watch: 10:09. "Radio him back and tell him I may be late."

"Will do. Oh, he also wants Mayor Sadler there, too. I'll call the mayor's office."

"Tell the mayor a riot comes first. Out." O'Brien saw the big store ahead. Maybe fifty people, bundled up against the wind and cold and sleet, were clustered at the center doors. Six of his deputies stood in front of the doors, holding shotguns. There was some arm waving going on.

He took the parking-lot driveway too fast, slewed, skidded in a long, graceful slide, finally regained control, and blared his horn as he approached the crowd.

When he stepped out into the blasting sleet, some of the

242

people came over to yell at him, "I need milk for my kids!" What the hell is going on?"

"Sheriff, my husband is on a special diet, and he has to have salt-free food! This is the only place that has any now!"

"We're all out of food!"

"There's no meat anywhere but here, and they won't let us in!"

O'Brien noted some rifles and shotguns in the crowd. There were frightened faces among the Safeway personnel inside the store. His deputies were uneasy.

He held up his hands for quiet and moved, bareheaded, into the crowd. "Listen! Listen, now! The store will be open at noon. Everybody will get some of what you need, but rations are being cut thirty percent effective today. And—wait a minute! Listen! You'll only be able to draw one day's rations at a time!"

A series of outraged, complaining shouts went up. He waited for a lull, then said loudly, "We have to do it! We're cut off here, and it may be weeks before the highways are cleared to Roseburg and Eugene. We have to stretch what food we have. We're in for tough times out here, and the only way we'll make it is by cooperation."

More shouting.

"I hear you. But I didn't create this situation. We're all going to be a lot thinner before we get out of the woods. I'm as hungry as you are."

Questions.

"Every buyer of food will have his or her hand stamped with indelible ink. The ink stamp will change every day. If you're buying food for more than one person, you'll have to show ID from that person, and that ID will be stamped every day."

Objections.

"Let me remind you people we're living under martial law! Looters will be shot on the spot. No questions, no explanations. Anybody who tries to steal food or fuel or clothes or blankets will be shot! My men have strict orders. . . . Yes! That's what martial law is! Your constitutional rights are on ice for a while."

243

O'Brien felt crowded. He was being jostled and shoved. He made his way back to his jeep and climbed up on the front bumper. He was a target but had to take a chance. The men with weapons in the crowd were friends, some of them. He thought he had a few more days of grace before things got really ugly.

He shouted, "I know, I know! Everybody is working at things they hate! I know there are foul-ups! But we all of us have no choice! It's work like dogs or die! Forget the old laws! Get this through your heads—the rules have changed! There isn't any such thing as social security anymore. No more welfare! No more SSI."

He finally gave up and climbed into the Jeep. He wondered how much longer he could control the town, even with a hundred new volunteer deputies. The food reserves were shockingly low.

After about another week there'd be small, vicious gangs going from house to house at night, killing, stealing food, pumping out heating oil, siphoning gas . . .

As he drove away, O'Brien cursed helplessly. A year from now he didn't think Grants Pass would have one-twentieth its present population.

He reached the airport ten minutes late. There was a big Oregon National Guard copter sitting close to the still-standing airport control tower. The copter's vanes were feathered and in neutral because of the strong wind. He could hear the engine running, probably to keep it warm and maybe to provide heat for the cabin. Bureaucrats and politicians liked their comfort.

The main building of the airport was a shambles inside from the winds ten nights ago that had blown out the big plate-glass windows and thrown debris through the gaping holes.

O'Brien drove up to the helicopter and parked next to the mayor's Pontiac. A national guardsman slid open the copter door and waved him over. He ran through the stinging sleet and climbed in.

He recognized the man sitting with Mayor Sadler at a small

fold-down table behind the pilot's compartment. It was the lying FEMA man who had come into his office with Captain Ferris. Ernie Wallace.

O'Brien decided to get in the first broadside. He said angrily, "Wallace, when do we get all that food you promised us over the radio?"

Wallace flushed and bridled at what he considered the sheriff's insolence. "That's secondary right now."

"People starving to death is secondary?"

"Shut up! I've just been to the FEMA Emergency Crisis Center at Wolf Ridge. They didn't respond to our coded radio messages as we approached, and when we landed at the ridge pad, somebody started shooting at us!"

O'Brien laughed. The mayor looked uncomfortable.

"You think that's funny?" Wallace made an outraged gesture at the skin of the helicopter. "Look at those bullet holes!"

There were several stitchings of ragged little holes. O'Brien estimated an automatic rifle had done the job.

Wallace continued. "Three men came out of the freight elevator building and opened fire on us! And they weren't our guards! They were—common citizens!"

O'Brien waited. He knew all about the take-over.

"Some group, some band of armed extremists, local survivalists, I'm sure, have gotten into the center and usurped it!" Wallace was puffed, eyes wide, flushed. "We were lucky to get away."

O'Brien asked, "Is that why you're here? An emergency landing?"

"I'm here, Sheriff O'Brien, to order you and your men to retake the center from those traitors. Clear them out! It must be done immediately."

O'Brien looked to Joe Sadler. The mayor said, "I told him there were still thousands of trees down on 199, but—"

Wallace's face contorted. "March on foot to the center. It isn't far! The president is waiting to set up the federal government in the center. It must be ready for her very soon, and for all the others who will follow."

"Including you?"

Richard Elliott

"Well, of course, including me! I'm a district director of the Federal Emergency Management Agency!"

"I see." O'Brien exchanged glances with Mayor Sadler.

Wallace continued. "And while I'm thinking about it, because the seat of the federal government will be so close, all local travel must be restricted. All shortwave receivers and transmitters in this area must be confiscated, including all CB radios. We cannot allow the location of the Wolf Ridge center to be broadcast or disseminated in any way. There is a continuing danger that a Russian submarine might send in some nuclear missiles if they learned the government's new location."

The mayor said, "So that damned center of yours is nothing but a target—and us with it."

"It could be if its location isn't kept secret."

O'Brien suggested, "Why not use this chopper to transport a force to the ridge?"

"No, no, that's out of the question. It's my only means of transportation. I can't risk losing it."

O'Brien stared at the man, baffled by Wallace's incredible, self-important stupidity. Talk about the dangers in giving a small man big power! He said, "I'm missing four deputies as it is. I don't know if they're dead or just quit. I sure as hell don't have enough trained men to take that place back for you, especially since I don't know a damned thing about it, don't know who's in there with how many guns . . ." He made a disgusted sound. "Listen, in a week, this town is going to be a war zone. If I went out there to Wolf Ridge with my best men, we'd probably end up joining those people."

"You— You're a traitor to your country! I could have you shot. You probably told those extremists about the center. You're probably responsible for all this!"

The mayor stood up from the table. "Mr. Wallace, Jackson O'Brien is the best sheriff Josephine County has had for thirty years. If you want that place back, you'd better bring in the army or the marines. We can't do it."

Wallace rose, too, shaking with anger. "Those people are rebels. We're in a state of war! You cannot refuse a direct order from a superior."

246

O'Brien went to the helicopter door. "You are a superior asshole, I'll give you that."

"You're refusing a direct order?"

"I don't have an order from anyone authorized—"

"I am authorized! Under Executive Order 369001-7W, I am authorized to command conscription of any citizen age sixty and under to age ten, wherever and whenever needed, and to call upon any existing law enforcement people to implement my orders. I am also authorized to requisition all supplies and equipment necessary for the carrying out of my orders."

"But you're asking the impossible. Get the army to take back your precious hideout . . . if you can."

Wallace screamed, "O'Brien, you're fired! You're dismissed from your office as of now, this instant! You're no longer sheriff. Give me your badge!"

"I was elected sheriff. You can't fire me."

"The Emergency Powers Act gives the president, and those she delegates, the power to remove from office any local or state official, for cause. Only Congress and governors are immune from that power."

O'Brien stared at the man for a second, then threw his badge to the metal floor of the helicopter. It bounced away, out of sight. "You just did me a favor."

"And your gun!"

"This gun is mine. The county-issue .38 is back in the office." O'Brien turned to the mayor. "Good luck, Joe." He then quickly climbed down out of the chopper.

O'Brien's sense of relief and freedom was astonishing. He took deep, joyous lungfuls of the cold, damp Oregon air. He knew exactly what he was going to do now: get on his bike and join his friends out on Wolf Ridge.

CHAPTER 38

PORTLAND, OREGON
January 18, 1992

SANDRA TIMMONS YAWNED AND STRETCHED LUXURIOUSLY, sensually. Her gaze drifted to the bedside clock radio. "My God, it's past two!"

John Norris rose up on his right elbow and leaned over to kiss one of her small, pert breasts. "We have all day." He eased a big, strong hand onto her flat, velvet-skinned belly.

She watched him suckle her erecting nipple. "I can't resist the president's new special assistant."

He smiled. "A proper attitude for the special assistant of the new special assistant of the new president." A blast of rain drew his eyes to the window of the Holiday Inn room they shared. The inn had survived the hurricane winds and was now the stopover headquarters of the president and the growing, migrating federal government.

It was raining a monsoon outside. The large window ran with water from hundreds of fat raindrops per second blown heavily against the thick glass.

The view of the vacant land, overgrown with grass and wild shrubbery, to the east of the main runway of Portland's International Airport, was warped and wavery in the gray light. Swiftly moving low, dark clouds loomed overhead as they dumped moisture accumulated from the North Pacific. The same air masses had dried over Asia two days before. Storm patterns were reasserting their usual west-to-east movement after the initial shocked heat madness from the micro-radiation flare from the sun. But the storm tracks were wild and swift, the fronts much more intense, and the highs distorted, providing only a few hours of respite.

The land and sea masses of Eurasia, Africa, and the Indian

Ocean continued to give off vast waves of warmth nine days after the one-hour holocaust.

Sandra hugged his hand against her belly. She yawned again. "I feel guilty as sin for being so well off while everybody else is fighting for their lives."

"We've done our share. We'll be working like galley slaves again once this storm breaks for a few hours and we get to southern Oregon."

"You've certainly done your share." She gently ran a fingertip over one of his crusted-over burns. "You heal amazingly fast."

"I give great scab."

"You!" Sandra pushed him onto his back and moved to kiss him. After the long, sweet, sexual kiss, she whispered, "At least as an official special assistant to the president you won't have to go on any more wild, dangerous missions."

"Don't be too sure. I think she sees me as a fount of unbiased advice and an ace troubleshooter."

"The trouble with trouble is that it sometimes shoots back."

"Sandy, you're hopelessly security oriented."

"And you're hopelessly danger oriented!"

Their phone rang. John reached for it. "Yes? . . . Of course, Mrs. President. We'll need five minutes. . . . No, it's no imposition. Your priorities must always override ours." He smiled at her reply and said, "I'm flattered. . . . Yes, fine." He hung up and said, "President Waggoner will be visiting us in five minutes."

"You're kidding!" Sandra sat up quickly, knowing he wasn't kidding. "We can't get dressed and make it to her office in five minutes!" She left the bed for the bathroom.

"I said she's coming here."

"What?"

As Sandy showered, John slipped into briefs, a blue pull-over sweater, and a pair of gray slacks. He was pulling on socks when Sandra burst from the bathroom to step into clean pantyhose. She delved in a suitcase filled with new clothes provided by FEMA, which had requisitioned clothing from a nearby shopping mall. She asked, "Why is she coming here? We should go to her suite or a meeting room."

"She didn't say. Maybe she wants to get away from all those advisers and aides and FEMA types."

Sandra wriggled into cream-colored pants and, after an agonized glance at the bedside clock, pulled on a green-flowered tunic. "Will you please make the bed?" she hissed.

John pulled on black loafers and threw the covers into reasonably neat order. He was flipping the bedspread into position when a quick knock came at the door.

Sandra toed into shoes and went to the door. She opened it and said, "Mrs. President."

Julia Waggoner entered. She appeared hagridden, worn out. She smiled and pressed Sandra's hands. "I know I'm intruding, but several things—" She turned and motioned her secret service escort to stay in the hall. She personally closed the door. When she turned again, she said, "John, I'm afraid I respect your judgment more than I trust the advice of my inherited Cabinet, especially that of Sterling Foster." She walked slowly to the large, rain-splattered window. "Dear God. This endless rain and wind is wiping out the winter wheat crop."

John turned on a small radio. Classical music quietly filled the room. He joined the president at the window. "How may I help you?" He unobtrusively gestured for Sandra to come closer.

Julia said, "When we got here three days ago, that ground out there was covered with ice and snow. Now it's all melted off in this damned rain." She turned to face Norris. "Why did you turn the radio on?"

"To make it more difficult to hear us if there are any bugs in here."

Sandra looked startled.

Julia stared at him. She sighed. "Now you've added another layer of worries in my mind."

John smiled wryly. "I'm a spy. I think in those categories."

"I know. I appreciate the precaution. I need to hear your thoughts, and Sandra's thoughts, too, about the secretary of the treasury. Foster wants me to go on an all-net hookup and announce a phased program for reopening the banks, the stock and bond markets, and other exchanges. He also thinks a return to the gold standard is in order.''

Norris said, "I'm not an expert in that area, but as I understand it, the government is requisitioning everything in sight and paying for it with IOUs."

Julia nodded. "To keep from flooding the country with money."

Sandra said, "Mrs. President—"

"Julia! For God's sake, it's Julia in private."

"I forgot. What I want to say is, I took a lot of economics in college, and I've picked up a lot in my work in the CIA, the rough, no-holds-barred kind of money games the international banks play, and what goes on in the underground economy, high and low. I can tell you that those promissory notes we're issuing are being used as money right now. They are assets. They probably have a full-faith-and-credit backing by the treasury, don't they?"

"Of course."

"Then, Julia, they're being bought and sold—and spent. I imagine hoards of old silver coins and gold coins are coming into circulation, too, alongside the regular currency and tokens. The economy—"

Julia asked, "Tokens?"

"Yes. Those sandwiched base metal coins the government has been issuing aren't really money. They are, strictly defined, tokens. Coin money is silver and gold. Our money has been so debased over the years—"

"I don't want a lecture on past inflation. I want to avoid inflation now."

Sandra nodded. "Yes. And those IOUs are terribly inflationary. And they don't draw any interest, do they? So they'll be discounted every day, and they'll lose value every day until they're paid off. So people won't hold them. They'll spend them or trade them for real money—gold or silver. There's no way to beat the real markets which are made by people trying to protect themselves from being cheated."

Norris said, "Julia, the prices of gold and silver will go through the roof. Whoever has a lot of it will make a huge killing."

"Foster wants me to set the price of gold at three thousand dollars per ounce."

Sandra frowned. "No, the only thing to do is suck up all that IOU money with stiff, almost confiscatory taxes and forced purchase of government savings bonds. Print as much money as needed and spend as much as you need, but drag it back out of the economy as quickly as possible. That's what was done during World War Two."

Julia smiled. "I see what you mean. It's a good thing I've got supreme emergency powers. That sort of tax program would never get through Congress. As it is, if I take your advice, they'll scream bloody murder."

Norris said, "At least those who have been bought by big money will scream on cue."

Julia made a face. "It's happening already. Just listen to the news or pick up one of the newssheets being published. I think Bradford Stoneman wants his country back."

Sandra laughed.

Julia turned away from the window. She tiredly wandered around the room, touching surfaces, trailing fingers, repositioning a calendar, a lamp, the clock. "Foster is one of Stoneman's people. They're all over me to do things their way, which is Stoneman's way. I'm trapped. I can't fire them because they know their jobs, and they do have great intelligence and executive ability, and they all have been working day and night to get the country back in operation. There's no conflict of interest in that area."

She sat on the edge of the bed and idly smoothed the hastily thrown bedspread. "Members of both houses of Congress are gathering in Washington. They'll have quorums soon and will demand a return to constitutional government. But it's too soon."

Sandra said, "The worst is yet to come. The food—"

Julia said in an aggrieved, resentful tone, "They're calling me a coward for deciding to move out here. They're calling me a dictator."

Neither John nor Sandra said anything.

Julia seemed distracted, almost talking to herself. "I'm afraid to turn the megabanks loose again. All that interlocked power. They could end up owning ninety-five percent of this country by the time the crisis period has passed. I wish I could think of a way to destroy them . . . break them up. . . . I suggested something like that to Foster, and he nearly had a coronary on the spot.'' She smiled.

John changed the subject. "Have you thought about naming a new vice-president?"

"Yes, but the Senate must confirm, and that means a return to the old system. It's too soon."

Sandra suggested, "Perhaps you could appoint a new vice-president on an interim basis and confer with House and Senate leaders on a—well, on something you might call a National Consensus for a New America."

"Even if I wanted to, I couldn't. Not now. We don't have the facilities here. The broadcast towers are all down. The satellite links are gone. There were wind gusts over two hundred miles per hour here. Some of the older bridges even went down. All the microwave receivers were blown away. All I can do is go on shortwave radio while I'm stuck here."

Julia shook her head as if to clear it of cobwebs. She looked up at John, her pale blue eyes haunted. "Calling me a dictator after only nine days! That's not fair."

John said, "The real danger is from FEMA. You've got to keep those bastards from digging in too deep. They're all career bureaucrats, and they instinctively build empires for themselves. They're arrogant, control-minded, anal-retentive sons of bitches who have a vested interest in keeping the national emergency in existence for as long as possible."

Sandra nodded. "That's right. They're your ally now, and they'll help you against Congress. But down the line they'll become so entrenched in running everything it'll be almost impossible to return to a free economy and free society."

Julia nodded. "I know, I know, I know." She sighed. "I wish Bill had sent me to Geneva in his place."

The room phone rang.

John strode to the bedside table and answered it. "Yes? . . . Just a moment." He turned to Julia. "Howard Salisbury needs to speak to you."

Julia took the phone. "Yes, Howard?" She listened for a

long moment, frowning. "All right. But before we do that, I'm going to send John Norris down. . . . Yes, I do. . . . Coordinate transportation immediately. I'll be up in a minute." She handed the phone back to John. "We have a problem at the Emergency Crisis Center. The local FEMA man can't handle it. I have to ask you to fly down and take care of it. I was going to get around to asking you in a few minutes, anyway. I didn't expect him to make any progress."

John asked, "What's the nature of the problem?"

Julia rubbed her eyes. "Two days ago, we received a strange report via the CIA com center that the ECC was being flooded by an underground stream and was being abandoned. There was no contact after that. Just one printout message. No voice contact from Schweitzer, no first alarm . . . nothing.

"So Salisbury alerted his local FEMA director in Eugene and sent him to look into it. We just received his report."

Julia sighed again and stood up. "John, the crisis center has been invaded and taken over by armed locals. Radical survivalists. And the county sheriff can't or won't do anything about it. Nor will the mayor of Grants Pass."

Sandra turned her back on Norris and the president.

John said, "I'll do what I can. What kind of authority will I have?"

"Carte blanche. I'll back you all the way. We *have* to have that place!"

Sandra spun and said, "How can he fly in this kind of weather?"

Norris said, "There is one all-weather G-16 copter on the base that can probably get me there."

The phone rang again. Simultaneously, someone began knocking urgently at the door.

Sandra rushed to open it. One of the secret service men, holding a walkie-talkie, blurted, "Mrs. President! A nuclear missile has just struck near Atlanta!"

CHAPTER 39

WOLF RIDGE, OREGON
January 18, 1992

T HE BIG, ARMORED ARMY CHOPPER SETTLED HEAVILY ONTO the debris-littered landing pad and sat rocking in the strong wind, its vanes feathered, engine idling. Waist gunners hung in their harnesses, ready with their machine cannons.

John Norris peered out a small window. At least it wasn't raining. He unstrapped from his metal bucket seat.

Beside him, Ernie Wallace said, "We'll have to be firm with this rabble, Mr. Norris. They're ideologues. They simply—"

"I'll talk with them alone."

Norris rose and signaled the crewman to open the door. There were five heavily armed national guardsmen in the chopper, too, rising, checking their heavy-weather jackets, their equipment and arms.

Wallace was aghast. "But, Mr. Norris! I'm the district director of FEMA here. It's my duty to accompany you."

Norris turned and put a big hand on the front of the man's yellow rain slicker. He pushed him back and down into his seat. "I have full presidential authority to conduct this meeting any way I like. I picked you up in Eugene to get the details of your encounter with these people and to learn more about this place. You've served that purpose. Now, you stay here."

"I must insist on being present. This is a FEMA facility! I am responsible—"

Norris said to one of the national guardsmen who had accompanied him from Portland, "Sergeant, this man is not to leave this helicopter, nor is he to use the radio."

"Yes, sir!"

Wallace's mouth tightened. His eyes showed hate for an instant. His lips twisted in a smile. "As you wish, Mr. Norris. Obviously, you think you know best."

John ignored him. He flipped up the fur-lined hood of his heavy, hip-length jacket and climbed down to the snowy concrete. Small limbs and twigs blown from the nearby fir and pines skittered on the pad. He remained in awe of the chopper pilot for managing the landing in such high winds.

A metal door opened in the large freight-elevator bunker, and two men emerged dressed in heavy camouflage jackets, jeans, and boots. They wore army sidearms. They waited for him to approach.

When he was near enough to hear them clearly, one of the men said, "First thing you got to know, mister, is that there are guns trained on you. And that landing pad is mined. Anything happens we don't like, you die, and that copter goes up in pieces."

John nodded. "Okay. I'm unarmed. Can we go inside and talk?"

They nodded and moved back inside. He followed them in. The heavy steel door clanged shut behind him.

He was frisked for weapons. The large freight bay held a scattering of crates. A dozen armed men stood around. It was bitterly cold in the echoing room.

Two of the men came forward. One was Darrell Beales, the other David Russell. Darrell asked, "What do you have to say?"

"First I need to know the condition of your prisoners."

"Everybody's okay except the lieutenant. He got shot in the shoulder, and he's down in the hospital. The nurse says he'll be all right."

"Fine. Now I need to know what it'll take to get you people out of here."

David Russell laughed. "This place is an ark for us. We aren't going to move out. We took it, and we're keeping it. You fucking government leeches can starve. It's what you deserve."

The watching, listening men agreed, laughing.

Norris asked, "Are you two the leaders? Who am I talking to?"

"You can call us spokesmen. Our names don't matter."

"All right. My name is John Norris. I'm a special assistant to the president. I'm here to make a deal with you, if possible."

Russell shook his head, grinning. "You didn't hear me. There'll be no deals. We're staying. You can tell your new lady president to go back to Washington, D.C., where she belongs. Let her take her chances with the rest of the people back there. This is now the free state of New America, independent of what used to be called the United States of America."

The other men agreed. One of them was Jackson O'Brien.

Russell put his hands on his hips. He glared belligerently up at Norris. "We've got teams out on the way to block the passes. We're going to isolate this area from you pretentious, arrogant federal bastards, and we're going to survive the starvation and diseases and rioting that will wipe out you and your kind."

Darrell said, "We deserve to live, and you and your fat-ass government don't. You've lied to us and cheated us and fucked us over for the last time. Go on back and face the mess you've made of the world."

A stairwell door opened, and Kimberly Beales entered the freight bay. She wore a heavy ski jacket with its nylon hood up. The heavy door clanged shut behind her, sending metallic echoes through the big, drafty room. Every eye turned to her for a moment. Her bandaged cheek made her instantly recognizable.

Darrell said, "It's too cold for you up here, sis."

"I'm okay." She stared at John Norris. "Who's he?"

"Some jerk from the president, trying to make a deal."

John Norris slowly took some printouts from his parka pocket. "Read these. Pass them around." He handed them to David Russell. He raised his voice to reach everyone. "You're all living in a wish world. In the real world, a Russian sub has just lobbed a nuclear missile into Georgia and nearly vaporized Atlanta. That Russian sub was destroyed by one of our subs before it could launch more missiles."

David Russell contemptuously passed the military-report printouts to the man on his left. He said, "That proves my point."

Norris continued. As he spoke, his gaze shifted from man to man, judging, studying. He knew about Kimberly. "In the Atlantic, all but one other known Russian Y-class attack submarine has surfaced and radioed surrender or declared neutrality. All but that one are heading for East Coast ports to accept sanctuary and freedom."

Kimberly had come forward to stand next to Darrell. She asked bitterly, "So what? What's that got to do with us?"

"Let me finish. In the Pacific, eighteen Russian missile-armed subs are on their way in to Seattle, Portland, San Francisco, Los Angeles, and San Diego."

Russell said acidly, "I'll tell you something about the 'real world': The military are going to be the ones who eat best and last. Some general is going to take over your phony paper government and shoot the lot of you! Every fucking senator and representative and special assistant to the president is going to be executed for 'crimes against the state.' And I'll bet the first one to get a bullet will be Julia Waggoner. That's the historical pattern, Mr. Norris. The United States will be the disunited states in a month! The country will be Balkanized. "You're going to have little fragmented armies fighting over scraps of food."

Russell contemptuously looked Norris up and down. How he hated these tall, strong, self-assured government sons of bitches! "But you won't be alive to see it."

Norris said grimly, "That's a possibility. But right now there are at least three Russian subs unaccounted for and a very real danger that those subs will nuke every major city on the East and West coasts."

Darrell Beales shook his head in mock sadness. "Awww, that's too bad. That's just what we've been saying would happen, one way or another, for twenty years. We were right!"

Norris said loudly, "My point is that there's a great urgency for the president and for the Congress to make their way here and for the government to function as best it can with all the facilities available to it here. This crisis center is absolutely vital to the government and to the country.''

Russell said defiantly, ''Tough shit!''

Norris let anger into his voice. ''Can't you people understand? *The president will have this place!* She will order it taken at any cost! Immediately! And don't think for an instant the army won't obey her!''

He glanced at his watch. ''I have only a few minutes left in which to negotiate with you. If I am killed and my helicopter out there is destroyed, the president will order in army, marine, and national guard units, and there will be no mercy! This country is under martial law, and this little escapade of yours is an act of insurrection.''

Darrell Beales paled. Kimberly whispered, ''Hey . . .'' Some of the other men shifted uneasily.

David Russell sneered, ''We went through icy hell to take this place. We're committed—''

Norris overrode him, continuing in an iron voice. ''You will be shot on sight if you are still here when they arrive. No prisoners will be taken. If you have families down below, they'll be killed, too. You, and they, are traitors, looters . . . and no mercy will be granted, no surrenders accepted. The government hasn't the time or resources to bother with trials or prisons. *Is that clear?*''

David Russell pulled his sidearm, a new .45 automatic. ''Is it clear to you that we can trash this place if we're attacked? We can destroy all that fancy electronics equipment . . . all those computers and communications stuff. We can wreck all the machinery. We can total the generators, the pumps, and the air-conditioning system. We can fuck up those deep wells— poison them for good. And we can pump diesel oil into the food-storage levels and set it on fire. How would your president like that? She could retake this place, but it wouldn't be worth shit!''

Norris shifted position slightly. He nodded. ''Do that and you sign your death warrants. If that's what you want, you'll die happy. Are you speaking for everybody here?'' Norris looked around at the other men, at Kimberly, making full eye contact. "Is he deciding for all of you and your wives and children?"

Russell yelled, "Just a minute! We decided before you—"

Norris raised his voice and easily overpowered the tenor voice of the smaller man. "I'm empowered to offer you all full amnesty if you'll pack up and leave immediately. I have it in writing from the president." He took an official document from inside his parka. He unfolded it and handed it to Darrell Beales. "You won't be identified or harassed in any way. The government will simply forget this happened. It's in both our interests to handle this situation this way."

Darrell nodded. Kimberly, reading, asked, "Can we take some supplies with us?"

David Russell was furious at having control of the situation taken from him. He was suddenly facing a total loss of prestige and power in the group—from hero and leader to . . . nothing. He'd be back to his hanger-on, survivalist groupie status of preflare days. He knew himself to be a small-time journalist who would be desperately freeloading, begging for food and shelter from Darrell and others. He had no land, no cabin, no animals, no hidden food stocks. He had only a small, cheap apartment in Grants Pass that might not now exist. He had lived a marginal existence on subscriptions from the readers of *The Survivalist Newsletter,* and now that was gone.

He cocked his .45. "You goddam lying son of a bitch!" He raised the heavy gun in his shaking right hand and aimed at Norris.

John dove instantly to the left and rolled into a startled, dark-bearded man in a red plaid mackinaw who held a shotgun.

Russell's .45 boomed, and the heavy slug smacked into a crate of heavy machinery behind Norris and the fallen man.

Nearby survivalists lunged away. Everyone began shouting at once. Darrell Beales struggled for Russell's gun.

Norris didn't stop moving. He wrenched the shotgun away from the man he had brought down and snaked swiftly between two crates. He pumped a shell into the chamber and crouched, ready, waiting, hoping the shooting was over.

Finally the tumult quieted to a few shouting voices. Norris

peered over the top of the crate and saw that the survivalists had separated into two groups. David Russell, holding a rifle given him by a cohort, stood with four other armed men by the stairwell door.

Facing them were Darrell Beales and seven men. Kimberly stood at her brother's side, hands fisted at her sides.

A big, solid man stood behind Kimberly, his left hand full of a .357 magnum held high in a professional manner. He boomed, "Don't be fools. You guys don't have families, so you don't have all that much to lose. But if you junk this place, we all die."

Russell screamed, "The fucking government isn't getting this place back! You fucking cowards! O'Brien, I thought you were committed!"

The big man shook his head. "I'm not committed to suicide."

Norris stood up and moved out from behind the crates. Everyone watched him. He held the 12-gauge shotgun with casual precision. He said, "There are other consequences if this center is trashed. If the government falls, we won't quite get the anarchy you think. We'll get a bastard set of rulers who take orders from the Stoneman empire. They're setting it up now. Big money is going to own this country like it never has before, and it'll all be legal, with new sets of laws passed by whores and cowards."

There was a short silence.

Darrell Beales said bitterly, "So we can't win, eh?"

"No. Not the way you want. All you can do is choose the lesser of two evils."

Kimberly called to one of the men in Russell's group. "Dean! I don't want to die. Even if I have to look like— You don't want to ruin everything, do you? We could move your trailer onto Darrell's land. Maybe . . ." She liked him, and he had shown some interest in her in spite of her damaged face.

The young man wavered. He smiled, meeting her eyes. "That's a good idea."

Russell exploded with rage. "What the fuck is the matter with you? Thinking with your cock again? I'll take my chances with Stoneman! Maybe the old bastard'll reward us.'' Without warning, he hip aimed a rifle shot at Norris and grabbed for the stairwell door.

The bullet tore splinters from the top edge of the crate and smashed into the concrete wall beside Norris's shoulder.

Dean threw his rifle away and dropped to the floor.

One of Russell's men shot wildly, hitting Darrell in the hand.

O'Brien's magnum came down and roared. Simultaneously, Norris's shotgun boomed. Russell and his three remaining followers were caught in the doorway. The last of them caught both blasts. His insulated jacket shredded, and a fist-sized hole showed mangled red flesh as he fell. An instant later, Russell and the other two had veered out of the line of fire, and the spring-closed metal door was sighing shut. A second magnum slug thudded into it.

When Norris reached the door, he discovered it had been locked. O'Brien was at his side. ''How do we get down?''

O'Brien pointed, ''Passenger elevator over there.'' They sprinted for the cage. O'Brien shouted to the others, ''Stay up here!'' He instinctively knew John Norris could handle any weapon, kill any man. The two of them could take Russell and the two others.

As they sank past level after level, O'Brien identified himself and said, ''Some FEMA asshole fired me. I hope Waggoner has sense enough to weed out shits like that.''

''We'll try. They protect each other like— Which floor are we going to?''

''Ten. Communications level. I'll take that. I think they'll split up. You should go down to the power level. Twenty-two.''

Norris accepted O'Brien's reasoning. ''Will we reach ten before they do?'' This elevator wasn't particularly fast.

''Dead heat, I think. You'll beat whoever goes on down to twenty-two. The generators—''

The elevator stopped at level 10. The doors opened. O'Brien grinned at Norris and leaped out. He dashed to the right.

Norris punched for 22 and waited impatiently as the elevator doors closed. He heard the loud roar of O'Brien's big revolver an instant before the doors sealed and the elevator began to descend.

O'Brien hadn't reached the communications room before the stairway door burst open and a man emerged with a high-powered rifle at the ready.

O'Brien was better prepared, better trained. He crouched, aimed, fired in a split second. The big, high-velocity slug shattered the man's arm and spun him down. The rifle went flying. Blood spattered the beige walls. The man screamed with pain.

O'Brien crouched, waiting for another of Russell's men, or Russell himself. Seconds ticked by. He ran to the stairwell door and flung it open. He heard echoing, descending foot sounds. Norris would have to face two men.

When the elevator stopped at level 22, Norris stepped out into semidarkness. A low, powerful humming permeated the too-warm air. A thrumming vibration penetrated his boots from the steel grating floor.

He moved quickly to the stairwell door and jerked it open. No sound! He looked up and saw only empty, spiraling steps. Then, far up, he heard someone coming down. He called, "O'Brien?"

An echoing "Yo!" was the response.

"They didn't come out on twenty-two."

"Go down. Tanks. Other stairs."

Norris cursed and ran around the freight-elevator housing. Of course Russell would have anticipated the elevator could beat him down this far. He'd left the stairwell and was coming down to 22 or 23 or 24 by means of one of the blockhouse elevators or another stairwell. And the monster, multithousand-gallon full-up diesel fuel tanks were probably located two levels below.

Norris found a metal stair and clattered down into deeper gloom. He was on a catwalk between two huge whining generators. Steam pipes loomed close overhead as he ran. He ran smoothly, the shotgun ready, but he didn't know where he was going.

A light ahead showed a platform with a large windowed

office containing three walls of controls, dials, switches, meters. Two engineers were inside, monitoring.

Norris snatched open the door, startling them. "Where are the oil tanks?"

One of the engineers said, "Hey, you don't want to mess with—"

"They're going to be sabotaged! Where are they?"

The man mutely pointed to his left.

Norris ran in that direction. The underground maze of pipes, conduits, and machinery seemed endless. The omnipresent power hum receded. The metal walkway rang with the impact of his boots. He was signaling his approach, but he dared not slow down.

Ahead, in the gloom, he saw towering, curving steel surfaces. The tanks. They were enormous. He searched for some sign of Russell.

It came with a sharp report and a ringing impact on the railing next to him. Then Norris saw two shadowy figures on a lower level, at the base of one of the huge tanks where a spaghetti of pipes fed oil to distant boilers.

One man was aiming at Norris. The other, smaller, Russell, was swinging a sledgehammer at a narrow-diameter pipe, trying to rupture it.

Norris threw himself to the metal decking of the narrow walkway and sent a booming fist of lead at the two men. He scrambled to his feet and pumped another shell into the shotgun chamber as he ran forward. He was too far away. Where was a down ladder?

Another rifle shot ricocheted away. A wrapped pipe abruptly sprayed a fan of live steam.

Norris couldn't see a way down. He was too easy a target on the walkway. He dodged to the right side railing and swung over. He dropped to a married six-way nest of conduits, then jumped to a bone-jarring landing on the concrete floor below. He grunted and rolled. He came up with a clear shot at the two men.

Russell had succeeded in breaking the pipe. Diesel oil gushed, spreading in black ripples on the concrete. Russell and his companion were retreating.

Norris took a chance and leveled a blast at them as they melted into darkness. He was rewarded with an anguished cry.

He crept forward, past a hulking pillar, and became aware of stepping in sloshing oil. Hundreds of gallons must already have been lost. A touch of flame to this stuff—

He saw a glare of light. In the sudden illumination, he saw Russell holding aloft a road flare. The small man's face seemed maniacal in the sputtering light. He stood on the second step of a metal stair, ready to throw the deadly flare into the surging, onrushing tide of oil.

Russell's only follower lay face down, silent, his blood creeping to meet the black fluid.

As Russell drew his arm back, Norris pulled the shotgun's trigger. The mass of lead pellets shredded the flesh of Russell's right hand. The flare was disintegrated, blown out. Russell howled and stood in shocked agony for frozen seconds.

Norris rushed forward in the returned darkness. He nearly fell in the slippery, cascading oil. When he reached the stairway, Russell was gone. He heard the man climbing, sobbing with excruciating pain.

Norris climbed after him, heard a door clang shut, and spent the next few minutes fruitlessly searching for that door.

He found it as O'Brien called to him. But the door was locked.

Norris later learned Russell had escaped via one of seven secret escape passageways through Wolf Ridge to Wolf Creek half a mile away. The designers of the crisis center had considered that possible need.

CHAPTER 40

Erica Stoneman luxuriated in her hot, foamy bath. She half floated in the steamy, scented water and wondered why her nipples were so much larger than other women's. Was it a vestigial survival trait? Was it intended that her babies could suckle better and gain nourishment more quickly, permitting her to give more time to possible fight-flight situations? Had some monkeylike ancestor—far back in time—gained a slight advantage for that reason? The trait had survived through millions of years of evolution.

She smiled. She had no children and would have none. Except— Her children were huge banks, corporations, holding companies . . . Her problems were the stubbornly enduring federal government headed by President Julia Waggoner!

Erica's mood changed for the worse. Was it all just a matter of luck? Events had been moving her way so beautifully until that stupid Russian submarine commander had attempted to nuke Washington after learning another Russian sub had been destroyed after sending a nuclear-armed missile to Atlanta. His missile had misfired and self-destructed fifty miles up. He hadn't tried again. But he was still out there.

And the gathering, controlled Congress had panicked and scattered again, leaving Waggoner in full control, unchallenged.

Erica reached for the phone beside her marble tub. She punched Lane McDermott's number. He answered on the second ring. She said, "Lane, come down here." And she hung up.

She rose from the water and took a large pink towel. As she dried herself and slipped on a white Antron robe, she wondered if McDermott was oral, too. Older men often turned in that direction, she knew, because intercourse became too much work for them.

Sometime she'd give Lane a try. But for now there were more important things to occupy her mind. She toed into white slippers and walked through the large bedroom to the living room.

The fake windows didn't fool her, even subliminally. She was tired of living in this fancy hole. Her eye was caught by a fluttering little telltale attached to the fresh-air duct near the ivory wall-to-wall carpeting. Another reminder.

McDermott stepped out of the elevator. He was big and fleshy from weight gained in the past six weeks, but he wore his slacks and shirt and sweater nicely.

Erica asked, "What's the latest? About that woman."

"She's assigned Fennley to work in the Virginia FEMA office allocating fuel rationing stamps. The White House has been closed down. Everything is now coming out of what they're now calling the Far West White House."

"Damn!"

McDermott said, "She was right to get out there to Oregon. She's shrewd in her fashion and can make a fine speech; she comes across as a loving, gutsy mother."

"With two hundred sixty million starving children!" Erica crossed her legs angrily. "I think she's hollow! A phony!"

"We did manage to pressure her to name a new vice-president."

Erica smiled. "Yes, that was beautifully finessed. We push hard for good old Roland Lewis, whom she hates, and use our hidden people to offer the man we really want in." Erica caught Lane watching her naked thigh where her robe had parted. Well, let him look! She commanded his eyes to hers. "Now that Gary Ember is next in line, how do we get rid of that woman?"

Lane became very serious. "There are two options that Mr. Stoneman prepared. The most dangerous is the military. We have high-ranking friends—generals, admirals—who might be willing to mount a coup. But frankly, Waggoner is too popular with the people, and among the armed forces, for that to be viable now."

Erica reluctantly agreed. "That's a genie I don't want to let out of the bottle. That's a last resort."

"The other option is . . . assassination."

Erica sat very still. "Go on."

"Mr. Stoneman, over the years, indirectly funded a variety of small organizations of idealists. Fanatics, if you will. They cover the spectrum of extreme political, social, racial, and even cultural beliefs. Whenever a new 'cause' sprang up, he fed it and controlled it and in so doing kept alive its inevitable lunatic all-or-nothing minority."

Erica nodded. She waited.

"Over the years, some groups were dropped, some wore out, some disbanded of themselves. But we managed to keep a sufficient variety of nuts available." McDermott noted that Erica was not in the least shocked. Her blue-eyed gaze was steady and keen. She had in the past few weeks matured and hardened. Here, indeed, was Bradford Stoneman's rightful successor.

He continued. "When necessary, a group, or a fanatic lone member of the group, can be manipulated—indirectly, of course—through a series of agents, by various pressures and lures, to do certain things consistent with their beliefs. It's all relatively simple."

"Who are you thinking I should use, now?"

"There is a small, fanatic cell of anarchistic survivalists remaining in southern Oregon. To them, President Julia Waggoner is the devil incarnate, and her underground FEMA White House is her lair, a terrible sore on the body of their natural land."

"Is that the group that tried to take over that place before she arrived?"

"The radical remnant. Two or three men. The leader I've managed to keep hidden for possible later use. Now might be the time. He's the perfect combination of bitter hatred, idealism, and cynical opportunism. Every level of his character is engaged."

Erica said softly, "I see." She felt creepy and exhilarated. Her full lips curled into a slow, evil smile. "Do it."

CHAPTER 41

ASHLAND, OREGON
March 2, 1992

Ernie Wallace peered distastefully into David Russell's smelly little room. "I think our conference would be better located elsewhere. Perhaps a short walk?"

"Who are you?" Russell was suspicious and afraid. This was the first time the man whom he had come to know as his mysterious benefactor had sought a personal meeting.

"That isn't important now." Wallace was also repelled by the small man's scraggly beard and moustache. "Come along."

Russell was compelled to follow. He was dead tired from a ten-hour shift in the huge emergency greenhouses built on the high school's football field. His bandaged, gloved right hand—what was left of it—ached constantly.

But this man had taken care of him, gotten his shredded hand treated, gotten him away from Grants Pass, and had arranged fake ID papers, a change of name. Now he wanted something in return.

Russell awkwardly put on his damp coat and followed the man down the narrow hall of the community residence—formerly the Lithia Hotel, built in 1906—and down the back stairs to a side door.

Wallace led Russell down a dark side street. There were no streetlights. The community couldn't spare the power, and there was no need: Few people went out after dark for fear of having their homes or apartments robbed of their remaining possessions. Everyone still alive huddled together in the scattered whole buildings and houses. There were no private cars running; all gasoline and oil were reserved for the Priority Community Survival Effort.

Russell sighed with weariness as he slogged along, waiting

for the man to speak. His new-grown beard itched from dried sweat.

Finally, Wallace said, "I'm a kind of recruiting agent for a large corporation."

"Huh. I thought corporations were outlawed by our fearless leader."

"Temporarily. There will come a time when the old property relationships will be in place again. The large corporations still exist on paper, and the people who control them want to be ready. They need good, skilled, talented men . . . like you."

"Sure. I'm great with a trowel."

"I mean your writing and editing talents. They know of your publication, *The Survivalist Newsletter,* and your expertise in those areas is their major interest."

"Why did you save my ass? Why did you get me over here to Ashland?"

"I can't tell you. Nor should you want to know."

"You've got to be pretty high up in government. Are you in FEMA?"

Wallace ignored the question. "There is being organized a new publishing firm, New Age Publications, in Eugene, and the people funding it are very interested in hiring you to be the editor of a line of survival books. New Age Living will be the imprint."

Russell laughed sourly. "Sure. The postal system is still a wreck, and the railroads and trucks are locked into federal priority freight forever. And it'll be decades before the airlines are reestablished. How do you distribute books?"

"Ah, they won't be distributed physically. The texts will be transmitted by code via satellite to thousands of local printers and distributors. Before the flare, this system was being set up, and the synchronomous satellites overhead are still in place, still operating. Only a few on the East Coast were affected by the flare. There are amazingly computerized duplicating machines capable of turning out a single copy of a perfect bound soft-cover book at the keying in of a code and the push of a button. Those machines are locked in warehouses all across the country, waiting to be franchised out to printers and distributors and bookstores. The postal service as we knew it may never return; most mail will travel electronically from now on."

Russell had heard of these developments before the flare. He began to hope. This man seemed to know what he was talking about. "When is all this going to get off the ground?"

Wallace didn't answer directly. "This is planned as a very large operation, a very large publishing house, and you could become very important in the corporate structure. Further, your salary would be paid in gold, initially, until the money markets and the confiscatory tax rates in effect now are changed.

"The people I represent are willing to pay you ten thousand dollars in gold, per month, as soon as the president signs new executive orders allowing corporate life again and allowing equity and debt markets to return."

Russell felt his hopes shatter. He said bitterly, "You've heard her speeches. Waggoner won't let big business take over again till hell freezes over. She's talking five years or more."

"Yes, unfortunately, she is. But it is in the interest of the country as a whole that her draconian economic dictatorship be ended as quickly as possible—by any means."

Russell stopped walking. Wallace stopped. They were very much alone beside a burned-out furniture store.

Wallace said, "Vice-President Ember is secretly very sympathetic to the cause of a return to normal business structures and practices. He is, of course, next in line to be president."

Russell whispered, "Yeah. He is."

"He would convene Congress very quickly and act to normalize the country."

"Great. Talk is also cheap."

"Of course I have quite a large advance on your salary for you . . ." Wallace delved in an inside pocket of his bulky overcoat. He dropped a handful of marvelously heavy Krugerrands into Russell's left hand.

Russell pocketed them quickly. He began to tremble. He said, "I don't know how I could—"

"Do you have a friend or two who would also like employment and who believe as you do?"

"Maybe."

Wallace said, "It's a shame the president stays holed up in the crisis center all the time. She should come out and be seen once in a while. It would help her image, and it would give the common people some access to her."

Russell said, "I know a couple men who would like access to her."

"Umm. I'll see what can be done."

CHAPTER 42

GRANTS PASS, OREGON
March 31, 1992

JOHN NORRIS STOOD UNEASILY NEAR THE STAGE-RIGHT CURTAIN, observing the townspeople of Grants Pass assembled in the high school auditorium. They were attentive, but a few raucous loudmouths were trying to provoke the president.

President Julia Waggoner was addressing them in person and the nation over broadcast and cable nets, which were nearly back to normal. Cameras and lighting had been moved into the auditorium hours ago.

Julia was relaxed behind the portable, armored lectern and smiled often. She wore a dark gray suit and a frilly pale blue blouse. She wore no jewelry except her wedding ring.

Julia finished her initial statement and was enthusiastically applauded.

Norris grudgingly admitted to himself that this "surfacing" of the president had been a good idea of Ernie Wallace's. Good public relations but a hellish security problem. All the people in the audience had passed through a metal detector. There wasn't a gun out there, but he had a hunch something nasty was in the works.

The town-meeting format had been chosen for its informality and effectiveness. Julia said, "Thank you. Now I'll answer some questions. If you'll—"

A heavy man in the balcony wearing overalls and a heavy plaid jacket, seated close to the balcony holocamera, bellowed, "When're you gonna stop being a dictator?"

Julia laughed and ran fingers through her graying blond hair. "As soon as I can, believe me! I'm as much a victim of martial law, FEMA, the emergency restrictions on travel, money, and all the rest as you are. I have to work twelve- to sixteen-hour days trying to keep all our efforts on the right track.''

More shouts: "Give us back our freedom!'' "Let nature take its course!'' "End rationing!''

She shook her head vehemently. "No! No! Listen to me! Listen! It's only been a month and a half since the sun went crazy and killed half our world. We lucky ones still have terrible storms and completely unpredictable weather. We have to be able to make sure the best planting areas have all the seeds, fertilizer, machinery, water, and fuel and labor they need. We're battling for our lives now! This is the crucial period. If we let nature take its course, nine-tenths of us would starve to death by summer, and the rest would be savages.''

A man in a business suit in the front row stood up and said, "There's no justice in the government moving in out of nowhere, taking everything in a man's store at the point of a gun, giving him a check in payment which he cannot cash! —and then taxing that 'transaction' at a ninty-five percent rate!''

"I agree. But we had to have control of every bit of food, fuel, certain equipment, tools, supplies. . . . We couldn't just steal it. But we couldn't flood the country with three trillion dollars of new debt money. The inflation— So we had to take that money right away from you. We had to think of the greater good, the overriding public interest. We had to—''

A thin, fiftyish man called, "What about forced labor? I'm a painter, not a damned lumberjack! When is this universal conscription going to end?''

Voices rose in agreement.

Julia overrode them. She had a volume control for the public address system. The engineers kept her national-broadcast voice within a moderate level. Her voice boomed. "We can do without painters in certain areas for a while. Our first priorities are food growing, conservation, rebuilding, and caring for the injured. Everything we have and everyone able to work above the age of ten must be put to those tasks! What some of you still don't realize is that we truly are in a terrible crisis—a life-and-death crisis! Those pictures taken by satellites and our long-range planes of the monstrous death and destruction in Europe, Asia, and Africa *are real!* It happened!''

She paused. The auditorium audience was quiet for a moment. She continued at lower volume. ''We're fighting to save civilization. And we have to do that together, with central organization, coordination, and, necessarily, local compulsion. I know! I know! I hate it, too! And at the earliest moment I will very happily turn you all loose, and I will very happily retire.''

''Communist! Socialist! Dictator!'' The bull-voiced man in the balcony was livid.

Julia nodded wearily. ''I know the arguments. I've heard them a thousand times. But I could not stand aside and allow tens of millions of children to starve to death. I could not stand aside and allow armed gangs to murder, rape, steal—do anything they want. And so I am, I suppose, temporarily a 'dictator.' I am guilty of severely limiting the wealthy from using the world disaster for their own greater advantage, as if they didn't have enough advantage before. I have struggled, and I have battled, and I have fought like hell to hold this country together, to save every life possible, and to assure our best chance for survival, to assure this great nation's future! You can call me names—anything you wish—*but I will continue on this course!*''

She received a roar of applause.

But John Norris went tight and alert. He had just spotted a man in the balcony who looked like David Russell. Take away the beard and moustache, cut the straggly hair poking down from that ear-flapped old hunting cap . . .

Russell had never been found after his escape from the crisis center over two months ago. It was thought he'd bled to death somewhere in the dense forest.

If he had lived—would he have the guts to come to this event, knowing security would be on like a blanket?

The man was sitting in the extreme right aisle seat, fifth row from the rear of the balcony, next to the high, narrow auditorium windows.

Norris couldn't see the man's right hand.

As the cheering and applause faded and as President Waggoner took another question, Norris slipped off the stage and headed for the balcony stairs in the lobby.

A man shouted, "What about the stories that you had President Barr assassinated in Geneva?"

Julia responded, "The Swiss army did not find any evidence of anything of that nature. Those stories and rumors are spread by those who want me out of the way. They want . . ." She recited her stock answer to that accusation.

"What about your conspiracy with the CIA to take over the government?"

"There's absolutely no substance to that . . ."

Norris reached the stairs and bolted upward. When he emerged at the top rear of the balcony, he glanced out through the windows at the heavily guarded Lockheed Z-36 army helicopter sitting in the high school's football field, the only field in southern Oregon not converted to greenhouses. The copter's five huge vanes swept slowly around and around as the engine was kept running.

Norris looked for the man he'd spotted from the stage.

There. But still the man's right hand was hidden.

The president was answering at top volume, "The fact is, ninety-eight percent of all businessmen have eagerly accepted . . ."

Norris started down the balcony steps toward the man.

The man looked around nervously and saw Norris. His eyes dilated. This close, full face, Norris recognized David Russell, and Russell realized it. He raised his gloved right hand as if to ward off a blow.

Norris pulled his gun, a Benelli, his favorite.

From the stage, President Waggoner was saying, "Food rationing will have to continue until late fall at the earliest. We must have a good harvest. We . . ."

Norris motioned people from their seats. "Security! Get out of the way!" He started along the row toward Russell, who seemed frozen with fear.

A bulky old man rose up before Norris. "Who do you think—"

An upper, left-side auditorium window shattered inward and rained deadly shards of glass on the people seated below.

Norris instantly looked to the president. She was startled but unhurt. He looked at the wall opposite the shattered window and saw a small hole gouged in the green-painted plaster where a rifle bullet had hit.

He realized instantly that the bullet had come from a tree line a quarter mile away. Screaming and shouting filled the school auditorium.

The president was surrounded by Secret Service men. Norris could barely see the top of her head. They were herding her toward the guarded double-door exit at the side of the auditorium by the stage.

He could see purposeful activity around the big army helicopter. The giant vanes began to speed up.

Norris knew something else had to happen. Whoever put that slug through that high window at that distance hadn't a chance of hitting the president; she had been below the lowest window level.

Was the only purpose of that shot to stop the speech and send the president scurrying back to her luxurious hole in the ground? Then why was Russell—

Russell was standing, as was everyone, but he was staring intently at the large exit door. His left hand worked at something in his jacket pocket.

Norris understood in that instant. The real purpose of the shot through the window had been to panic the president's security men to get her to the army helicopter immediately— and the shortest route was through that guarded side door!

Norris raised his gun, but there were still too many standing, moving people in the aisle between him and Russell.

The clot of men protecting the president surged down the stage steps and approached the side door. Army guards on either side of the wooden doors warily watched the crowd.

Russell pulled a small, palm-size object from his pocket. He looked at Norris. Their eyes locked for an eternal second.

The people in the aisle had seen Norris's raised gun. They were scrambling away from his line of fire, exposing Russell.

Russell lunged forward and tripped on a seat back. He fell in the aisle but protected the object in his left hand. Norris recognized the object as a miniature triggering radio transmitter.

Russell struggled up to see the progress of the president.

Norris shot Russell in the back as the president's knot of protectors entered the exit doorway.

Russell screamed and collapsed. He choked on blood but convulsively pressed the button on the transmitter.

The doorway below exploded. The hollowed, plastique-packed frame disintegrated into thousands of deadly, bullet-swift splinters. The concussion shook the building.

CHAPTER 43

WOLF RIDGE, OREGON
April 2, 1992

DEBRA WILEY, THE PRESIDENT'S APPOINTMENTS SECRETARY, smiled when John Norris entered the FEMA center's hospital on the fifteenth level. She had a temporary desk outside the president's hospital room. "Right on time. You have three minutes, four tops. Please?" She waved him into the room.

When Norris entered, he saw Julia Waggoner listening to a cassette. She was bandaged at the right shoulder and wore a full-skull bandage on her head. She looked up as he approached her bed. She smiled and winked a blue eye. "Sit down, John. I've been listening to your report. Amazing how you keep saving my ass." She clicked off the player and took the tiny speaker from her ear.

"I almost didn't this time, Mrs. President. You're damned lucky."

"Julia, when we're alone. I only wish we'd had sense enough to search everyone at the entrance. We should have had photos of him and all the other crazies provided to the guards at the metal detectors. Too many fine men died."

He nodded. Four Secret Service agents, one army guard, and a civilian had been killed by the blast of wooden splinters. Three agents were in serious condition in other rooms in the hospital. Ten civilians were in the Grants Pass hospital.

He said, "You survived. That's the important thing."

Julia grimaced. "If you call this surviving. It hurts to breathe with three cracked ribs. Those brave, dying men pushed me down and fell on me like tons of bricks!" She gestured carefully at her bedside table. "That jar stays with me till my dying day. After that, some museum can have it. Just look at the wood they cut out of me!"

The jar held a myriad of splinters—some up to three inches long—in a clear gel.

Julia added ruefully, "Most of them came out of my scalp. They had to sheer me like a sheep before surgery. Now I'll be using wigs for a year or two."

"How soon before they let you out of here?"

"Tomorrow, maybe." Julia paused and said, "I really am grateful to you, John. You're an amazing man. And by the way, I've given you a ten-thousand-dollar raise and a new title: From now on you're my personal troubleshooter. The official title is senior special assistant to the president."

He smiled. "Thank you. Now tell me where I can spend the five hundred dollars left after taxes."

Julia shifted slightly, painfully, on the canted hospital bed. "Do you think there'll be more attempts?"

"Yes. But you'll have to risk more public appearances."

"I know. I'm going ahead with the new three-year renewal plan, too. It all has to be done. The trouble is there are so many variables . . . so many things we can't foresee or control."

"Like hundreds of thousands of starving Mexicans swarming north across the border."

She sighed and nodded.

"And sending expeditions to the dead lands for the rare metals needed for certain high-tech manufacturing."

She said, "I never realized before how dependent we are on some foreign raw materials."

"Well, it's all there for the taking, now. Europe, Asia, Africa—they are the new frontier. And there are reports already of free-lance scavenging expeditions to Europe. The Stoneman interests are recruiting private armies to send over to go about looting in a big way."

"That's disgusting!"

"Greed will conquer disgust any day."

"But didn't old Stoneman die?"

"Yes, but I hear stories that his new wife, Erica, is tougher and smarter and more ruthless than he ever was." He paused as Debra Wiley opened the door. He stood up. "We have been cursed to live in interesting times."

President Julia Waggoner smiled faintly. "There's another old Chinese saying if I can remember it: 'The superior man knows from whom comes the evil. His position is perilous, but there will be good fortune. It will be advantageous to cross the great stream.' I'll be seeing you in a few days, John."

"Yes, Mrs. President."